To murder thousands, takes a specious name,
'War's glorious art', and gives immortal fame.

Edward Young

PART ONE

ASSASSINS

Arm! Arm! It is – it is – the cannon's opening roar!

Lord Byron

One

Murder

The atmosphere in the small room was heavy. The shutter over the single window was open only a crack, less to allow the fresh October air to enter than to enable the waiting people to hear what was happening outside. Though the only sound at the moment was the generalised hum of the city of Belgrade at early afternoon work.

The four people sweated with nervous apprehension of the coming minutes. They were an ill-assorted group. Maric, the Serb, was short and squat. He wore a black moustache to go with his black beard, and looked far more sinister than he was actually known to be. Kostic, the Croat, was a big man, young, powerfully built and clean-shaven. Ruggedly handsome, he *was* far more dangerous than he looked; his every action in this war was born of vengeance. Sandrine Fouquet, the Frenchwoman, was short and fair; she wore her straight yellow hair loose, and it fluttered from beneath her sidecap as she moved. Her soft features were close to beauty, and although like her companions she wore blouse and pants and boots, that she had a good figure was obvious; her very presence was affecting the two soldiers as much as what they were about.

If the Englishman Tony Davis, tall and dark, his aquiline features usually enhanced by his saturnine humour, was less affected by Sandrine, it was because that good figure and lovely face and flowing hair were all his, whenever he chose to exercise his right to them. But for that very reason he was more concerned at her presence than either of the others. He would have preferred his mistress to remain in the comparative

3

safety of the mountains. But Sandrine had too great a desire for vengeance on the men who had killed her best friend – who also happened to be Svetovar Kostic's sister – ever to accept being left behind, and she had, over the six months since Yugoslavia had become sucked into this greatest of wars, proved herself time and again as good a guerilla as any man. Besides, she would never willingly let Tony Davis out of her sight; he was her sole reason for living. Now she smiled at him. 'Listen . . .' she said, speaking Serbo-Croat. The wail of a train's whistle cut cross the morning.

'Do you know, Wassermann,' General von Blintoft remarked, 'that I know Belgrade very well?'

Frau von Blintoft, seated beside her husband in the first-class compartment, giggled. 'We honeymooned there. In 1922. I even learned to speak the language.' She switched to Serbo-Croat. 'So did Antoni. I sometimes think that was the reason he was given this job.' Her husband cleared his throat, loudly; even after nineteen years of marriage, he had not got used to his wife's indiscretions.

'How nice,' Major Fritz Wassermann commented, preferring to stick to German. Himself a semi-professional soldier – he wore the black uniform of the SS – at thirty-six his hair was already speckled with grey, and his coldly handsome face seemed set in a permanently angry sneer, caused at least partly by frustration at being repeatedly passed over for promotion, or even a place on the Russian front, which he would dearly have liked. He was still trying to come to terms with the fact that his new superior was only two years older than himself, and was a general. That was thanks to the Russian front, not his ability to speak Serbo-Croat. Of course, there was a downside to everything. Antoni von Blintoft was actually in Yugoslavia because he had been severely wounded during the summer, when the German drive on Moscow had still been in full gear before being slowed by the autumnal rains. After several weeks in hospital he still walked with a limp. But he had had the time to prove himself both a leader and a hero; his

4

Iron Cross First Class revealed that. He had no more worlds to conquer, enjoyed total domestic bliss – as the presence of both his extremely attractive wife and the slim, dark-haired and quite exquisite young woman beside her, the Blintoft's only child, attested – and was also reported to be one of Hitler's favourite people. He was certainly a man to be admired.

Yet Wassermann resented him. He resented the so-evident aura of success that surrounded the general. He resented his being placed in a position of such inferiority to a man so close in age to himself and not, he was certain, any more talented. And most of all he resented the fact that in 1922, when as a seventeen-year-old boy he had been reduced to begging in the street, this man, or his family, had been wealthy enough to marry and honeymoon on a lavish scale . . . and that had been before the Nazis had even been widely known, much less gained power.

'That was before the country was even known as Yugoslavia,' Magda von Blintoft reminisced. 'Then it was the Kingdom of the Serbs, Croats and Slovenes.'

'You will find it has changed, Frau von Blintoft,' Wassermann said.

'Was Belgrade badly damaged?' Angela von Blintoft asked. She had a low and what Wassermann considered an enchantingly musical voice.

'I'm afraid it was, Fräulein.' Wassermann smiled at her. He might resent her parents, but that was no reason not to find the daughter attractive, or even to flirt with her; rather it encouraged her desirability. And she was the most attractive young woman he had seen for a long time. Her features were finely etched, her eyes blue and clear, her hair a glowing dark brown; she wore the fashionable garb of a female member of the Hitler Youth – white shirt buttoned to the neck and the wrists, ankle-length black skirt, black stockings and shoes, black tie – and looked both trim and severe, as she no doubt intended. But the shirt was well filled, and the skirt sat on slim hips, while the slender ankles suggested that her legs would be on a par with the rest. He had a strong desire to see her in evening dress, when much of what was now concealed might be revealed, although equally, if she was a typical representative of the youth of this new Germany, she would no doubt indulge in such pastimes as hiking or cycling or swimming, wearing shorts or a bathing costume – or even less. It would be his duty to escort her. 'But the governor-general's house – it used to be the royal palace – has been repaired,' he assured her.

'Has not the entire city been repaired?' Blintoft asked. 'It is six months since the occupation.'

'There have been other priorities, Herr General. And obtaining labour has been difficult. While the guerilla groups—'

'Have these thugs not been dealt with by now?' the general asked.

'It is our intention to deal with them, certainly, Herr General. But it is a long, slow business. Owing to the shortages we have been suffering in men and materiel' – he paused to give his new boss a censorious glance; the shortages had been caused by the necessity to have every available man and gun on the Russian front – 'they have been allowed to develop their strength. In the mountains to the west they occupy whole towns, control large areas of the country.'

'And we permit this?'

'They are difficult to contain, sir. They infiltrate the cities. The problem is identifying them. As they do not wear uniform, they simply meld into the population – and, of course, they are widely supported and, where necessary, concealed *by* the population. We employ informers, agents, but they are not of great value. And if they are discovered by the guerillas, well . . .' He gave Angela von Blintoft an apologetic glance. 'It is really too horrible to talk about.'

'My information is that the guerillas are commanded by a regular soldier, a former chief of the Yugoslav General Staff,' Blintoft said.

'That is correct. General Draza Mihailovic. But actually he commands only a portion of the rebels. They are divided into several groups. Mihailovic commands the rump of the old Yugoslav army. They call themselves Cetniks. Frankly, my estimation is that Mihailovic is less concerned with our occupation of the country, which he accepts as a concomitant of the war, than with what happens afterwards. He seeks a restoration of the monarchy and the status quo ante.'

'But as there *is* a war on, and the country has been occupied, he is still in arms against the properly constituted authority,' Blintoft pointed out. 'What does General Nedic think about this?'

'With respect, Herr General, General Nedic is a puppet. He pretends to be acting for us in ruling Serbia, and to be in control of the Yugoslav army, but he has no authority beyond the suburbs of Belgrade – except where we enforce it – and very little even within the city. Mihailovic is far more important. And he is a man with whom we can do business. With whom we have done business.'

'You have done business with a guerilla leader?'

'These things are sometimes necessary, Herr General, in such areas as the exchange of prisoners, or the establishment of safe areas.'

'Safe areas?'

'Places where our people can move freely without the risk of being murdered by these Cetniks.'

'And presumably where these Cetniks can move freely without the risk of being arrested by our people. Well, I must say, that sounds very civilised.'

'Yes, sir. Unfortunately, not all the guerillas are Cetniks, or pay more than lip service to Mihailovic's authority.'

'Ah,' Blintoft said. 'The Ustase.'

'No, sir. The Ustase are very helpful to us.'

'They were described to me as a terrorist organisation.'

'Well, I suppose they are a terrorist organisation.'

'Did they not carry out the murder of King Alexander in 1934?'

'That is correct, sir. But they would describe themselves as patriots. They are composed of Croats, you see, who have never accepted the union with Serbia.'

'And now they have been given their independence, by the Reich.'

'Croatia has been given its independence, Herr General. But not all its people are prepared to accept it, under our auspices. For example, this man who calls himself Tito is a Croat, and yet he commands one of the most vicious of the guerilla groups.'

'Tito! Yes,' Blintoft said. 'I have heard of this man. He is a Communist.'

'He is the secretary-general of the Communist Party in Yugoslavia.'

'And why has he not been arrested?'

'Simply because we have not ever caught him. He lives in the mountains to the south-west and has a devoted band of followers. Men like the Englishman, Davis . . .'

'Davis,' the general commented. 'Yes. I have also heard of this man. Was he not a British officer? Is he not wanted for murder? He and some woman . . .'

'A Frenchwoman, Sandrine Fouquet. Yes. They both took part in the shoot-out with the Ustase outside the village of Divitsar in the summer, and then were prominent in the raid on Uzice. We believe Davis was wounded in that battle, but he appears to have recovered; he has been identified as being involved in several terrorist acts, with his French girlfriend. As I have said, they are two of Tito's most devoted followers.'

'Hm,' Blintoft observed. 'I assume you have some ideas, Major, on how these people should be dealt with?'

'They should be hanged,' Wassermann said.

'Just like that?' Frau von Blintoft asked. 'If this man is a British officer—'

'He is a renegade. He was engaged to be married to a Croat girl, Elena Kostic, when we occupied the country. Instead of leaving with the British embassy staff – he was an attaché – he fled the city with this woman, and the Frenchwoman, and began engaging in terrorist activities.'

'How romantic!' Angela von Blintoft exclaimed.

'You would not think so, Fräulein, if you knew some of the things they have done.'

'And they too have never been caught,' the general remarked.

'We captured the Croat woman, and executed her, but Davis and the Frenchwoman got away and linked up with these Partisans.'

'Partisans?'

'That is what Tito's people call themselves.'

'And you have been unable to capture them,' the general said.

'Given carte blanche, I could do so,' Wassermann declared, looking at Angela in search of admiration.

'You have an entire army of occupation,' Blintoft pointed out.

'It is too small an army for the job. Also, we – that is, our superiors in Berlin – do not seem as yet to have made up our minds how to deal with these people, sir. I think it is time to do this. I have said that they move about the country, and even into the towns, with impunity, because of the support given them by the local population, into which they can merge. I think if we were to make it our policy to shoot their supporters in groups if the guerillas refuse to surrender we would soon bring them to heel. Certainly local support for them would dwindle.'

'That sounds barbaric,' Angela von Blintoft said.

'War is a barbaric business, Fräulein,' Wasserman said, disappointed in her reaction. 'As you would understand if you were ever to see one of our people after being captured by these brigands.'

'Please, Major,' Magda protested.

'I apologise, Frau von Blintoft. But I regard the situation as serious enough to require serious methods.'

'But if we started shooting men indiscriminately,' Magda said, 'would that not simply drive more of them into joining the guerillas?'

'Oh, we would have to shoot their women as well, and their children.'

'Oh, Papa!' Angela exclaimed.

'Yes,' Blintoft said. 'It all does sound very barbaric. I was sent here to pacify this country, Major, not turn it into a desert.'

'Yugoslavia can never be pacified as long as men like Tito and this Davis are allowed to roam free, sir.'

'I understand that. And I understand that they can best be defeated by undermining the support they are receiving from the common people. But I doubt that wholesale shooting of men, women and children is going to accomplish this. People are easier conquered by kindness than by cruelty.'

'Kindness?' Wassermann did not seem able to believe what he was hearing.

'Kindness,' the general repeated emphatically. 'If we treat these people with dignity, rewarding those who accept us and even support us, while punishing, but not too severely, those who oppose us and give shelter to our enemies, we will achieve far more. Win the hearts and minds of the people, Major, and you have won the war.'

'I was under the impression that we have already won the war, Herr General,' Wassermann said coldly.

'A war is won when the last shot has been fired,' Blintoft said firmly.

'There are houses,' Angela said. She had been looking out of the carriage window, and now sought to ease the tension between the two men. 'How much farther is it?'

'Five minutes, Fräulein,' Wassermann assured her.

Sandrine Fouquet stood to one side of the window, looking down on the station forecourt. 'So many men,' she said. Beneath her the guard of honour was assembling, shuffling to and fro, watched by a surprisingly large crowd, curious to see their new master. General Nedic was there, as well as several other high officers in the rump of the Serbian army. 'Will we get away?' Sandrine asked.

'Yes,' Tony Davis said with more conviction than he perhaps felt. He was aware of a sense of unreality. But he had existed in that sense for six months now. In April

10

he had been a young man with hardly a care in the world, the horrors and humiliation of the abortive British campaign in Flanders and Belgium, and of the wound he had suffered which had hospitalised him for several months, submerged in the relative peace and quiet of Belgrade, a city he had loved at first sight. His appreciation of Belgrade, and of Yugoslavia in general, had been encouraged by the fact that he had also fallen in love with Elena Kostic. Elena, earthy and enthusiastically amoral, could never possibly have been envisaged as the wife of a captain in the Buffs, as he had then been – and probably still was, at least in the Official Gazette – but she had been the most perfect mistress for a young man who believed in living life to the hilt.

It had been his determination to make sure that she survived the unheralded bombing attack that had introduced Belgrade to war. Her rescue had caused him to be absent from the British embassy when the staff had been evacuated, and launched him into this bandit-like existence, in the course of which he had discovered that very little in Yugoslavia was as it seemed, that the rivalries and fears shared by Serbs, Croats, Slovenes, Montenegrins, Macedonians and Albanians transcended anything he could have imagined possible. He had learned to survive, by turning himself from an officer and a gentleman into a ruthless killer. That determination to carry the fight to the enemy had cost Elena her life, but at the same time had brought him the amazing devotion of the little French journalist who had escaped Belgrade with him and who had learned to be as ruthless as himself, with equal reason – Elena Kostic had been her best friend.

Neither of them would have survived, he knew, had they not joined forces with Tito. In many ways the big Croat was the antithesis of everything they stood for. He was a Communist who took his orders from Moscow, and he was unashamedly looking to the formation of a Communist government after the war. But he never forced his beliefs or his ideals on any of his followers, and although he was a Croat and his country had been given a form of independence by the Germans, he was continuing the fight against the invaders of Yugoslavia – which was more than Draza Mihailovic, who was a Serb and who therefore should have had more reason to wish the Germans expelled, seemed prepared to do.

Tito and Tony Davis had taken to each other on sight, and Tony felt they were friends. Yet here he was, crouching in an attic bedroom, preparing to commit murder and thus risk his own life, and that of Sandrine, because Tito considered it necessary – and because he considered that Tony's exceptional ability with a rifle made him the best man for the job.

'I see it,' Sandrine said.

'Check your weapons,' Tony told them.

The other three were armed with tommy-guns and pistols, and each had a string of grenades round his or her waist. Tony also had a tommy-gun slung on his shoulder, but in his hands he held a high-powered Mauser rifle with telescopic sight, and this he now loaded. He reckoned it might just be possible to get in two shots, but he was fairly sure he could settle it in one. From his tunic pocket – like his companions he wore a species of uniform, not that any of them supposed this would do them much good were they to be captured – he took a folded newspaper sheet, and opened it for a last look at General von Blintoft's photograph; there were now a lot of officers gathering in the station yard, and he did not wish to kill the wrong man. But Blintoft's big, bland, not unhandsome face would not easily be mistaken.

He moved to the window. Sandrine had opened the shutter just sufficiently for him to slide the gun barrel through when he was ready. Which would not be until the official party emerged from the station and into the yard; the station roof prevented him from seeing the actual platform at which the train was now stopping. Tony did not doubt that there were security guards watching all the buildings overlooking the railway terminus; given enough time one of them might well spot a rifle barrel projecting from a supposedly empty room. He listened to snapped orders, watched the guard of honour come to attention and present arms. He was tempted to keep his shot

12

until the general commenced the inspection of the guard, which would take place in the fullest possible light. But then Blintoft would be moving, and unexpectedly stopping from time to time to chat with one or other of the soldiers. Whereas as soon as he emerged from the building, he would stand still while the anthem was played. That was the best possible moment.

The bandleader raised his baton, and Sandrine gave Tony a quick squeeze of the hand. She knew as well as he that the next few minutes might well be their last on earth. Several people emerged from the station doorway, coming from the shade into the light. None was the general. But now Blintoft appeared, a commanding figure. Tony knew the man beside him: Major Wassermann, who headed both the German military police and the Gestapo in Yugoslavia. Tony would in fact far rather have been aiming at Wassermann, who had made himself feared throughout Yugoslavia by his mistreatment of those even suspected of subversion who might be unlucky enough to fall into his hands, while the general's only crime, so far, was the mere fact that he was the newly appointed governor-general.

Blintoft stood to attention on the station steps, Wassermann immediately behind him. Tony slid the rifle barrel through the open shutter, and checked in consternation. If he had noticed the fluttering hair and skirts behind the general, it had only been half-consciously, so hard had he been concentrating. But now Blintoft turned and put an arm round each of the two women standing behind him, bringing them forward to stand in front of him for the anthem. 'Shit!' Tony muttered. Both women were fairly tall, and though one was bareheaded, the other wore a big hat. Together they quite obstructed a clear view of either the general's head – the best target – or his breast. If he fired, one of them would certainly be hit.

'What is the matter?' Svetovar Kostic stood at his shoulder.

'No one said anything about women,' Tony muttered. He had seen women die, violently, as when he had led the assault on the Gestapo headquarters in Uzice a few months ago, but he had not enjoyed it. So, it seemed he still retained some of the attitudes of an officer and a gentleman after all.

13

The band struck up. Everyone in the station yard was standing to attention. 'You must shoot,' Svetovar said.

'I will hit the women,' Tony said.

'So what is one German woman, more or less?' Svetovar snatched the rifle from Tony's hands, threw the shutters wide, aimed and fired almost in the same instant.

Sandrine gave a little shriek, as she was inclined to do in moments of stress, and banged the shutter closed again. This prevented Svetovar from firing a second time, and before he could react Tony had regained the gun. 'That was a bloody stupid thing to do.'

'You would not shoot.'

'Now we are all scuppered,' Maric said.

Sandrine was peering through a crack in the shutter. 'They are pointing. We must get out.'

'If we can.' Maric opened the door at the back of the room.

'Hurry,' a voice said from down the stairwell.

'Go,' Tony commanded. The two men ran to the door. Sandrine hesitated. 'I am right behind you,' Tony promised. But he paused to look down at the station yard. As he had suspected, one of the women had been hit, and was now lying on the ground, surrounded by standing or bending or stooping people. As a target, the general – also crouching – was even more concealed than before. Meanwhile the guard of honour was certainly looking up at this building, and there was considerable activity to either side.

He considered the sniper's rifle he still held. It was useful only for murder, would not in any way assist in facilitating his escape. Nor would it matter when it was found by the Germans; they would already know what sort of weapon had been used to fire the fatal shot. He laid it on the floor and ran out of the doorway on to the landing, where Sandrine was waiting. The footsteps of the two men rumbled from beneath them.

'That bastard has ruined everything,' Sandrine complained. 'I knew we should not have brought him. He is too riddled with hate to be reliable. He should be shot himself.'

'Let's get out of here first, and worry about him later,' Tony recommended. He grasped her arm and hurried her down the stairs.

On the next landing a middle-aged man waited. He wore a suit and looked prosperous, but also highly agitated. 'You have five minutes,' he said.

Tony nodded, and he and Sandrine went down to the first floor of the house. Here Maric and Svetovar waited. 'We got one of the bastards, anyway,' Svetovar said.

'We got no one of the least importance,' Tony told him. 'And your throwing that window wide has told them exactly where to look for us. Mr Brolic . . .' Brolic, who had followed them, gestured at a bedroom. Here a woman and two teenage children, a boy and a girl, were lying on the floor. They were already bound and gagged. Brolic lay beside them, indicating the waiting cords. It took only a matter of seconds to bind his wrists and ankles and stuff a gag into his mouth, but the gag was deliberately badly secured so that it could quickly be got rid of. 'Good luck,' Tony said.

They ran down the last flight of stairs, and now could hear the tramp of feet and the barked commands of the approaching soldiers. 'Here . . .' Maric said. He was an old friend of Brolic, and had set this up. Now he held the cellar door open for them. They reached it just as there was a crashing knock on the front door.

Svetovar led the way down into the gloom while Maric closed the door behind them. He did not lock it, as that would have indicated someone was down here. They reached the foot of the steps, and Tony flicked the switch of his flashlight. 'Over there,' Maric said.

Above them they heard shots as the front door was forced. They ran to where Maric was pointing, Svetovar turning round to look at the steps, tommy-gun thrust forward; the soldiers could be there at any moment. But now they heard Brolic shouting; he had got rid of the gag as planned. 'Help me!' he yelled. 'Help us!'

Predictably, the footsteps now sounded on the upper stairs.

Maric pulled away several barrels of wine to indicate a small doorway; this he opened to reveal an even smaller passageway.

'Will they not find this?' Sandrine asked.

'Of course. We must be out of it before they do,' Maric said.

'You first,' Tony told Svetovar.

Svetovar slung his tommy-gun, dropped to his hands and knees, and crawled into the aperture. Sandrine followed, and then Tony. Maric meanwhile was rearranging the barrels as best he could to make them look undisturbed, then he too crawled into the passage, closing the door behind him. 'How far?' Sandrine whispered.

'A hundred feet,' Maric said. 'Then there is another door. You are not afraid of rats?'

Sandrine blew through her teeth, contemptuously, and resumed crawling behind Svetovar, almost bumping into his backside when he suddenly stopped. 'What is the matter?'

'I have reached the door.'

They listened to the sound of rushing water, and now inhaled a most unpleasant odour. 'Shit!' Sandrine commented.

'That is exactly it,' Maric agreed.

'Will they not simply seal off the sewers?' Tony asked.

'Only when they are sure we are down here. We have a few minutes yet.'

Svetovar opened the door, and now the stench was overwhelming, while the shrill barks of the rats rose even above the swish of the water. 'Remember to stay on the shelf,' Maric said. 'It is quite deep in the middle.'

Svetovar crawled on to the ledge, and kicked a rat into the water. 'Will they attack us?'

'Only if they think you are attacking them.'

Sandrine crawled through. 'You spend a lot of time down here, Maric,' she suggested.

'It has been necessary, from time to time,' Maric agreed equably.

Tony climbed through and Sandrine squeezed his arm. 'There is a rat standing on my foot,' she whispered, her voice trembling to belie her earlier declaration. 'I think it is trying to get up my trouser leg.'

'Kick your foot,' he recommended.

Sandrine did so, and the rodent flew off and into the water with a squawk.

'Haste,' Maric said. There was now a great deal of noise from behind them, although whether it actually came from the cellar they could not be sure.

Svetovar was already moving along the ledge, ankle-deep in water, kicking rats left and right as he did so. Sandrine followed, every so often reaching behind her to make sure that Tony was at her shoulder. Now Svetovar reached a ladder leading up. 'Where do we come out?' he asked.

'Not here,' Maric said, bringing up the rear. 'It is the fifth ladder.'

Svetovar splashed on, followed by the others. Tony wondered if they were going to make it. Maric had been confident of it when the plan had been laid. But they had also counted on an extra few minutes caused by German uncertainty as to where the shot had come from. He was angry about what had happened, both because of the added danger it had placed them in and because it had involved a bystander rather than the principal. He certainly intended to have Svetovar punished – even if the young man had very nearly been his brother-in-law – for such a blatant disobedience of orders.

'Two,' Svetovar said as they passed the next ladder.

But now, suddenly, there was noise in the sewer. 'Shit!' Sandrine muttered.

'You in there!' a voice shouted. 'Come back and surrender. You cannot escape.'

'We are done,' Svetovar said.

'We'll use the grenades,' Tony said. 'Carry on.'

'I will stay with you,' Sandrine announced.

'No,' Tony said. 'I am giving you an order.'

'And I am disobeying it.'

'I will stay,' Maric said. 'I know these sewers. I can find my way out by another route.'

'You cannot get out,' the voice called. 'All the exits are sealed.'

'Is he right?' Tony asked.

'No. There are secret exits. The fifth ladder does not go to the surface. It exits in another cellar, another safe house. They are expecting you.'

'And you?'

Maric's teeth showed in the gloom as he grinned. 'I will be there.'

Tony squeezed his hand, then turned back to the others. 'Let's go.'

Antoni von Blintoft knelt beside his wife, watched the blood welling from the wound in her chest. With every breath she also expelled blood from her mouth and nostrils. 'Magda,' he said. 'My God, Magda!' He raised his head. 'A doctor. We need a doctor.' He gazed at Angela, who was kneeling on the other side of her mother, staring at the dying woman. Her face was composed, and there were as yet no tears, but the little muscles at the base of her jaw were jumping as she clamped her mouth shut.

'You heard the general,' Wassermann snapped. 'Hurry. She should not be moved,' he added as hands reached for the woman. 'Wait for the doctor.' His eyes were already scanning the buildings around the station yard.

'Wassermann . . .' Blintoft said.

'I will see to it, Herr General,' Wassermann said. He looked at the girl, almost as if he wished to say more, then thought better of it and strode towards his men.

The wail of an ambulance siren could be heard, and already soldiers were moving towards the onlookers, using the butts of their rifles to push the crowd back. A tremendous hum of comment rose out of the yard. An officer saluted, and then pointed. 'That window, Herr Major.'

'Follow me,' Wassermann commanded, and set off at the double. The captain signalled his sergeant, who followed with a dozen men. Wassermann drew his Luger pistol as he crossed the open space. His mind was a jumble of mixed emotions. He enjoyed action, the chance to hit back at the guerillas, to vent his spleen upon the wretches who sought to make life difficult for the Reich. He was not overly concerned for Frau von Blintoft, but his blood boiled at the thought of how easily the bullet could have struck Angela, the mental picture of that white shirt and superb torso torn apart by the flying lead. What kind of man would have done such a thing?

More disturbing than any of those considerations, however, and more irritating, was the fear that he might be blamed for what had happened, for inadequate security. No matter that he had ordered all of these houses to be searched this very morning; as it had been the general's command that he should be met at the border by his police chief, he had not been here personally to oversee the search.

He reached the steps leading up to the front door; this was on the street adjacent to the station yard, and he was therefore out of sight of the tragedy, although he could still hear the shouting. 'Name?' he demanded.

'Brolic,' the captain panted at his elbow. 'He has a general store in the city.'

'Any record?'

'None. He has always been a supporter.'

'Those are the worst.' Wassermann banged on the door. 'The house was searched?'

'Yes, Herr Major.'

Wassermann banged again. 'The time?'

The captain looked at his sergeant. 'At eight o'clock this morning, Herr Major.'

'Who was inside?'

'Herr and Frau Brolic, and two children.'

'Herr Brolic had not yet left for work?'

'No, Herr Major. There is another son, older, who works for his father. He had already left the house.'

Wassermann nodded, and stepped away from the door. 'Break it down.' The sergeant beckoned two of his men, who

19

levelled their rifles and shot into the lock. Wood splinters flew, and the lock disintegrated. But it was still held by a bolt. More shots were fired, and the wood shattered sufficiently to be dug out by a bayonet, exposing the bolt. This was forced back, and the door hurled in.

Wassermann stepped into the gloomy hall. 'Check the cellar,' he commanded, and was himself checked by a shout from upstairs.

'Help me! Help us!'

Wassermann took the steps two at a time, followed by the captain and several men. The sergeant and the remainder of the squad waited in the hall, the order to check the cellar on hold for the moment. The major reached the landing, threw open the bedroom door, and gazed at the four people lying on the floor. 'Thank God!' Brolic said.

'Untie them,' Wassermann commanded, and surveyed them while they were being freed by his men. A middle-aged man, a younger woman, and two rather overweight children – brother and sister, in their early teens, he estimated. About as average a family as one could think of. And then there was Captain Ulrich's opinion that they were willing acceptors of the German occupation. That made him suspicious, for a start. 'What happened here?' he asked.

Brolic was sitting up and rubbing his wrists where the bonds had been released. 'We were having breakfast, just after your men had been here, when these people appeared.'

'What people?'

'Three men and a woman.' He knew he could not lie about this, just in case the Partisans were to be captured.

'You knew these people?'

'I had never seen them before. But they were armed, and said they would shoot us all if we made a noise. Then they made us lie on the floor and tied us up.'

'Where are these people now?'

'I do not know.'

'You mean they may still be in the house?'

'It is possible.'

Wassermann turned to the captain. 'Search the house. Begin with the cellar.'

'The shot came from the attic, Herr Major.'

'They are hardly likely to have stayed there, waiting for us to come for them. But send two men upstairs anyway. The rest to the cellar.'

Ulrich saluted and hurried off, beckoning his men to follow.

'You mean these people have been shooting?' Brolic asked.

Wassermann regarded him for several seconds. Then he said, 'You say they came here at eight o'clock this morning?'

'Well, perhaps half past.'

'It is half past two. You have been tied up for six hours.'

'Good Lord!' Brolic commented.

'You must need to go to the toilet.' Wassermann looked at the rest of the family.

'Yes,' Mrs Brolic said. 'Yes. With your permission, Herr Major.'

'You have my permission. Not you,' he told Brolic. 'Hold out your arms.' Brolic obeyed, frowning. Wassermann pushed back his sleeves. 'There is no mark. You were tied up for six hours, and you made no effort to get free?'

'Well, there did not seem any point.'

Wassermann went to the bathroom door, and threw it open to a chorus of alarm and embarrassment. 'Come here.' Mrs Brolic came into the room, hastily adjusting her clothing. 'And you,' Wassermann added to the children behind her. They followed their mother, exchanging anxious glances with Brolic. 'Hold out your arms.'

They obeyed, obviously frightened. Brolic licked his lips.

Wassermann examined each wrist in turn. 'None of these are chafed. I do not believe you have been tied up for six hours.'

'I told them it was no use trying to escape,' Brolic said.

'I think you are lying. You will come to headquarters.'

'But . . .' Brolic looked at his wife and children.

'Oh, they had better come too. Sergeant!' The sergeant clicked his heels.

The Brolics looked at each other, and Mrs Brolic opened her mouth, but was silenced by a quick shake of the head from her husband. The exchange was noted by Wassermann, but he made no comment, especially as at this moment Ulrich came hurrying up the stairs. 'There is a door from the cellar into the sewers, Herr Major.'

Wassermann nodded. 'Have all exits from the sewers blocked, and then take a squad and flush them out.'

Ulrich gulped; he was a fastidious man. 'From the sewers?'

'Yes, Captain. From the sewers.' Ulrich hurried back down the stairs.

'Do you still wish us to come to headquarters, Herr Major?' Brolic asked optimistically.

'Indeed, Herr Brolic. I wish you to tell me how these assassins knew that your cellar leads into the sewage system.'

The ambulance pulled into the hospital forecourt. A surgeon sat beside Magda von Blintoft, whose face was covered by an oxygen mask, which inflated and deflated regularly. But he had not been able to stop the bleeding. The general sat on the other side of his wife, holding her hand. The surgeon wished he wasn't there. His presence was inhibiting, and his repeated question – 'Will she live?' – unanswerable. There was absolutely no chance of Frau von Blintoft surviving; she had clearly been shot through the lung. Even more off-putting was the presence of the daughter, seated at the back of the ambulance, incongruously still holding her mother's hat. Unlike her father, her face was calm, but it was also closed, and she did not take her eyes off her mother for a moment. Dr Scholl wondered what thoughts were going through her mind; he was not sure he wanted to find out. He did not doubt he was going to have to treat her for shock soon enough.

The ambulance stopped, the doors opened, the stretcher bearers were waiting. The girl stepped out of the vehicle and stood to one side, ignored by her father as Magda's body was lifted out and carried into the building. Angela trailed behind the group, past anxious nurses and orderlies standing to attention. Dr Scholl muttered something to one of the sisters, who waited while the stretcher party went past her, then went to stand next to the girl. 'Fräulein?' Angela's head jerked. 'A cup of coffee?' the sister asked.

Angela shook her head.

'Well, a brandy?'

'Will my mother be all right?'

The sister turned her head away from the overhead light, so that her huge starched hat cast a shadow across her face. 'We must trust in God.'

'God!' Angela said. 'Will they catch the people who did this?'

'I should say they will,' the sister said.

'What will happen to them?'

'Well, it is not really something a nice young lady like you should think about.'

'I want to see them hang,' Angela said in a low voice.

Two

Involvement

The sound of the exploding grenades seemed to make the sewers shake, and sent the rats scurrying for safety, now totally ignoring the humans. But the humans were hurrying as well, splashing through the water. 'Will he escape?' Sandrine panted. She kept slipping, to be dragged back to her feet by Tony.

'If anyone can escape, it will be Maric,' he reassured her. 'It is the others that worry me.' They spoke French, as was their custom with each other.

'All for nothing,' Sandrine said. 'Because that bastard—'

'Number five,' Svetovar said from in front of them. 'I am going up.'

Sandrine and Tony reached the foot of the ladder, watched his feet disappearing into the darkness. Sandrine put her foot on the bottom rung, and Tony held her arm. 'Just let's wait a moment,' he whispered.

She leaned against him, and they listened to the sound of Svetovar's feet on the ladder. Then there came a bang, and another. They heard a scraping sound. 'Thank God for that,' Svetovar said. 'I was beginning to think—'

'Get him out,' said a voice in German.

Sandrine seemed to freeze against Tony. He listened to a gasp from Svetovar, then grasped Sandrine round the waist and stepped off the ledge, at the same time putting his other hand over her mouth, as he knew her weakness for shrieks. They went down into the rushing water, and were carried several feet beyond the ladder while he fought to regain his balance.

The noise above them was confused, but he could hear voices, loud enough to suggest that the Germans were peering through the manhole. 'Sssh,' he whispered as Sandrine endeavoured to speak. He was now neck-deep in the torrent, still being forced forwards, holding Sandrine up and against him – he knew she couldn't swim. 'Hold your breath,' he whispered into her ear, and went below the surface, just before there was a loud explosion, and then another.

They surfaced again, Sandrine gasping and spitting; Tony could only hope she hadn't swallowed any of the evil-smelling liquid. Now they were some thirty feet from the ladder, beyond the range of the flashlight beams which were scouring the darkness. 'My God,' Sandrine said. 'My God.'

'Sssh.' He held her mouth again, for the Germans were coming down the ladder. By their flashlights he could see that quite a lot of the ceiling masonry had been dislodged by the explosions, and now lay in great chunks in the water which bubbled about them. Three men stood on the ledge, sending their beams to and fro, while the rats squealed louder than ever. The Germans were shouting; Tony spoke the language fluently, but it was difficult to make out what they were saying against the flow of the water. After a few minutes they climbed back up, and the manhole clanged shut.

'Were we betrayed?' Sandrine asked.

'Looks like it. But they either don't know how many of us there were, or they reckon we're dead.'

'Aren't we dead, Tony?'

'Not while we're breathing. Let's get back on to the ledge, and keep going. This will eventually take us to the river.'

'Eventually.' She shuddered, but allowed him to push her up on to the ledge, then gave him a hand up. 'Will we ever be clean again?'

She had a fetish about bathing and keeping clean, which had not always been easy to do while surviving in the mountains. But he did not suppose either of them had ever been as filthy as this before. 'Sure,' he said. 'When we get to the river.'

25

'I meant, really. Have you ever heard of a man called Marat?'

'I think so. Jean-Paul, wasn't it? He was a bigwig in your revolution. Got himself murdered by Charlotte Corday while sitting in his bath.'

'Why do you suppose he was sitting in his bath?'

'To receive a charmer like Charlotte? Imagination boggles. Wasn't it something to do with a skin disease?'

'That's right. Years before, when escaping from the police, he had to flee through the sewers. He had to spend some time down there, up to his neck in it. Just like us. So he contracted a ghastly skin disease, and had to spend the rest of his life sitting in a bath of water to stop the itching from driving him mad. If that were to happen to me . . .'

'We'd find you a nice bath,' Tony said. 'But maybe the Paris sewers are dirtier than these here in Belgrade.' She blew a raspberry.

They waded for a long time, past several ladders leading up, without being tempted to try one. 'Will Svetovar betray us?' Sandrine asked.

'Yes.'

'The bastard.'

'So would you,' Tony reminded her. 'If the Gestapo ever got to you.'

'Where is she?' Wassermann asked the sister.

'In there, Herr Major.' She nodded at the waiting room.

'And Frau von Blintoft?'

'She is still on the table, but I do not think there is any hope.'

Wassermann blew through his teeth, and opened the waiting-room door. Angela's head came up with a start. 'I'm sorry,' he said. 'It's only me.'

'Mother . . . ?'

'Is still in the operating room. So there is still hope,' he lied. He laid his cap on the table and sat beside her. 'How are you?'

'I am alive. Have you got the people who did this?'

26

'Yes.'

'You have?' Her face filled with passion. 'What will you do to them?'

'That depends on your father. What would you like us to do to them?'

'Oh . . .' Several expressions flitted across that so pretty face. 'I hate them. I want them to suffer for what they did. But . . .' She bit her lip.

'As I said on the train, war is a nasty business. You did not agree with me.'

'I agree with you now,' she said fiercely. 'May I see these people?'

Wassermann frowned. 'I do not think your father would approve of that.'

'Why not? Is it possible for them to harm me? Are you going to let them go?'

'No,' he said. 'We are not going to let them go. But they are under interrogation. People under interrogation are not very pretty.'

'I don't want them to be pretty. I want to see them suffer.' Her voice was quiet, but filled with suppressed emotion. She was clearly on the edge of a breakdown.

Wassermann hesitated, wondering how transient this spasm of pure hatred was, and, if he dared to do as she wanted, just what her reaction would be – whether she would be shocked or titillated, whether it would bring them closer together or drive them apart. He so wanted to get close to this girl.

The waiting-room door opened. The sister stood there. 'Your father wishes to see you, Fräulein.'

Angela got up out of the chair and glanced at Wassermann, who had also risen. 'I will wait here,' he said, and took the broad-brimmed hat from her hands.

Angela did not attempt to prevent him; she looked at the hat, as if surprised that she should still be carrying it, then followed the sister along a corridor and up a flight of steps. Nurses gazed at her, anxiously, but she was not really aware of them. She was not really aware of anything, even of herself. Reality had fled the moment her mother had collapsed at her feet. She had not even heard the shot, had been unable for some moments to understand what had happened, only slowly had realized that the rock on which she had built her life had somehow disintegrated.

Angela had been born in 1923 into a Germany that was in chaos, a once proud Reich that had been humbled in war and brought to its knees, reduced to begging for economic survival. But even then, before she had been aware of it, Grandpa's money, so carefully invested before the Great War, had sheltered them from hardship. And by the time she was old enough to observe and understand what was going on about her, Hitler was already in power, and the dark years had become history – at least for those who were prepared to worship the new god. Papa and Mama had always been prepared to do that. Just too young to fight in the Great War, Papa had always been determined to fight in the next – the war everyone knew was coming, the war of revenge – and Mama had been equally determined to take her part and share in the new Reich. They had made sure that their only daughter was properly educated, read only the right books, made friends with only the right people. Angela had never questioned any of their decisions; it had not been her place to do so.

Besides, life had been so excitingly full. Quite apart from school, where she had been taught only of the greatness of Germany's past, there had been the nature holidays, when she and her friends had frolicked through the woods like nymphs, encouraged to go naked by their schoolmistresses to free their bodies as they freed their minds; the athletic meetings and the dances; the long bicycle rides; and above all, the rallies, when they had listened to the Führer and cheered themselves hoarse. As the daughter of an up-and-coming member of both the party and the Wehrmacht, she had even been presented to the great man, and received a squeeze of the hand and a kiss on the cheek, even if he had seemed disturbed by her name. Mama had explained it; Hitler's niece had also been named Angela, and had committed suicide, some said after receiving unwanted attentions from her uncle. 'Silly child,' Mama had said, firmly excluding the Führer from any blame.

Not even the coming of war, which had begun shortly after her fifteenth birthday, had interrupted Angela's life; Hitler did not consider that women had any prominent part to play in the conflict, and as the Blintofts' home had been in the country she had never even been subjected to an Allied bombing raid. There had been a mutually shared spasm of apprehension when Papa had marched off, but in fact he, and the Wehrmacht, had made it all seem so totally easy. As with Caesar of old, the Germans came, they saw, and they conquered, whether faced with the French, British, Belgians, Yugoslavs, Greeks, or now Russians. Meanwhile Papa, always enthusiastically efficient, had moved steadily up the professional ranks, from captain to major to colonel to general, and, since his wound, to governor-general. That wound, not in itself serious, had merely put the lid on his career. Mama had even been pleased, because, as she had said, he would now be out of harm's way. Oh, Mama!

The only downside to Angela's carefree existence had been the increasing implications that women – especially young women – *did* have a part to play in the success and perpetuation of the Reich, not by taking part in the war itself, but by producing lots of healthy babies, preferably male. As Angela had completed her schooling, there had been suggestions from both her teachers and the local party officials that it was time she followed the example of her friends and got married. But this was something she had absolutely no desire to do. For one thing, she had no wish to leave her home and the constantly reassuring presence of Mama, always so gay and so elegant, so comforting and so encouraging. Equally, she had no desire to 'belong' – an utterly distasteful word when used in this context – to any man, much less the arrogantly brash youths who surrounded her whenever possible. The thought of having sex with any of them was repulsive.

Mama, dear Mama, had recognised her feelings, and thus had insisted that she accompany them to Belgrade – just for a month or two, she had said – to get used to being no longer a schoolgirl, and to think about things. Which she did, constantly. The man she wanted to marry needed to be much older, experienced, away from the first flush of youthful exuberance, someone who would always think as much of her as of himself. Someone like Major Wassermann? The very thought made her blush, because he was very obviously taken with her. But he was indeed much older than her – just about twice as old – and she knew absolutely nothing about him, apart from Papa's opinion that he had not had a very successful career. Getting to know him, and perhaps even allowing him to flirt with her, had promised to be quite exciting. But now . . .

The sister knocked, and opened the door. Angela stepped through, and gazed at her father, who sat by the bed. Then she looked past him, at the bed where Mama lay. The sheet was pulled to Magda's neck, and she looked quite peaceful. Only the absence of colour in that normally ruddy complexion jarred. Angela moved forward to stand beside Blintoft, and the general put his arm round her thighs to hug her against him. 'She never regained consciousness,' he said.

Angela continued to stare at the dead features. She felt she should be having screaming hysterics, or at least cry a little. But she felt only anger. 'Major Wassermann has the men who killed her,' she said.

'Good,' Blintoft said. 'That is good.' He stood up. 'I must attend to it.' He turned. 'Sister . . .'

'We will handle it, Herr General.'

'Thank you. I would like . . .' He hesitated.

'Of course, sir. You will see her whenever you are ready.'

'Thank you.' Another hesitation, then he stooped and kissed Magda on the forehead. He straightened, and looked at Angela, waiting for her to do the same. But she did not move forward. 'I will arrange a car to take you . . . to the palace.'

'I do not wish to go there, Papa.'

'You must. That is where we are going to live. Believe me, you will be perfectly safe. I will see to that.'

'I am not afraid of being attacked. I just do not wish to go there without you. What are you going to do now?'

'I am going to find Wassermann, and interview these people he has arrested, to find out if they really are the guilty ones.'

'Major Wassermann is waiting for you downstairs.'

'Oh, right. Well . . .'

'I would like to come with you, Papa.'

'I don't think that would be proper. I don't think you would enjoy it.'

'These people killed Mama, Papa. They are our enemies. They are *my* enemies. I wish to look upon their faces.'

The general looked uncertain. He did not know his daughter very well; military duties had kept him away from home for much of the time throughout the last eight years, and he had been content to leave Angela's upbringing to his wife. He knew his offspring only as a somewhat serious young woman, but certainly a devoted member of the family. Which had now been torn apart. Angela might well need psychiatric counselling to cope with such a traumatic event. He hated the thought of that, because he hated the very idea of psychiatry; a man, or a woman, did their duty and that was that. But the only duty ever required of Angela, up to this moment, had been to love and obey her mother. Thus if she wanted to develop a personal hatred for the guerillas – at least those who had committed so terrible a crime – he did not wish to stand in her way. He was beginning to feel that way himself.

'I am exhausted,' Sandrine said. She certainly looked about to collapse, and Tony caught her round the waist to hold her up; to him she was the most valuable thing in the world. Their relationship was still fresh enough to be exciting, even if they had now been utter intimates for several months, and lovers for most of that time. Before then she had been no more than a most attractive acquaintance, a close friend of Elena Kostic's and also the girlfriend of a German officer who, like Tony, had been an attaché at his embassy in the then neutral Yugoslavia.

Looking back, that world, where four people of different nationalities, backgrounds, religious beliefs and, most important of all, political ideologies, had been able to meet in bars and at parties, and become friends, seemed entirely unreal. The bombing of Belgrade, and the subsequent invasion of Yugoslavia in April, had ended all that, abruptly. Suddenly, at the behest of their various governments, they had become enemies, the requirements of their national identities distorted by their personal involvement with each other. Thus Sandrine had found herself abandoned by Bernhard, who had been ordered away to join his army and had returned as a member of the invading forces. He had commanded her to leave the country, but Sandrine, with her Vichy-France passport and her job as a sub-editor in the Belgrade office of *Paris-Temps*, had preferred to stay where the news was, only to see her office destroyed and her colleagues killed in the bombing. Then she had sought to escape the burning city in the company of her friend Elena and Elena's lover, Captain Tony Davis.

Tony recalled that at that time he had regarded her as a nuisance – very pretty, but still a nuisance. Brought up in French sophistication, concerned at least as much with personal appearance and hygiene as with ethics or politics, holding down what had been a soft and undoubtedly family-obtained position in a romantic city, she had been totally unsuited for the situation in which she had found herself. In addition, her feet had been badly cut and she had had to be carried most of the time, while her very attractiveness had caused problems with the various men who were fleeing with them. From the beginning, even while wishing she wasn't there, Tony had had to admire her courage and determination to cope with a series of misfortunes which were both painful and embarrassing.

But he had also encountered problems which far transcended those of protecting a helpless woman from rape. He had only been in Yugoslavia for six months before the invasion, and while he had become aware that there were many tensions running beneath the surface of Yugoslav life, he had not understood how deep some of these tensions were, nor had he anticipated how violently they would disrupt that surface once the central authority had been destroyed.

Thus when he had sought refuge with the predominantly Serbian guerilla army called the Cetniks – commanded by General Draza Mihailovic, erstwhile chief of the Yugoslav General Staff – he had been welcomed, but to his consternation Elena, as a Croat, was regarded as an enemy. Indeed, it had been all he could do to save her from being shot. They had escaped the Serbs and sought refuge with a Communist enclave in the village of Divitsar, only to be caught up in the savage attack by the terrorist group Ustase. The situation had not been improved by the fact that the Ustase were Croats who were working with the Germans for the establishment of a separate Croatian nation state.

The Divitsar massacre had turned Sandrine from a nuisance into a heroine. Although the Ustase had not included them in the massacre, simply because Elena was a Croat, their commander, Ante Pavelic, had yet intended to hand both Sandrine and Tony, as enemies of the Reich, over to the Germans – and in the meanwhile they were not to be treated with any regard for their comfort or well-being. There Sandrine *had* suffered rape and mistreatment, but she had yet helped them get free, and in doing so proved herself as ruthless a fighter as any man. By then, as a result of their forced intimacy, she had already shared Tony's bivouac. Elena, totally amoral, had not objected, providing there was always something left over for her. Tony, brought up in the manners and morals of middle-class 1930s England, had in the beginning been appalled by the situation in which he had found himself, but which had been irresistible. It had ended in tragedy, with Elena's capture by the Germans and her death during the otherwise successful raid on Uzice. By that time they had linked up with the Partisan army of Colonel Josip Broz, code name Tito, officially subordinate to Mihailovic's overall command, but determinedly acting on his own when the Cetniks dragged their feet.

Tito, indeed, was beginning to have considerable doubts as to how seriously Mihailovic was prosecuting this war, and whether he was entirely to be trusted; his determination to assassinate the new governor-general had been less to harm the Germans – who would, presumably, have other potential governors-general waiting in the wings – than to force Mihailovic to take a more positive stance, as the Germans were certain to react violently.

But he had never had the slightest doubt about the commitment of at least two of his people. Tony had been wounded in the attack on Uzice, and had been offered an escape route by both Tito and the British in Alexandria. He had declined. This had become *his* war, and he wanted to see it out. Alexandria had not demurred. They had just been beginning to understand that guerilla activities against the Germans in Yugoslavia could be of considerable value to the Allied cause, and having a 'built-in' liaison officer with the Partisans was important. What they did not seem able to understand as yet was that there was a growing divergence between the Partisans and the Cetniks, a divergence exemplified by their appearance – the Cetniks wore their hair long and sported beards, while Tito's people cut their hair short and were clean-shaven, a situation which reminded Tony of the Roundheads and Cavaliers from English history. Unaware of this divergence, the British continued to communicate with, and send such supplies of arms and ammunition as were available to, Mihailovic, as the senior officer on the ground. So far that had merely been an irritant to Tito. What would happen now, as this particular disaster – the recent assassination attempt – had not been authorised by Mihailovic, was a matter for some consideration.

Sandrine's commitment had been a little more unexpected. Although he knew they had fallen in love with each other, he had still been as surprised as gratified when she too had chosen to stay – despite being offered a way out as well – not necessarily to fight with the Partisans, but to be with her man. Over the several months since Uzice they had shared more and more, of their minds as well as their bodies. And she had always wanted to be with him when he was called into action, even if he suspected this was at least partly caused by her desire to avenge Elena – the two women had been very close. But for all the brutality to which she had been exposed since fleeing Belgrade she remained a sensitive and, wherever possible, cultured woman. His woman.

She leaned against him, gasping, while the water and the rats flowed by; the rats were almost old friends by now. 'How long have we been down here?'

Tony studied the luminous dial of his watch; using the flashlight was risky, and, in any event, he did not doubt that the water had got to the batteries by now. 'Just gone six. Say four hours, all but.'

'Four hours! I am so hungry. And thirsty. And cold. How much longer?'

'It can't be long now. Anyway, we don't really want to get to the river until dark. That won't be before seven.'

'My fingers are all crinkly.'

'They'll recover. Come along – we must keep moving.'

Sandrine resumed wading. 'Will we ever get rid of this smell?'

'Yes.'

She waded on for several minutes, then asked over her shoulder, 'Do you think that woman died?'

'She was hit in the chest by a high-velocity bullet. If she survived it was a miracle.'

'Who was she, do you know?'

'Something to do with the general. Either his wife or his daughter.'

'How do you feel about that?'

'Like shit.'

'They killed Elena. And all those women and children in Divitsar.'

'I know,' Tony said. He supposed the Divitsar massacre, carried out by the Ustase in the summer, was the worst experience of his life; a hundred people, men, women and children, had been mown down by sub-machine guns for no other reason than that they were Communists. 'But we don't know if that woman had ever committed any crime.'

'She was a Nazi,' Sandrine said.

'We don't even know that for certain.'

'She was married to a Nazi.'

'Are you going to marry me, when the war is over?'

'Probably. If you ask me nicely.'

'Will you then automatically become English?'

'Don't you like me being French?'

'I adore you being French. But that's the point. Your marrying me will not automatically make you English any more than that woman marrying Blintoft would automatically have made her a Nazi.'

Sandrine blew a raspberry. 'Are you sure you were not a lawyer before the war started? Anyway, we do not know it was his wife who got hit.'

'It would be even worse if it was his daughter. She can't be very old.'

'But I will bet you what you like that *she* is a Nazi . . . . What's that?'

'Daylight. We're there. Let me go first.'

Sandrine pressed herself against the wall, and he wriggled past her. The light was still some distance away, but he unslung his tommy-gun. The weapon had been immersed so often he could only hope it was still serviceable. He looked back at Sandrine, now almost visible. She also was unslinging her gun. He could not stop himself from grinning.

'What's so funny?'

'You have lost your cap, and you look like . . . a drowned rat.'

'Snap. Let's get on with it.'

He waded towards the light, which every moment grew brighter.

'There's a grating,' Sandrine said.

'There would be.'

'Then how do we get out?'

'It's not actually a grating. Just bars. We squeeze through.'

Sandrine studied the bars as they came closer. 'The bars are horizontal.'

'That'll make it easier.'

'My tits are too big. I'll never get them through.'

'How big is your bust?' He found it odd that he had never discovered that before; however generally small she might be, she certainly had a magnificent figure.

'When last I measured, it was thirty-seven inches.'

'Hips?'

'Oh . . . thirty-five.'

'Tremendous. I always knew I was on to a good thing. My chest is forty-two, uninflated. So if I can get through, so can you.'

'I am always inflated,' she pointed out.

They reached the bars, and peered through. Several feet below them, the river surged by. On the far bank there were houses. 'Not too close,' Tony told her. 'Someone might see you. We have to wait till it's dark.'

'Another hour,' she sighed, and leaned against him.

Wassermann and the Blintofts drove to the military head-quarters in the governor-general's car. Wassermann was conducting this investigation himself, excluding both the local police and the Gestapo, at least for the time being, although he was using the Gestapo offices at the headquarters building, since it was the most suitable place both to hold and to interrogate prisoners.

It was now late afternoon, and several hours since the shooting, but the streets were still filled with agitated people gathered in groups amidst the many buildings reduced to rubble by the April bombing, busily gossiping about the events of the day, wondering what was going to happen next, and glancing nervously at the German soldiers, who were present in some numbers.

'There is a dusk-to-dawn curfew,' Wassermann explained. 'These people will soon be gone.'

He sat on the jump seat facing Blintoft and Angela, who were together in the rear of the car. He remained uncertain how to handle the situation, the like of which he had not encountered before at this level. Obviously, neither had the Blintofts, but he found the way they had both withdrawn into themselves disconcerting. He had no doubt that there was an immense surge of angry despair lurking behind those two fixed expressions; he had no objection to that, but he would have liked to know when the explosion was likely to happen, and what form it was likely to take. And whether or not what they were about to see would trigger it.

The car turned through the arched gateway and stopped in the yard. Armed guards stood to attention, and a lieutenant hurried forward to open the door. Wassermann got out first, waited for Angela and the general to emerge. The lieutenant saluted, but looked at the girl in a mixture of surprise and alarm.

'We wish to see the prisoners,' Wassermann said.

'Ah, yes, Herr Major. If you will allow me one minute—'

'We wish to see them, as they are, now,' Wassermann said.

The lieutenant licked his lips, and looked at the general. 'Now,' Blintoft confirmed.

'Now, Herr General.' The lieutenant clicked his heels, gave Angela another anxious glance, and gestured at the door, which was opened by one of the sentries. Wassermann led the way inside, the lieutenant bringing up the rear. They walked along a wide corridor, past several open doorways, each of which became filled with people standing to attention, anxious to gain a first glimpse of their new commander-in-chief. Although everyone in the building knew what had happened, none of them had ever seen either General von Blintoft or his daughter before.

Wassermann led them along the corridor to the end, where there was a staircase going both up and down. From below them, a radio played music, loudly; it sounded something like a medley from Wagner. 'Sometimes the people we have down here make a good deal of noise,' Wassermann explained. 'The music helps drown it out. Mind the step.'

He was looking at Angela, waiting for her to say 'Enough!', but her expression remained unchanging, save for a slight flaring of the nostrils at the variety of odours, dominated by disinfectant, that came up the stairwell. Wassermann led them down the stairs and into a small lobby, off which, on the right, a corridor emerged. On the left there was a room in which there were a dozen backless benches, arranged in two rows and facing a desk, at which there sat a sergeant. In front of him, sitting on the benches, backs absolutely straight, were several people.

At the sight of the officers, the sergeant stood up, heels clicking as he gave the Nazi salute. 'Up,' he shouted. 'Up!' The people in front of him hastily tried to obey, but it was easy to see that they were stiff from sitting down, and they stumbled as they rose. One of them, a rather plump teenage girl, fell over the bench in front of her, and had to grasp it to push herself up. 'Swine!' the sergeant shouted, picking up a rubber truncheon from his desk, and striding forward. But then he checked, looking at Wassermann. Wassermann nodded, and the sergeant swung his club, catching the girl a blow across the thigh. She uttered a scream, and instinctively clutched at the injury, only to receive another blow, this time across the fingers, which had her wringing her hands in pain while tears rolled down her cheeks.

'We call this the tram,' Wassermann explained, speaking loudly to make himself heard above the blaring radio, which was situated on a table against the wall. 'This is where these people wait for interrogation. They are required to sit to attention, and are not permitted to speak. Any transgression is severely punished.'

I can see that, Angela thought. She felt degraded that human beings should be so humiliated, especially as she could see that at least one of the men had wet his pants. On the other hand . . . 'Are any of these people involved in the shooting?'

Wassermann glanced at her, surprised by the calmness of her voice. 'Perhaps not directly, Fräulein. But two of them' – he pointed at the girl who had fallen over and the boy standing beside her – 'are the children of the people from whose house the shot was fired.'

'Then why are they not being interrogated?' Blintoft asked.

'They will be, Herr General. When we have finished with the parents. But keeping them here for a few hours is in itself a form of interrogation. When they are finally called upon to answer questions, they are often so terrified and uncomfortable, and hungry and thirsty – we do not feed them in the tram, you see, nor are they allowed to drink – that they tell us anything we wish to know without persuasion. But in fact, we are doing quite well without their assistance . . . Ah, Captain Ulrich.'

The captain, short and inclined to plumpness, had approached from the corridor. Now he stood to attention. 'Heil Hitler!' He had been at the station, and looked more surprised than anyone at the sight of Angela in these surroundings.

'The general wishes to see the prisoners, Ulrich,' Wassermann said.

Ulrich gulped. 'To see . . .' He looked at his superior for confirmation.

'All of them,' Wassermann said.

'Yes, Herr Major.' He gave Angela another nervous glance, then led the way along the corridor, past a succession of iron doors that were closed and locked. But each door had a peephole. Ulrich paused before the third door. 'This is the man Brolic,' he explained. 'The shot was fired from the attic window of his house. It was their plan to say that he and his wife and family were attacked and tied up by the Partisans, but we proved that to be false.'

'I proved it,' Wassermann said with some pride.

'Yes, indeed, Herr Major,' Ulrich agreed unenthusiastically. 'But also through the actions of the other son.'

'Ah. You have arrested him?'

'Not yet, Herr General. And that is the point. He worked in his father's store, but at some time today he just walked out and disappeared. We have not yet found him. But the mere fact that he disappeared proves he knew what was going on.'

'And the father has confessed?' Blintoft asked. He was used to concentrating on essentials.

'Well, no, Herr General. He is tougher than he looks. But his wife has confessed.'

'Let me see them.'

'Of course, Herr General.'

Ulrich stood to one side and raised the flap on the peephole. Blintoft stooped to look through it for several seconds. Then he straightened, and took a handkerchief from his pocket to wipe his brow. 'Is he alive?'

'Oh, yes, Herr General.'

'He is not moving.'

'He is in a state of shock, Herr General. Prisoners often enter such a condition after interrogation, but it soon passes off. Would you like me to wake him up?'

'No. You said his wife has confessed?'

'Only a few minutes ago.'

'Let me see her.'

'Ah . . .' Ulrich looked at Wassermann.

'I wish to see this man,' Angela said.

Ulrich looked positively frightened. 'I do not think—'

'I would like to, Papa,' Angela said.

'Well, it is not a pretty sight.'

'I would like to.'

Blintoft hesitated a last time, then stepped away from the door, and Angela took his place. Wassermann moved forward to stand immediately behind her, as if to catch her if she were to faint.

Angela looked through the peephole. There was no furniture in the cell, save for a single naked electric bulb, which glowed brightly. Brolic was slumped against the far wall, half-turned away from the door. He was naked, and his body was a mass of bruises and cuts, some of them oozing blood. Clearly he was quite unaware that people were looking at him, although she wondered if he would respond even were they to enter the room. Oddly, she felt no emotion, perhaps because he was remote. If he had allowed his house to be used by Mama's assassins, he deserved to be beaten. But she no longer hated him. He was not even pitiable. He had become a thing, hardly recognisable as a human being. She had never seen a naked man before, and she did not feel she had looked at one now.

She stepped back, and found herself against Wassermann, who held her arm. 'Are you all right, Fräulein?'

'I am all right.'

'Show me the woman,' Blintoft said.

Ulrich attempted a protest. 'The Fräulein . . .'

'She wishes to see.' Blintoft's voice was suddenly harsh, and it occurred to Wassermann that the general was upset that his daughter had shown much less emotion at the sight of the beaten man than himself.

'Yes, Herr General.' Ulrich led them past three more doors, then paused before one that had no peephole. 'This is the punishment cell,' he explained.

'Open it.'

Ulrich licked his lips, then opened the door; it had not been locked. In the cell there were two women. The first one stood to attention when she saw who the visitors were. She wore the usual uniform of white shirt and black skirt, but had discarded her tie and unbuttoned the neck of her shirt. She was sweating heavily. She was allowed no more than a glance, as their attention was taken by the other woman, naked and suspended by her wrists from the ceiling. In early middle age, she was plump, with black hair which lay on her shoulders. From her shoulders to her thighs she was a mass of bloody weals where she had been flogged; the woman standing beside her still held the whip, its single thong also bloody.

Wassermann glanced at his two guests. Now he was more worried about the general's reactions than the girl's; the only sign of emotion revealed by Angela was again the flaring of her nostrils as she breathed. 'Anything new?' Wassermann asked.

'No, Herr Major. She keeps fainting.' The woman's tone was contemptuous.

Wouldn't you, Angela wondered, if you were humiliated by being stripped and then had your back torn to pieces? She could not imagine what it might feel like to be in that position . . . and to know that after all this suffering there would be only the hangman's noose. In public.

'What has she told you?' Blintoft asked, his voice heavy with saliva.

'She has confessed her family's part in the business. That they agreed to be tied up while the gunmen used their house.'

'But we already know that,' Blintoft complained. 'Can she identify these people?'

'She says they were definitely Partisans – that is, members of Tito's organisation. There were three men and a woman. Two of the men were Yugoslavs. As for the other two, the man was English and the woman was French.'

'You think the man was Davis?' Blintoft asked Wassermann.

'The presence of the Frenchwoman makes me certain of it, Herr General. They always work together.'

'Which of them fired the shot that killed my wife?'

'She does not know.'

'Then are we any further ahead?'

'Oh, indeed, Herr General. This woman is merely supportive evidence. We have one of the Partisans.'

'Where?' The general looked somewhat apprehensive.

'He is in my office, Herr General,' Ulrich said. 'Just along here.'

'Show me.'

'Yes, sir. Ah . . . I do not think it would be suitable for the young lady to accompany us.'

Angela had not stopped staring at the suspended woman. She was experiencing a strange sequence of feelings, the strongest being an intense desire to use the whip herself, to watch the woman writhe in pain and cry out in agony. But to do that would be to shock Papa, and the poor old dear had had sufficient shocks for one day already. Now she turned sharply. 'Why not?'

'Because . . . well . . .' Ulrich flushed and looked at his superior.

'The captain is afraid that you will be shocked, Fräulein,' Wassermann explained. 'This bandit is awaiting interrogation. He has already been prepared for it. And he is a young and, shall I say, virile man.'

'I will not be shocked,' Angela said.

No, Wassermann thought, I don't believe you will be shocked, my pretty little sadist. He felt a sudden sense of excitement. This girl might be everything he had wanted throughout his life. And at this moment he had a feeling that he was what she wanted as well. Him, and his powers.

'I wish to speak with this man,' Blintoft said.

'Of course, Herr General. Ulrich!'

Ulrich clicked his heels, and escorted the party to a large room at the end of the corridor. Here there were a desk, and a couple of chairs, and, in the very centre of the room, a peculiar piece of furniture, half stool and half chair, set very low to the floor and with a back. Seated on this chair was Svetovar Kostic. As with the other prisoners, he was naked, and because of the awkward nature of the stool he was in a very uncomfortable position. His ankles were secured to iron rings in the floor, set wide apart, so that his knees were actually on a level with his face. His wrists were also secured, to bolts set behind the back of the chair, so that his arms were pulled behind his shoulders, leaving him quite helpless. Two men waited in the room, one standing to either side of the prisoner, but as yet the man did not appear to have been harmed in any way, save for a bruise on his cheek and another on his chest. He breathed slowly and evenly, but caught his breath as he identified the general's uniform – and again as he saw Angela.

She was again aware of a surge of conflicting emotions. Svetovar was quite a handsome man, and he was the first man she had ever seen not only naked – she still discounted Brolic – but so totally displayed . . . and immediately reacting to her presence. And he was about to be destroyed. She did not doubt that.

'I'm afraid he stinks,' Wassermann said apologetically. 'We extracted him from the sewer. We did put him under a shower to get the worst off, but, well . . .'

Blintoft stood in front of the prisoner. 'You shot my wife,' he said in Serbo-Croat.

'No,' Svetovar said. 'No. I swear it. It was . . .' He bit his lip.

'Yes?'

'It was one of the others. I do not know which one. I was guarding the door.'

'You are lying.'

'I swear it,' Svetovar said again.

'What was your business there?'

'I was support only,' Svetovar said.

'How can we know if he is telling the truth?' Blintoft asked.

'It is very simple,' Wassermann said. 'Ulrich.'

Ulrich stood to attention. 'I think the Fräulein should withdraw.'

'Well . . .' Wassermann looked at Angela.

Who continued to stare at the man. 'I will stay.'

Wassermann looked at Blintoft.

'Oh, let her stay. This man is as guilty of her mother's death as if he pulled the trigger himself.'

'You heard the general, Ulrich. Proceed.'

'I must register a protest, Herr Major. The young lady should not be present.'

'Your protest will be noted. Now proceed. That is an order.'

Ulrich hesitated a last time, then nodded to the waiting men. One turned to the desk and reached for a square box, from which there protruded two wires. At the end of each wire there was an alligator clip. Also protruding from the box was a handle, such as that used to make a telephone call. The soldier placed the box on the floor directly in front of Svetovar, who gazed at it with wide eyes. The other soldier now grasped his knees and pulled his legs further apart, while his comrade knelt and forced one of the alligator clips into Svetovar's anus. No lubricant was used, and Svetovar gasped with discomfort. He found himself staring at Angela, who stared back. The second clip was opened and attached to Svetovar's penis, which was rising as he gazed at the fascinated girl. Now he again gasped with discomfort as the small teeth ate into his flesh, but also with fear of the coming moments. 'Listen,' he panted. 'It was the Englishman who fired the shot. The Englishman, Davis!'

The kneeling man looked at Ulrich, who looked at Wassermann. Wassermann nodded. The man cranked the handle on the box. For a moment nothing happened, then Svetovar uttered a tremendous shriek, and his body arched away from the seat – held as it was by wrist and ankle it *could* only arch, so much so that it almost appeared as if his spine had to break. But the crank was no longer turning, and Svetovar fell back to the seat with a dull thud and lay there, his body even more disorganised, while his chest rose and fell in great pants. 'One needs to be careful,' Wassermann explained, speaking principally to Angela. 'We can generate a considerable voltage, and to apply too great a charge at one time can cause death. But, properly used, it does have the property of bringing out the truth, and it leaves no discernible mark.'

Angela continued to stare at the man, lips slightly parted.

'Will he now tell us the truth?' Blintoft asked. 'I want to know exactly what happened. Why my wife was killed.'

'You heard the general, Kostic,' Wassermann said. 'Tell us exactly what happened.'

'Yes,' Svetovar panted. 'I will tell you. We were sent to assassinate the general.'

'Sent by whom?' Blintoft asked. 'General Mihailovic?'

'No,' Svetovar said. 'We were sent by General Tito.'

Blintoft and Wassermann exchanged glances, Wassermann's expression conveying satisfaction that what he had told the general on the train was being proved correct. 'Go on,' Wassermann said. 'How many of you were there?'

'We were a team of four.'

'Names.'

'Davis, Fouquet, Maric, and me.'

'Fouquet was the woman, eh?'

'Yes. She is a devil.'

'And the Brolics were expecting you?'

'It had all been arranged, by Maric.'

'What happened upstairs?'

'Davis had the rifle. He is a first-class shot. He was waiting for the general to stand on the platform steps. I was at his shoulder. When the lady stepped in front of the general, I tried to catch his arm. I told him he could not shoot because he would hit the woman. But Fouquet said, "Shoot, shoot, she is only a German." So Davis shot.'

Wassermann looked at the general, who was breathing deeply. 'Where are these people now? Still in the sewers?'

'We have found nothing, Herr Major,' Ulrich said. 'Someone was throwing grenades at us, so we opened fire, but he, or she, seems to have escaped.'

'That was Maric,' Svetovar said. 'He volunteered to hold you up with grenades. He said he knew another way out.'

'But did he not tell you to use the fifth exit from the Brolic cellar?'

'Yes. He told us that.'

'Did he not know that we had already sealed that exit some time ago? Or do you think he betrayed you?'

'I do not know,' Svetovar said. 'I do not know.'

'So where are the other two? Davis and Fouquet?'

'I do not know.'

'There is no way that they can have got out, Herr Major,' Ulrich said. 'We have sealed every exit.'

'What about the river?'

'There is a grill . . .'

'Do you think that will stop two desperate criminals?'

Ulrich gulped.

'I want them,' Blintoft said. 'I want them both. I want them *there*.' He pointed at Svetovar.

'You will have them,' Wassermann said. 'Captain Ulrich, I want those sewers scoured until those three assassins, or their bodies, are found. I also want the river exit sealed.'

'If they can get through the grill, they will have done so by now,' Ulrich said, looking at his watch. 'It is dark.'

'You had better hope they have not,' Wassermann said.

'Keep me informed,' Blintoft said. 'When they are caught, I wish to see them. Come, Angela.'

Angela looked at Svetovar a last time, then followed her father from the room. She looked as composed as ever, but Wassermann noticed that her fingers were twitching. He would have followed them, but Ulrich said, 'A word, please, Herr Major.' Wassermann raised his eyebrows, but waited. Ulrich stood close to him and spoke in a low voice. 'I have to inform you, sir, that everything the man Kostic has said is a lie.'

'What do you mean?'

'Simply that the rifle that fired the fatal shot was discarded by the terrorists, and recovered by us. I immediately had it tested for fingerprints. There were two sets, but the upper ones about the trigger guard and butt were clearly from the person who handled it last. I also had Kostic's prints taken, and they are an exact match. There can be no doubt that Kostic fired the shot. So, as he has lied about that, there must be serious doubts about everything else he said.'

'That does not mean that Davis and Fouquet are any less guilty,' Wassermann said. 'They were there. Anyone who was there is equally guilty.'

'Agreed. But do you not think that the general would like to know the truth of the matter?'

'No,' Wassermann said. 'Whether he would like to or not, I do not think it would be a good idea, Ulrich. This general is a hard man with a soft centre. Right now he is filled with anger, a desire for vengeance on the person who killed his wife. But it will not last. And if we present him with the actual murderer, he will no doubt feel a good deal of satisfaction at watching him hang, but he will also consider the matter – the murder of his wife – to be closed. Then he may well revert to some very peculiar ideas he has about dealing with these terrorists. But if we allow him to continue to think that the murderers are still at large, I believe he will give us what we want: the right to deal with these thugs as we choose. That is more important than the truth.'

'But . . . when we arrest Davis and Fouquet, or find their bodies, won't the general again feel that the matter is closed?'

'But you are not going to find them, are you, Ulrich? They have now been at large for more than six hours. They will surely have got out by now. If they have not, you see to it that they do.'

Ulrich gulped. 'You mean to let them go? Davis and Fouquet? When we have been trying to catch them for the past two months?'

'As I said, we are after bigger game. The right to destroy all the Partisans, our way. The general will give us that right, in order to catch his wife's killer.'

'But . . . suppose they are dead? When we find their bodies—'

'You are not going to find their bodies, Ulrich. Or if you do, you are going to bury them where only you will know where they can be found, just in case we need them at some future date. But as I have said, it would be best if they were to escape, at least for the time being. We can always catch up with them later.'

'I have to say that I do not like it, Herr Major.'

'But you will do your duty, which is less to the general than to the Wehrmacht.'

Ulrich clicked his heels. 'Yes, Herr Major. But what about that carrion?' He jerked his head over his shoulder.

'Lock him up for the time being. He may be useful. But make sure he is kept incommunicado. And endeavour not to ill-treat him more than necessary; we will need him to give evidence at the trial.' He clapped his subordinate on the shoulder. 'This will be our secret, Ulrich. And when we have cleaned up these Partisans, we will both be promoted. Remember that.'

Three

Decision

'Time,' Tony said. It was now quite dark beyond the grating.

'I don't think I can,' Sandrine said. 'I am frozen stiff. Anyway, those bars—'

'Have to be negotiated. So get colder yet. Strip.'

'Here?'

'I should have thought you'd be happy to get out of that gear.'

'I will be. But we can't get back to the mountains with nothing on.'

'We won't. Hang your clothes on the bars, and we'll collect them when we're through.' During the dying moments of daylight he had ascertained that there was a ledge beneath the flowing water, separating them from the river, which was at a level several feet beneath the grating. 'Let's get started.' He took off his tommy-gun and belt of grenades, unstrapped his revolver, and hung them on the bars, then did the same with his stinking clothes. Sandrine watched him for several seconds, then followed his example.

'My teeth are chattering.'

'And you have goose pimples.'

'So have you.'

'Mine aren't as big as yours. Now . . .' He peered into the turgid water rushing past their knees, as if looking for fishes, then suddenly thrust his hand down. 'Gotcha!'

'What in the name of God . . . ?'

'This will make you slippery,' he explained.

'You are not going to rub that stuff on me?'

'Only on your shoulders, breasts and hips,' he explained.

'That is obscene.'

'Not as obscene as being captured by the Gestapo. You can close your eyes.' She did so. 'Now me.'

'You will have to do it. I could not possibly touch it.'

'One day we'll laugh at this.' He coated himself in turn, and then passed a leg and an arm through the grating, straddling the bar he had chosen to negotiate.

'Be careful,' Sandrine said. 'That is a piece of you that I value highly.'

'Still?' Tony asked, lifting his genitals to the outside of the bar. 'Now for the difficult bit.' He laid his chest and his cheek on the bar, and began easing himself through. The iron closed on his flesh, and for a moment he thought he wasn't going to make it. He certainly knew he was tearing his flesh, on both chest and back. But then he was through in a rush, having to grab the bars to stop himself from tumbling off the ledge and into the river. 'Come on.'

'Shit,' she muttered.

'Absolutely.'

She thrust her right leg and arm through the bars as he had done, then lowered her body to lie on the steel, again following his example.

'Just remember that there are several bits of you that I also value highly,' he told her. Actually, it was easier for her than for him, because she could get her breasts through one at a time, wriggling her body to and fro, until she was standing beside him.

'Ooof,' she said. They dressed themselves while the water flowed about their ankles, holding on to each other in turn to put on their boots, Sandrine's nose wrinkling with distaste as she inserted her legs into her sodden knickers and pulled them up past her thighs. 'Don't you think we have been lucky?' she asked, slinging her weapon. 'It was very careless of them not to have blocked that exit right away.'

'Very,' Tony agreed. 'But I don't think now is the time for us to look gift horses in the mouth.'

'I am very sorry to have to tell you, Herr General,' Wassermann said, 'that the terrorists appear to have escaped.'

It was eight o'clock in the morning, and the general, still wearing a dressing gown, was seated before his breakfast in an upstairs room of the royal palace, called the Stari Dvor, or Old Palace, to differentiate it from the Beli Dvor, or White Palace, which stood in the same large estate situated in Belgrade's once well-to-do suburb of Dedinje, south of the rivers. The Stari Dvor was a large three-storeyed building, although the top floor was simply attics; the lower floors were dominated by huge, arched windows looking out over ornamental gardens. These had been damaged by the bombing, but, as Wassermann had promised, had largely been restored, although the work was still going on. On the other side of the table, also wearing a dressing gown, was Angela; Wassermann thought he had never seen a more attractive sight.

'How did this happen?' Blintoft asked.

'Carelessness. It appears they got through the bars leading from the sewers to the river. Why this was not sealed the moment they were known to be down there is a mystery. Ulrich says it was assumed that they had been killed by the grenades thrown by his people. But there is no evidence of this.'

'That is very unsatisfactory,' the general said. 'To think that my wife's killers are out there, laughing at us . . .'

'We will get them, Herr General. With your permission.'

Blintoft gazed at him for several seconds, then glanced at Angela, whose face was, as usual, impassive. 'It is something to be considered,' he said.

'With respect, Herr General,' Wassermann said. 'We must act immediately. Or they will indeed be laughing at us.'

'The first thing I need to do,' Blintoft said, 'is bury my wife. We will leave tomorrow morning. I will be gone three days, Wassermann. Only three days. And while I am in Berlin I will discuss the matter with our superiors. When I return we will know how to deal with these people.'

'And in the meantime?'

'In the meantime, Herr Major, you will hold the fort and carry on as usual.'

Wassermann clicked his heels. 'Will you come to the office this morning, sir?'

'Yes, I will. Wait here, and I will dress and come with you.' He got up, went to the door, and there checked. 'This man Ulrich, he does not seem to be very competent.'

'He is actually very good at his job. I think he, like all of us' – Wassermann looked at Angela – 'was so shocked by what had happened that he temporarily lost control of the situation. I have, of course, issued him a severe reprimand, but I do not think the matter should be taken any further. It would be bad for morale.'

'Hm,' Blintoft commented. 'Well, you are the man on the ground, so I will bow to your judgement in this instance. But there must be no more losses of control. Pour the major a cup of coffee, Geli. I will not be long.' He closed the door behind himself.

'Would you like a cup of coffee, Herr Major?' Angela asked.

'Thank you. That would be very nice.'

'Then do sit down.'

Wassermann laid his cap on the table, sat opposite her, and watched her pouring the coffee, the dressing gown for a moment drawing tight across her breast. When she suddenly turned towards him, holding out the cup, he flushed. 'How do you feel today?' he asked.

'I wish to cry,' Angela said. 'But I cannot. I feel . . . confused, I suppose. I'm not sure it's all happening.'

She was totally adrift, Wassermann realized, just waiting to be picked up. *Eager* to be picked up. If he allowed this opportunity to slip away from him he would never forgive himself. 'I wish it wasn't happening,' he said. 'Hadn't happened. Except . . .'

'Yes?'

'Well, despite everything, I am bound to say that meeting you has been one of the great moments of my life.'

'Thank you. That was very sweet of you.' Still there was no evidence of any response on the level he sought. Perhaps she was incapable of responding at this time.

'Will you be returning to Germany with your father tomorrow?'

'Of course. Oh, I shall come back with him as well.' She gave a half-smile. 'To look after him on the domestic front. He is not very domesticated.'

Wassermann had given a sigh of relief. Now he drew a deep breath. 'I am so happy that you are coming back.'

She gave him one of her disconcerting glances, so penetrating and yet so difficult to determine what might lie behind it. 'What did you feel yesterday when you were torturing that man?'

Wassermann reflected that her glances could never be as disconcerting as her sudden, probing, intimate questions. 'Ah . . . we were interrogating him,' he corrected. 'As for feeling, it is not my business to feel anything. He was an enemy of the Reich who was attempting to conceal information.'

'I should have felt pity,' Angela said, half to herself. 'But I did not.'

'Nobody could have expected you to.'

'I felt . . .' Her tongue emerged and circled her lips. 'What do you think *he* felt?'

'I would suppose, in the first instance, fear more than anything else.'

'I meant . . .' Another quick circle of her lips. 'When . . . well . . .'

Wassermann realized that what was bothering her was that she had been sexually stimulated by the sight of the naked man. This made him stimulated as well. 'Well,' he said, 'that is a very tender part of a man's body. I would say when the current passed through – and to get from his anus to his penis it had to pass through his intestines

54

and bladder as well – he felt extreme pain. His reaction indicated this.'

'But it was, well . . .' She bit her lip. 'Moving.'

'Had you never seen one before?'

'Not really. Never, well, to look at.'

'Yes, well, when it is handled, or aroused, it hardens. If it did not, it would not be able to perform its prime duty, that of entering the female. You do know about that?'

They gazed at each other. How incredible, she thought, that I should be having such a conversation with a man I only met yesterday, and not be totally embarrassed. But because of yesterday, she seemed to have known him all her life. 'I know about it, yes.'

'Well, you see, when it is hard, although it is then at its most sensitive sexually, it is also, oddly, at its least sensitive to pain, or at least discomfort. It is when the erection has diminished, either by ejaculation or because the erotic impulse has passed, that any pain inflicted becomes apparent. Of course, this does not apply in the case of an electric shock, but I would say that he did not feel the teeth of the clips so badly before the shock.' He smiled. 'He is more likely to be feeling them now.'

'Where is he now?'

'In a cell.'

'Will you . . . interrogate him again?'

'Perhaps. Would you like to watch it again?'

She shot him a glance and then drank some coffee. He realized she would, and his heartbeat quickened. But she continued to probe. 'Have you ever . . . ?'

'I have never been tortured, Angela. I am an officer in the Wehrmacht.'

'I meant, have you ever . . . Suppose it had been a woman? Suppose it had been the woman Fouquet? How would you . . . ?' She gazed at him with her mouth open.

'How I wish it could have been the woman Fouquet.' He gave a quick smile to conceal his very real desire to have Sandrine Fouquet naked and at his mercy; he had seen a

55

photograph of the Frenchwoman. 'She is a far deadlier enemy than Kostic.'

'But . . . how would you . . .' She licked her lips.

'In exactly the same way. Women are not so very different from men, you know.' He got up, came round the table, and sat beside her. 'When you come back . . .' He rested his hand on hers, and was concerned when she gave a little shudder. 'Do I frighten you?'

'No. It's just that I feel so terrible,' she said.

'Tell me.'

'My mother is lying dead. And I cannot cry. All I can think about is that man. And . . .' Another bite of the lip.

And of a woman suffering in the same way, Wassermann realized. Perhaps even yourself, my gorgeous little monster. Gently he squeezed her hand. 'You have been very brave. But you will cry. And then, when you have expelled your grief, you will begin to live again. I would very much like to be able to help you to do that.' She gave a little sigh, and to his surprise but utter delight her head sank sideways to rest on his shoulder. 'And together,' he said, 'we shall avenge your mother. Would you like that?'

'Yes,' she said. 'I should like that.'

'It has been an unfortunate business,' Tito said. He sat behind his desk in his office in the town of Uzice, and was not his usual smiling self.

Occupying Uzice, which was not all that far from Belgrade, had been the Partisans' greatest coup thus far. They had attacked it in the summer, and learned of its weaknesses – and its attractions: Uzice contained a bank full of money and a large printing press. Tito might not ram Communism down the throat of any of his followers, but he had immediately commissioned a history of the movement, so that his people might understand the benefits of such a regime. Then they had returned a month later, destroyed the German garrison, and taken over the town.

It had been a frustrating triumph, and not only because it

had failed to bring the main German forces in Yugoslavia into the open. It had also encouraged many people to suppose that even greater triumphs, perhaps even the recapture of Belgrade itself, might be just around the corner. That, of course, had never been a possibility. The Partisans had consumed a major part of their supplies of ammunition in getting this far, and they entirely lacked the necessary transport facilities to mount a major offensive. Repeated appeals to the Cetniks for support – if only logistically – had brought nothing; Mihailovic had indeed condemned the occupation of Uzice as an unnecessary provocation to the Germans. Attempts to appeal over the general's head to the British for aid to be dropped directly to the Partisans had also met with no response. In fact, very little aid was even being dropped to the Cetniks, but the mere fact that it was indicated, annoyingly, that the British continued to regard Mihailovic as the proper leader of the Yugoslav resistance. Hence the attempt to provoke the Germans still further by assassinating the new governor-general, along with Tito's decision to give Tony the task, was at least partly influenced by his desire to involve the British more closely; by having one of their officers named as the assassin, the British might be persuaded to take the Partisans more seriously.

Now Tito surveyed the two people standing before him. He was a big, heavy-set man, forcefully handsome. That he possessed both a dynamic brain and considerable charisma was immediately apparent. That he was already considering what might happen next was also obvious.

'I never thought that Svetovar was reliable,' Sandrine remarked.

Since they had regained the Partisan headquarters, after three days of hiding in bushes and crawling by night, fed by sympathetic villagers, both she and Tony had had a hot bath and changed their clothing. Sandrine's hair had been restored to its normal cleanliness, and lay on her shoulders like a golden mat, but she did not think she would ever get the stink of the sewage out of her system.

'And it appears you were right,' Tito agreed. 'You say he was taken. Alive?'

'We heard no shots at that time,' Tony said.

'Do you think he is capable of standing up to torture?'

'No,' Sandrine said.

Tito looked at Tony. 'I would say Sandrine is right,' Tony said. 'But he can't tell them much that they don't know already. Except the involvement of the Brolics. I feel very sorry about that.'

'Yes,' Tito said. 'It may interest you to know that one of our patrols brought in a Brolic yesterday. The eldest son. He was apparently at his father's dry goods store when the shooting took place, and made himself scarce. Very wisely, as it turned out; apparently the Germans were there within the hour, seeking to arrest him.'

'Does he know anything of his family?'

'Only that they were arrested. So we must suppose the worst. That is unfortunate, but there is nothing we can do about it. What we need to consider is what the Germans will do now. First of all, we must assume that Svetovar has identified Maric and yourselves as the other members of the squad.'

'Is there news of Maric?'

Tito shook his head. 'We must assume the worst there, also. What I find odd is that while the Germans reported on the radio the next day that the wife of the governor-general had been shot and killed, they have not yet named anyone, or even any group, as being considered responsible. But if Svetovar has confessed, they must know it is us, just as they must know you were in command. Do you not find that odd?'

'Perhaps they are waiting for you to claim responsibility,' Sandrine suggested.

'Will you do that?' Tony asked.

'It is a conundrum. A considerable problem, thanks to that idiot. While I have no doubt that the whole non-Nazi world would have applauded the death of the governor-general, there is going to be considerable criticism at the shooting of his wife.'

'Even if it was not intended?'

'The Germans are unlikely to agree that it was not intended.' Tito snapped his fingers. 'And that is why there has been no official reaction. They are waiting for us to make a claim. Because if we do, we shall be telling the world that we are the vicious murdering thugs they claim we are. No, we will not claim. We shall let them accuse.'

'And Mihailovic? He must know of it by now.'

'Oh, certainly. But he too is in a difficult position. Is he going to denounce us, and further split the resistance movement? And at the same time publicly reveal his sympathies with the Germans? As the Germans have not yet accused us of the incident, for him to step in now would be to indicate that he knew of our plan in advance. And that would not go down well with his Nazi friends. I think we will wait and see what happens next.'

'And when the Germans start shooting people as a reprisal?'

'Then we will shoot back. And hopefully Mihailovic will feel obliged to do the same. You are both excused from duty for forty-eight hours. You have had an arduous time, and it is not your fault that it has turned out badly. Rest up.' He grinned. 'Then go back to your women.'

In Tito's determination to create an army, the Partisan force sought recruits wherever they were to be found, and if at first suspicious both of Sandrine's ability as a soldier and the effect she might have on the morals of his people, Tito had rapidly come to respect her on both counts: she was as determined a fighting soldier as anyone in his command, and she was so utterly devoted to Tony that she never looked at another man and would permit no liberties from anyone. Thus she had been placed in charge of recruiting a regiment of women, as loyal and combative and, as regards sex, single-minded as herself. Her recruits, who already numbered some five hundred, had been formed into a regiment and placed under the command of Tony, with her as his adjutant.

Tito's entire army, which now numbered more than three

thousand, was divided into several regiments, which mostly operated on their own, although during the last few weeks everyone had been devoted mainly to recruitment and training, and in building defences both in front and behind the town to give them an alternate position should the Germans, as anticipated, begin bombing them. In recruiting, too, there was considerable rivalry with the Cetniks, as both groups sought to draw on the same human reservoir. But whereas the Cetniks would allow only Serbs into their ranks – and monarchist Serbs at that – and accepted no women, the Partisans welcomed anyone who would fight, be they Serb, Croat, Bosnian, Montenegrin, Macedonian, Albanian or Muslim, and regardless of sex. Nor was any recruit required to be a Communist. Tito, himself a Croat, did not trouble to hide the fact that he could see no value in restoring the monarchy after the war, but whatever happened after the war had to wait on the ending of the conflict first, and that meant the defeat of Nazi Germany. It was this pragmatism that had encouraged Tony and Sandrine, neither of whom had the slightest Communist inclinations, to join the Partisans, as it had also attracted large numbers of young people, equally uninterested in politics but determined to resist the Nazi invaders.

Tony being an officer, and Sandrine being his woman, they had been allowed a two-room apartment in one of the houses appropriated by the Partisans. It even had its own bathroom and kitchenette, although they usually ate at the communal mess hall just down the street. Sandrine sat on the bed to pull off her boots, and then stretched out on her back. 'Do I smell?'

Tony took off his own boots and lay beside her. 'I think you smell delicious.'

'I think I stink. I shall always stink. I think that shit is in my nostrils.' She sat up, got out of bed, and undressed. 'Look at me.'

'Happy to obey, ma'am.'

'Look closely.' She lay on her stomach. 'I am sure there is something.'

He traced his finger up and down the velvet skin. 'There are a couple of scratches from those bushes. Nothing else.'

She rolled over. 'I wish I could believe you. What about my front?'

'I like this bit better. But there really is not a blemish, save on this tit.'

'The bars did that. Will I get cancer?'

'Why should you do that?'

'My mother always said that if you got bruised on the breast you would develop cancer.'

'Who am I to argue with your mother? On the other hand, I promise to keep looking for lumps. Tell me, does your mother know what you're at?'

'My mother is dead,' Sandrine said.

'Hell. I'm sorry.'

'Both my parents were killed in a train crash. When I was sixteen.'

As he knew that Sandrine was roughly the same age as himself – twenty-seven – that meant she had been an orphan for eleven years. Which accounted for a great deal. One of the odd things about their relationship was how little they knew about each other.

He had met her as a sophisticated and even high-powered French journalist working in the *Paris-Temps* office in Belgrade. However attractive he had found her at first sight, the fact that she considered herself engaged to Bernhard Klostermann, and that he himself had become involved with Elena Kostic at the same time, had prohibited questions about the past. And since then, as their world exploded over and over again, what they had been before the explosion was no more important than what they would be when the explosions ended. Only survival mattered – and the growing certainty that they could trust each other and that they could find, in each other's bodies, some relief from the trauma in which they lived and with which they were surrounded.

Tony had always been quite sure, from the way she spoke, the way she acted, the way she had dressed before the war, and indeed the job she had had, that she was from at least a middle-class background, although if some of the occasional mentions she had made of her youth were true, she had always been something of a rebel. Perhaps the tragedy of her parents had played a part in that. But whenever he allowed himself to dream, it was of them both surviving the war, and her returning with him to the quiet Somerset village in which he had been born and brought up, and where *his* parents, so far as he knew, were still living.

So now he squeezed her hand, and she put her arms round his neck, and they both started when there was a knock on the door. 'Shit!' Sandrine said. 'We are off duty,' she shouted.

'May I speak with you, please?' a man replied.

They looked at each other; it was not a voice either of them recognised. 'I suppose we'd better,' Tony said. Sandrine rolled beneath the sheet, and pulled it to her throat. Tony straightened his clothing, and opened the door. 'Yes?' There was something familiar about the face.

'My name is Josef Brolic,' the young man said.

Tony had never met him, but like his father he wore a moustache, and now the resemblance was obvious. He became watchful, unsure of what the visitor's reaction was going to be. 'I am sorry about your parents,' he said.

'The fortunes of war,' Josef Brolic said, looking past Tony at the bed.

'Oh, let him come in,' Sandrine said. Only her eyes and her hair were visible, however suggestive the fact that she was in bed might be.

Tony stepped back, allowed the young man to enter, and closed the door. 'But you managed to get out,' he remarked.

'Yes. I . . .' Brolic licked his lips, and gave a short bow towards the bed. 'Madame.'

'You were lucky,' Sandrine observed. 'And it is mademoiselle.'

'I apologise, mademoiselle. I heard my parents speaking of what would happen. I am not very brave. I ran away.'

'But you know that your parents and your brother and sister were arrested,' Tony said.

'Yes. Yes, I know that.'

'Do you know if they are still in custody?'

'I think they would still be in custody.'

'And you know what that means?'

'Yes,' Brolic said. 'Yes. It is my duty to avenge them.'

'It is all of our duties to do that.'

'But mine more than any other. I would like to serve with you, Colonel Davis.'

'You mean you would like to serve with General Tito. I thought you were already doing that. And you must know that my command consists entirely of women, so it is not possible for you to join my regiment.'

'Yes, sir. But it is well known that you, and Mademoiselle Fouquet, carry out special missions for the general. Missions such as that of three days ago. I would like to serve on your squad.'

'Hm,' Tony commented. 'You understand that what we have to do can be very dangerous? As on this last mission.'

'I understand that, sir. But if it will help to avenge my parents . . .'

'You should also understand that anyone who lets his personal feelings override his judgement – again, as happened on this last mission – is a liability, and will not be tolerated.'

'I understand, sir. I will keep a cool head.'

'Well, I will discuss your request with the general.'

'Thank you, sir.' He bowed again towards the bed. 'Mademoiselle.'

Tony closed the door behind him, and Sandrine sat up. 'You're not really going to take him on board?'

'Don't you like him?'

'He gives me the creeps.'

'Why?'

She shrugged. 'I do not know. I just do not like him. I think it would be very dangerous to have him along.'

'Do you know, I agree with you,' Tony said.

'Then why did you not just throw him out on his ear?'

'Because there are several aspects of what happened in

Belgrade that I don't like, and that I think need explaining. Such as, just for starters, how did the Germans know that we would be using the fifth exit after the Brolic's cellar?'

'But . . . Maric told us to do that. And he died covering our retreat.'

'Actually, we don't know that he did die. But in any event, he had to have been told by someone to use that exit.'

Sandrine was frowning. 'It can only have been Brolic himself.'

'Yes. But it could have been arranged in front of the rest of the family.'

'And you think that that boy . . . But that was his own mother and father! His own brother and sister! That would make him a monster!'

'It would, wouldn't it,' Tony agreed.

Wassermann was on the platform to greet the returning general and his daughter. Angela wore a severe black dress, and looked, as always, quite superb. 'Herr General!' He saluted. As with the general's departure, there was no guard of honour this time, and a minimum of fuss, just the stationmaster perspiring beneath his silk hat.

Blintoft acknowledged the salute, and went straight to the waiting Mercedes. Angela sat beside him, and Wassermann, as usual, sat on the jump seat facing them. 'I trust you had a satisfactory visit,' Wassermann suggested.

'If a funeral can ever be satisfactory,' Blintoft remarked.

'Of course, sir. But . . . in Berlin . . .' He glanced at Angela. Her face was as unemotional as ever.

'Oh, yes,' Blintoft said. 'Berlin was very satisfactory.' Wassermann waited, but the general did not continue. Instead he asked, 'What has been happening here?'

'Ah. We have received a message from General Mihailovic, wishing to convey to you his deepest sympathy in your bereavement.'

'The treacherous, murdering swine,' Blintoft remarked. Again Wassermann glanced at Angela – he had not known the general in this mood before – but again there was no response from her. 'He has not even the guts to claim responsibility,' the general said.

'I do not think Mihailovic had anything to do with it, sir,' the major ventured.

'Is he not in overall command of the guerillas?'

'As I have explained, he does not necessarily know everything that is happening, or planned. Nor is he always obeyed.'

'That is not relevant. He claims to be in command, thus he must take responsibility for everything done by his people.'

Except that, as I have tried to explain, I do not believe that the Partisans are his people, Wassermann thought. But he decided against saying it.

'So who *has* claimed responsibility?' Blintoft asked.

'To this moment, no one.'

'Ha. And have you caught the murderers yet?'

'Not yet, sir, but we will. May I ask, have you, and Berlin, determined what is to be done about the general situation?'

'Yes.' Again Wassermann waited. 'We will discuss it tomorrow.'

'Ah . . . yes, sir. May I enquire what your plans for the evening are?'

'I am very tired. I shall have an early dinner and go to bed. There is much to be discussed, much to be planned. Tomorrow.'

'Yes, sir.' Wassermann looked at Angela, and at last got a response – a waggle of the eyebrows. 'Would it be in order for me to invite the Fräulein for dinner?'

'Ha ha,' Blintoft said. 'If you think Angela will tell you my plans, she will not, because she does not know them. Besides, I am sure she is as tired as myself.'

'I am not the least tired, Papa,' Angela said.

Wassermann took her to a small restaurant, exclusively reserved for the use of German officers. 'Are we safe here?' she asked. She still wore the black dress, and looked enticingly demure.

'Safer here, probably, than in any place in Belgrade, at least outside the army headquarters or the official residence.'

'But . . .' She glanced left and right at the other diners; the restaurant was almost full. 'Are all of these women German?'

'Very few of them, I would say. But they, or their families, have – what is the word? – Nazified.'

'Are they not afraid of reprisals?'

'Only if, for any reason, we ever leave.'

'Are we going to do that?'

'No. You are not afraid, I hope.'

'Not when I am with you.'

'Well then, you must try to spend as much time as possible with me from now on.' Was he travelling too fast? He was rather relieved when the maître d'hôtel arrived with the menu and wine list, and they could spend the next five minutes discussing the various dishes and ordering. 'Was it a terrible ordeal?' he asked when they were again alone.

'I was very close to my mother.'

'I understand. I am sworn to avenge her death.'

'I know this. And I am grateful, believe me. I would also like to help in any way I can. You know this.'

'I do. But all the help I need from you is the knowledge that you are always there, willing me on.'

This time the interruption of the waiters with their meal was less opportune, and they ate in silence while he wished he could gain even an inkling of what was going on behind that high forehead, those unfathomable eyes. He was totally surprised when, over coffee, she suddenly took the lead.

'Why have you never married, Major? Or am I being impertinent?'

'You could never be impertinent,' Wassermann protested. 'I have never married because I have never met the right woman. Until now.'

She did not respond to his last remark. Instead she said, 'You have been married to your job, perhaps.'

'You could say that. It has not been a very fruitful marriage, I am afraid.'

'It will happen. If you are thinking of Papa, he has been lucky. Always in the right place at the right time. And, you could say, under the right eyes. You are a member of the party?'

'Well, of course I am.'

'I never really supposed you were not. Tell me what you wish of me, really.' Once again he was taken completely by surprise. As he was so obviously lost for words, she smiled – a sufficiently rare occurrence for it to be almost frightening. 'I think you would like to take me to bed,' she suggested. Wassermann stared at her. 'Now I have been impertinent,' she said.

'No, no,' he said. 'I have said—'

'That you would never consider me impertinent. Well then, will you not answer my question?'

He drew a deep breath, still not sure whether or not she was playing some game with him. 'Of course I would like to take you to bed, Angela. I fell in love with you almost the moment I saw you.'

'Love?' she asked. 'Do you only fuck women you love? Then you must fall in love very easily, or you have a very sterile sex life.'

Once again he was left reeling, this time by her use of a word he had never heard from a woman before. But he managed to pull himself together. 'I was speaking of you.'

'Did you fall in love with me because you wanted to fuck me, or did you want to fuck me because you had fallen in love with me?'

'You are making fun of me.'

'I apologise. But it is important, don't you think, to know what is in a man's mind when you let him have the use of your body.'

Once again her choice of words distressed him. 'Is that what you are going to do? Let me have the use of your body?'

'Yes.'

'Just like that?'

'Don't you want it? You just said you did.'

'Oh, I want it.' He was regaining control. 'But surely you understand that it is equally important to the man to know what is in the woman's mind when she agrees to have sex with him.' He smiled. 'Especially when she is the boss's daughter.'

'You may not like it.'

'I cannot form a judgement until you tell me.'

She put down her coffee cup and gazed at him. 'Five days ago, I came to Belgrade with my mother and father. It was to be a holiday for me, before I decided what I really wished to do with my life, and it was to be in a place of which both my parents had fond memories. I was looking forward to nothing but happiness. And then, without any warning, I found myself kneeling beside my mother, watching her bleed to death.'

He squeezed her hand. 'I understand that you have been through a terrible experience, that you are perhaps still suffering from shock. I intend to do everything I can to help you. Just tell me what you wish of me.'

'All I have been able to think of since then,' she went on, as if he had not spoken, 'was that the bullet could easily have hit me. It was aimed at Papa, but struck Mama, who was standing next to him. But I was standing next to him as well, on his other side. Had the assassin aimed just a little to the right . . .'

'That thought haunts me too.' He was beginning to feel just a little uneasy.

'Should I not have felt grief? I was closer to Mama than anyone else in the world.'

'Well, the grief will come,' he suggested tentatively, as he had done three days before. 'Your immediate reaction was anger, a sense of outrage. That was entirely natural. I think we all felt that.' He peered at her. 'Perhaps you still do.' He realized that he might have made a mistake in suggesting that anger was no longer an emotion controlling *his* actions, but she did not seem to notice.

'Anger,' she said. 'Yes, I still feel anger. I want to hurt people.' Wassermann drank some brandy, unsure how he wanted this conversation to proceed, how he wanted this beautiful girl to turn out. 'But I also want to *feel*,' Angela said. 'I could be lying in that grave . . . What is that horrible word they use about the dead?'

'Disintegrating.'

'Disintegrating, without ever having *felt* anything in my life.'

'I'm sure that isn't so. A girl like you, all your boyfriends . . .'

'I have never had a boyfriend. I never wanted one.'

'Well, girlfriends . . .' He was nervous, venturing into unknown and, for him, uncertain territory.

'No girlfriends, either,' Angela said. 'I didn't want them.' Wassermann gave a soft sigh of relief. 'I didn't want them,' she repeated. 'I didn't want any emotional involvements, any feelings, to disturb my life. I felt there would be time enough for that when I was older . . . And now I realize that I could have died, without ever . . .' She gazed at him, eyes huge.

Another squeeze of her hand. 'I understand. I said I—'

'Would do anything to help me.'

'Yes.'

'Then will you help me feel?'

Sheer exultant desire raced through his system. But he remained uneasy. 'If you will tell me what you wish, I will do it.'

'Do you swear?'

'Ah . . .' But what did he have to lose? 'I swear.'

Her tongue came out and circled her lips. 'I want you to . . . pretend to hurt me.'

Wassermann finished his brandy in a gulp. 'I'm not sure what you mean.'

'You know how to hurt people, Herr Major. I have seen you do it. I want you to do the same to me. To pretend I am a guerilla, and interrogate me.'

'You can't be serious.'

'You promised.'

'You mean you want to feel electric shocks between your legs?' She was opening up a Pandora's box of anticipated pleasures . . . but Pandora's box had released endless disasters as well.

'I don't know,' she said seriously. 'I don't think so, really. But I would like to feel that it was going to happen, feel entirely at your mercy. Feel helpless. But alive. Can you understand that?'

'Of course,' he lied, making a mental note that before he got *too* close to this girl he simply had to get her to a psychiatrist. But more urgent considerations came first, while she was in this mood. 'And sex?'

'Make me feel, first, and do what you wish with me, afterwards.'

He gazed at her, and she flushed slightly. 'Please, Herr Major.'

'I think,' he said, 'that you should start calling me Fritz.'

'Ah, Wassermann,' General von Blintoft said. 'Good morning.'

Standing in the doorway of the general's office, Wassermann had to collect his thoughts; he hadn't expected his boss to be in quite so early – or in such a clearly good mood. 'Good morning, Herr General.'

'Sit down.' Wassermann seated himself before the desk. 'Tell me, what did you do with my daughter last night?'

Wassermann gulped. The one thing he had not considered was that Angela might have mentioned anything about last night to her father. He had not sworn her to secrecy, but if she had suddenly been overcome with a feeling of guilt, if only about losing her virginity . . . 'We had dinner.'

'She didn't come in until three. I was beginning to get worried.'

'Well . . .' Had the old goat seen her? 'We danced for a while, and then talked . . .'

Blintoft nodded. 'That was good. She needs to talk. And you know how it is – girls find it difficult to talk to their fathers.'

Wassermann felt a sense of relief. But he still didn't know how much, if anything, Blintoft knew. On the other hand, he reflected, he couldn't possibly be this affable if he had the

70

slightest idea that his only daughter had allowed herself to be placed in the chair in Ulrich's office and handcuffed to the floor, and then had her drawers pulled down and the electrodes clipped to her most private parts, to be made to feel, as she had wanted, before having sex. What had she felt when she had so willingly placed herself, and that splendidly shaped body, at his mercy? She had stared at him with an intensity that had almost been frightening. But then, he had been frightened himself as he had released her dress to pull it down past her breasts, to expose them and touch them, and then eased it up past her thighs, to uncover such a feminine wonderland. He had expected her to cry, but, as on her visit to the cells, she had not, while he had felt the strongest urge to turn make-believe into reality, been so tempted to turn on the current, but had resisted it. And then he had taken her, lying on the floor, and she had gasped softly as he had entered her. Even less could the general possibly envisage that she had appeared to enjoy every moment of it – or suspect that he had a severe mental case as a daughter. 'I understand,' he said. 'I am very anxious to help her.'

'Thank you,' Blintoft said. 'Still, you mustn't overtire her. She is still in bed. This is very unusual for her.'

'I apologise, sir. It is just that . . . she did not seem to wish to go home to bed.' Which was absolutely true.

'You must insist the next time. Now, I have the most tremendous news. As you know, while I was in Germany I went to Berlin. I had long meetings with both the Führer and General Heydrich, and they both agreed that we should do something about the Yugoslav situation, certainly in the light of this latest outrage.'

Wassermann's heartbeat quickened, but he could not resist asking, 'Have you changed your opinion of what is necessary, Herr General?'

'I have come to the conclusion that you may have been right, Major, that these people – these Partisans and their friends the Cetniks – cannot be treated as civilised human beings, but must be destroyed before Yugoslavia can possibly become a properly constituted colony of the Reich. This is not simply because I wish to avenge my wife and bring her killers to justice, although I certainly mean to do that. The overall picture requires that this business be settled as rapidly as possible. The eyes of the world are starting to look towards Yugoslavia. The fact is that we are already experiencing some guerilla activity behind our lines in Russia, as well as in Greece; these people undoubtedly have heard of the successes gained by the Cetniks and Partisans, and used them as their examples. So we, in turn, must make an example of them. Do you agree?'

'Entirely, Herr General. Although I still think it would be a mistake to lump the two groups together. Divide and rule, eh? I think if we denounce the Partisans as the murderers of your wife, thus discrediting them in the eyes of the world, and concentrate our efforts upon them, we may well find that the Cetniks will cooperate with us. And once we have destroyed the Partisans, then we can turn on the Cetniks.'

'It is certainly something to be considered,' Blintoft agreed. 'Although I am not sure that it will be necessary. I have been promised two divisions of front-line troops, together with a panzer brigade. They are on their way here now.'

'But that is splendid news, Herr General. We will at last have a proper army.'

'Together with all the air support we require. We will begin by regaining Uzice. Hopefully this Tito will attempt to hold on to it, and then we will destroy him.'

'Yes, *sir*!'

'And just to encourage the locals, I am empowered to offer a reward of ten thousand marks each for the capture, dead or alive, of this Captain Davis and the woman Fouquet.'

PART TWO

SURVIVAL

*When bad men combine, the good must associate;
else they will fall, one by one, an unpitied sacrifice
in a contemptible struggle.*

Edmund Burke

Four

Plans

'Déjeuner!' Tony Davis reeled in his line, pulled the flapping fish from the hook. Sandrine had been bathing in the stream, and was naked. Even after six months of utter intimacy, Tony remained fascinated by her body, by the whiteness of her skin – there had not been a great deal of time for sunbathing during the summer – just as he also always marvelled at its symmetry; she was a small woman, but perfectly formed; that her breasts were slightly disproportionately large only added to her beauty. 'What is it?' she asked.

Tony laid the fish on the ground. 'I have no idea. But it's a big one. What we call a whopper. Three pounds at least. Is that fire ready?'

She turned on to her knees and struck a match. A moment later the accumulation of twigs and dried leaves was alight, while Tony quickly gutted the victim and laid it in two strips on a small frying pan in which he had already placed a dollop of cooking oil.

Even in early November, it was a delightful day, both warm and sunny. The clouds gathering in the mountains to the west were still only a threat. It was a treat to escape the crowded bustle of Uzice for the peace of this lonely wooded hillside, with its bubbling stream and its still leafy trees. He knelt beside her to fry the fish, and their shoulders touched. 'On days like this,' she said, 'I am happy to be alive.'

'What about on other days?'

'I am surprised. Do you think we are going to survive this war, Tony?'

'Just let's keep on being surprised.' The fish was ready, and from his haversack he took a bottle of wine; they drank from the neck.

'If only there was some end in sight,' she said. 'Hmm.' They ate from the pan, and the fish was still very hot.

'There will be.'

She chewed thoughtfully. 'But the Germans are winning, are they not? Is it not true that the Russians are beaten?'

'It certainly looks like it.'

'Then there is nobody left to fight Hitler.'

'Except England.'

'England,' she said. 'I suppose they may hold out. But they cannot help us here. Especially if they lose Egypt as well. Then what can we do? We can never surrender. They would hang us.'

'So like I said, we keep on being surprised.' He stroked his finger up her arm and over her shoulder to touch her neck. 'We can get out, you know. You and I.' She turned her head. 'Alexandria would agree to that. They offered to take me out a couple of months ago, remember, when I was hit. If I were to tell them now that I wanted out, they couldn't object. We could go home to England.'

'And what then?'

'Well, we'd get married . . .'

'I'd like that. Where would we live?'

'You'd live in Somerset with my family, for the duration.'

'I do not speak any English.'

'I'd teach you.'

She considered. 'And you would stay with me?'

'Well, no. I'd rejoin my regiment.'

'And be sent away somewhere to fight.'

'That's what it's all about.'

'I would prefer to be beside you when you fight. As we are now.'

'I don't think they'd wear that in the British army.'

'Then I would rather stay here. Anyway, how could we desert these people?'

'There's a point.'

She finished her fish, and lay down with her arms beneath her head. 'But I think it would be a good idea if you were to start teaching me English. After we have made love.'

'The heat from the sun is going,' Tony said. 'We'd better pack it in.'

Sandrine pulled on her clothes, looking down the hill. 'Who is that?'

Tony shaded his eyes; from their position they overlooked one of the minor roads, hardly more than a track, that led towards the town. These approaches were always under surveillance by Partisan patrols, but clearly no one had thought it necessary to challenge a lone cyclist. 'A man on a bicycle.'

'Pedalling very hard.' She picked up her tommy-gun. Before the day they had escaped Belgrade last April, Tony knew that she had never fired a weapon, never, in fact, handled one. But in that desperate adventure she had found herself in possession of a tommy-gun, and since then she had never been without one.

He picked up his own weapon as he watched the man. The slope of the road had now grown sufficiently steep to force him to dismount, but he was still pushing his bike as quickly as he could. His clothes indicated that he was, or was pretending to be, a Serbian peasant, but what he was doing out here in the middle of the afternoon all by himself was a question that would have to be answered, whether the sentries thought it necessary or not. 'Cover him,' Tony said, and stamped on the still glowing fire to put it out. Then he took the frying pan to the stream and rinsed it before stowing it in his haversack. Sandrine meanwhile moved forward to the edge of the copse, and was standing behind a tree; the road passed immediately beside the little wood. For the moment the man was out of sight, but she knew he would soon appear over the brow of the hill. Tony joined her. 'No shooting,' he said.

The man came in sight, and Tony decided that he was unarmed – although he did carry a satchel in which there could be a weapon – and also that he was middle-aged and did not in any way suggest a combatant, whether regular or irregular; it was difficult to determine whether the stubble that coated his cheeks and chin was the result of an unsuccessful attempt to grow a beard or from merely forgetting to shave for a couple of days.

Tony stepped out from the trees. 'Stop,' he commanded, switching from French to Serbo-Croat. The man's head jerked, and he nearly let go of the bicycle. 'Where are you going?' Tony asked.

'I am going to Uzice.' The man's eyes rolled as Sandrine also emerged from the trees, her yellow hair fluttering; her sidecap was tucked into her waistband.

'What business have you in Uzice?' Tony asked.

'I am to see General Tito. And . . .' He peered at Tony, and then looked at Sandrine again. 'You!'

'Do you know me?' Tony asked.

'You are Colonel Davis.' He turned back to Sandrine. 'And you are the Frenchwoman.'

'Ha!' Sandrine commented. 'I do not even have a name.'

'Your name is here.' The man opened his satchel, and checked as both tommy-guns were levelled. 'I have no weapons. I have these.' He took out two large rolls of stiff paper, and unfurled one of them. 'You are Sandrine Fouquet.'

Sandrine looked at the enlarged photograph of herself, head and shoulders, smiling at the camera. 'Elena took this, last Christmas. Where did they get it?'

'I would say from your apartment in Belgrade,' Tony said. 'Didn't you leave everything there?'

'I had no choice, we left in such a hurry. But . . .' She studied the poster, which was in both Serbo-Croat and German. 'Ten thousand Deutschmarks! Is that not a hundred thousand francs?'

'It was once,' Tony said. 'Could be worth more now.'

'I am worth more dead than I am alive!'

'Actually, it says dead *or* alive.' He read over her shoulder. 'For the murder of Frau von Blintoft and other crimes against the duly constituted authority of the Reich. I have an idea they'd prefer you alive.'

'Ha!' she remarked again. 'And what are *you* worth?'

Tony unrolled the second poster. 'The same. I make it a thousand pounds, at pre-war rates.'

'But there is no photograph. That is just a drawing.'

'That's because I didn't leave anything behind,' Tony pointed out. 'It's not too bad a likeness. I wonder who did it for them.'

Sandrine turned to the man. 'And you have come to collect this money, eh?'

'No, no,' the man said. 'I have information. For General Tito.'

'We are General Tito's friends,' Tony told him. 'Give us the information, and if we think it is important enough, we will take you to the general.'

The man licked his lips, and looked at Sandrine, who smiled at him. 'If you do not, we will decide that you are a spy, and shoot you,' she said. 'But we will keep these posters. It is a nice picture of me.'

'Are you not afraid?'

'Not of two pieces of paper,' Tony said, and released the safety catch on his gun with a loud click.

The man panted, 'The Germans are coming!'

'Makes a change. When, and with what?'

'They are being reinforced. Two divisions. A panzer brigade. Aircraft. They are coming to destroy you.'

Tony looked at Sandrine. 'It had to happen some time,' she said.

'When is the assault due to begin?' Tony asked.

'I do not know, sir. They say it will happen as soon as all the troops have arrived. That could be any day now.'

'How do you know this? What is your name, anyway?'

'My name is Boris. Boris Malic. My daughter is a maid at the royal palace, which is now the home of the governor-general. She overheard them talking, the governor-general, von Blintoft, and his chief of police, Major Wassermann.'

'And she told you. Do you realize how dangerous it is for you to have come out here to tell us? Dangerous for both you and your daughter.'

The little man drew himself up. 'I wish to serve Yugoslavia.'

'But you have not taken this information to General Mihailovic.'

'Bah. He is a traitor. Besides, Uzice is closer.'

'And you can come and go as you please.'

'My daughter is Fräulein von Blintoft's personal maid.'

Tony looked at Sandrine, who shrugged. 'I think we will take you to Colonel Tito,' he decided. 'But we will blindfold you, eh?'

'Tony!' Tito said, as boisterously as ever. 'You are back just in time. I have someone to see you.'

Tony turned in surprise, which grew as he took in the man seated at the side of the desk; he was wearing the uniform of a British officer, and had all the neatness as well as the little moustache that went with it. Now he stood up, and Tony saw that he wore the crown of a major. 'Captain Davis. Bob Curtis.'

'My pleasure, sir,' Tony said, shaking hands. He could not salute, as he was not wearing a hat.

Tito did not intend that there should be any doubt about their respective ranks, at least in Yugoslavia. 'Captain Davis is actually a colonel,' he remarked slyly.

Curtis raised his eyebrows.

'I shouldn't think it has ever been gazetted,' Tony said. 'I hold the rank in the Partisan army, not yet the British.'

'Major Curtis is from Alexandria,' Tito said. 'And this is Mademoiselle Fouquet.'

Curtis looked tempted to kiss her fingers. But he shook hands instead. 'The famous Sandrine.'

Sandrine showed him the poster. 'The Germans think so too.'

'Major Curtis has come from Mihailovic,' Tito explained.

'I was actually sent to see the situation on the ground,' Curtis said.

'I'm sure you will be of great assistance,' Tony said. 'May we have a word, General?'

Tito looked at Curtis. 'If you will excuse us, Major.'

Curtis looked distinctly put out, but he gave a brief bow. 'I would like a word with *you*, Captain,' he said. 'I beg your pardon, *Colonel*. When you have the time.'

'Five minutes,' Tito said. Curtis left the room, and Sandrine closed the door. 'Let me see those,' Tito said. The two posters were laid on his desk. He inspected them in turn. 'So they have decided to lay blame.'

'That is the least of it.' Tony told his commander what Boris Malic had said. 'He's outside if you wish to question him.'

Tito stroked his chin. 'Do you believe him?'

'I have a gut feeling that he is telling the truth. On the other hand, the information could be a plant, just to let him have a look at our dispositions. That's why I blindfolded him to bring him in.'

'Very sensible.' Tito grinned. 'But even if he is a traitor, Tony, he can do us no harm. The Germans know we are here, and they must know that we are prepared to resist an attack. They must also have a fairly good idea of our numbers. Even were he not blindfolded, he has nothing of value to tell them. As for the information, we will act on it anyway. I suspect it is genuine. It is the reaction I expected after the killing of Frau Blintoft. Two divisions and a panzer brigade, with air cover. That could prove too difficult for us to handle.'

'What about Mihailovic? Now that we have a British liaison officer . . .'

'Yes,' Tito said. 'I would be interested to hear what you and Major Curtis have to say to each other.'

Tony raised his eyebrows. 'Problems?'

'There could be. Major Curtis has arrived with certain

81

preconceived ideas. I would say that they originated in London, but Mihailovic has added a few. Now, this information you have just obtained may alter the situation, but we cannot be sure of that.'

'What do you intend to do?'

'That will have to depend on Mihailovic. How much time do we have?'

'I would say not more than a few days.'

'Very good. Go and discover what Curtis has to say to you. Find out if Mihailovic will support us, and, indeed, if Curtis will recommend that he does so. Then report back to me, and we will form our plans.'

'And the informant? Do you wish to see him yourself?'

'Does he have anything more to say?'

'I don't think so.'

'Then give him some money, and tell him to go back to Belgrade. Tell him we look forward to hearing from him again, as his daughter is in such a useful situation. But you had better again blindfold him until he is outside the town.'

'And you say I am to tell Major Curtis?'

'Oh, indeed.' Another grin. 'At times like this, we must all hang together – or we may hang separately.'

Tony saluted; the rules were different in the Partisan army.

He paid Malic a hundred dinars. 'We are most grateful to you,' he said.

'I did not do this thing for money,' Malic protested, but he took it anyway.

'You said your daughter is a servant in the governor-general's house?'

'She is personal maid to the governor-general's daughter.'

'What is her name?'

'Rosa.'

'I meant the name of the governor-general's daughter.'

'That is Angela.'

'Has your daughter told you how this Angela has taken her mother's murder?'

'She says she does not appear to grieve. But she spends a lot of time staring into space.'

'That figures,' Tony said. 'I suspect she does grieve, but inside.'

'I will come back when I have anything more to tell you.'

'Don't chance your arm,' Tony advised. He summoned a sergeant and told him to escort the little man out of the town, and not to remove his blindfold until he was.

'You are sorry for that girl,' Sandrine remarked.

'Yes, I am.'

'Someone you have never seen.'

'I am sorry for her because I regret what happened to her mother. Let's have a go at Curtis.'

They took the major to their apartment. 'I must say,' Curtis commented, 'that you seem to have made yourselves very comfortable.'

'One learns to do the best one can with what one has,' Tony agreed, switching on the lights; it was now dark outside, but the town's generating plant had been repaired. Sandrine drew the blackout curtains. 'Drink? Local beer,' Tony explained, opening the large, vacuum-sealed bottle and filling three glasses. 'There isn't anything else. Now, sir, sit down and tell me what you have for me.'

'Well . . .' Curtis looked at Sandrine, who had gone into the kitchenette, only a few feet away.

'Anything you have to say to me can be said to Sandrine as well,' Tony told him. 'We are a team.'

'So I have heard,' Curtis commented disparagingly.

'So?'

'Well . . .' Curtis drank some beer. 'I was sent here to report on the general situation, and on yours in particular. I may say that, down to a short time ago, GHQ was very happy with the work you were doing here. I'm afraid I'm not so sure that they still are.'

'What is the official reaction to Frau von Blintoft's death?'

'I'm afraid I don't know. I was already here when the, ah, incident took place.'

'But presumably you're in touch?'

'Sadly, at the moment I am not. My transmitter got damaged in the drop . . .'

'And General Mihailovic is reluctant to let you use his.'

'Well, he feels it may be monitored by the Jerries.'

'He has been afraid of that since day one.'

'Of course, you were with him at the beginning.'

'Briefly.'

'May I ask why you left him so abruptly?'

'He wanted to shoot one of my companions.'

'Was there a reason?'

'She was a Croat.'

'You're not serious. *She?*'

'She. And I am very serious. I don't know how long you have spent in Mihailovic's camp, but you must have noticed that his people are entirely composed of Serbs.'

'Under his immediate command, yes. But he is in contact with other Yugoslav elements – apart from this one, of course. We were visited only last week by some people I understood to be Croats.'

Tony frowned at him. 'Did you meet their commander?'

'Oh yes, a fellow named Pavelic. Quite a character. Out of the Wild West. All moustaches and two revolvers on his hips. He has something of a reputation, I believe.'

'Ante Pavelic is a cold-blooded murderer,' Tony said.

Sandrine left the kitchen to join them. 'And a rapist,' she said. 'He raped me.'

Curtis gulped.

'And he commands an outfit called the Ustase,' Tony said. 'They work for the Germans, killing Yugoslavs they don't like.'

'But he and Mihailovic seemed on the best of terms.'

'Yes,' Tony commented.

Curtis looked from face to face, and finished his beer. Sandrine refilled his mug.

The major regrouped. 'I suppose you know that General Mihailovic has been made a member of the Yugoslav

government-in-exile, and, as the man on the spot, has been placed in command of all the Yugoslav resistance forces.'

'I would say that indicates that the government-in-exile is out of touch with the true situation here.'

'Well, certainly that is one of the reasons I have been sent here,' Curtis agreed. 'To find out what is the real situation on the ground, and report on it. The fact is, as I said, that while GHQ is pleased with the way the resistance movement here is carrying the fight to the enemy, it is also disturbed at the reports we have been receiving of the splits that appear to be developing between the various guerilla groups. And I am bound to say that much of this has been confirmed by General Mihailovic himself.'

'Well, that's entirely natural. The general has lost control of events.'

'Because sizeable groups like this one have hived off and refuse to obey his orders.'

'Because there have been no orders, sir, except to sit tight and stop provoking the Germans. It may interest you to know that he did not authorise the seizure of Uzice, and in fact expressly forbade it.'

'Well, he feels it will be impossible to hold when the Germans decide to retake it.'

'I'm afraid the real reason is that he does not wish the Germans to be defeated until and unless he can guarantee a monarchical restoration and, in fact, a reversion to the status quo of 1939.'

'Well, isn't that what we are all seeking?'

'I would have thought we should be seeking something better.'

Curtis looked down his nose at him. 'Are you a Communist, Captain? Or perhaps' – he glanced at Sandrine, who had returned to the kitchen – 'Mademoiselle Fouquet is.'

'Neither Mademoiselle Fouquet nor I have any politics, Major, except that we are opposed to Fascism.'

'But you are aware that this is a Communist group?'

'No, sir, it is not. General Tito is a Communist, certainly.

He does not deny it. Nor does he deny that he would rather have a Communist government in Yugoslavia after the war than a royalist one, as this has not proved very successful in the past. But his overriding concern is to win the war, and then start worrying about the peace. I believe I am correct in claiming that I am obeying Mr Churchill's own behest when I say that I would rather fight with someone, anyone, against Nazi Germany than with someone who shows no desire to fight, and whose motives for not doing so are at best suspect, and at worst treasonable, if what you say about his entertaining Ante Pavelic is correct.'

Another stare down the nose. 'I think I should remind you, *Captain* Davis, that it is not for you to be lecturing me, but rather the other way around. When I am able to regain contact with GHQ I will be obliged to make a full report on the affair of Frau von Blintoft, following which I imagine that you will be recalled – I will certainly recommend it – when you may well be faced with a murder charge.'

'I assume you will also report that I did not fire the fatal shot.'

'Who did?' Another glance at Sandrine.

'One of my command. Against my orders not to shoot. In any event, that the bullet struck the lady was an accident.'

'You expect me to believe that?'

'Yes. Because I am an officer in the British army.'

Curtis cleared his throat, embarrassed. 'There will have to be supportive evidence.'

'Mademoiselle Fouquet was there.'

'Mademoiselle Fouquet. Ah. Yes.' This time his glance was apprehensive. 'But . . . well . . .'

'I am Tony's mistress,' Sandrine said. 'Does that mean I cannot tell the truth?'

'It might be considered that the evidence would be prejudiced. What about the other members of your command? The man who fired the shot?'

'He is, or *was*, in German custody. He may well be dead by

now. The other man was probably killed during our escape; we have not seen him since.'

'Hm. Not very helpful. Well, I will have to consider the matter, and see what can be done.'

'Dinner is ready,' Sandrine announced.

'Excellent wine,' Curtis remarked.

'Like the beer, it too is locally brewed,' Tony said.

'Very locally,' Sandrine added. 'I think I would give half my life for a bottle of decent claret and a piece of decent cheese.'

'I imagine you two must have had quite a few adventures during the past six months,' Curtis suggested.

'If you think it is an adventure to have to watch a hundred people, men, women and children, shot down in cold blood.'

'That was done by Mihailovic's friends the Ustase,' Tony said. 'Led by Pavelic.'

'That was before he raped me,' Sandrine said. 'Actually, he buggered me. That is worse, you know.' Curtis appeared to choke on his wine. 'If I ever see him again,' Sandrine went on, 'I am going to shoot him in the balls.'

Curtis blew his nose, and drank some more wine. 'And she means it,' Tony said.

'Ah . . . well . . . yes.' Desperately Curtis tried to regain control of the conversation. 'What would really be helpful is if you were to bring about some kind of reconciliation between Mihailovic and Tito. Have them working together. If you could do that, well, all other matters could be forgotten.' He looked at Tony almost appealingly.

'I doubt that is really possible,' Tony said. 'The only way it could happen is if Mihailovic got off his ass and started to fight. He'll never have a better opportunity than right now.'

'Why right now?'

'Because I have just received information that German reinforcements are being poured into Yugoslavia, with a view to an all-out assault designed to destroy the guerilla movement.'

87

Curtis frowned. 'Does General Tito know this?'

'I have just told him.'

'But . . . My God!'

'Exactly. That they are doing this is precisely because of Tito's successes against them.'

'But . . . reinforcements? In what numbers?'

'We have been told two divisions of infantry, a brigade of panzers, and aircraft support.'

'Good God! They'll wipe you out.'

'Whether they do or not, we still consider that we have scored a triumph. Those troops have had to be withdrawn from the Russian front.'

'Do you suppose that is the least relevant? What are we talking about? Sixty thousand men and a couple of dozen tanks? Our latest estimates are that there are three million German soldiers in Russia, and three thousand tanks. They are going to have Moscow by Christmas.'

'That may be so, Major. But the fact is that if the Russians were to surround and capture – that is, remove from the battlefield – two divisions and a brigade of panzers, it would be trumpeted as a great victory. That is what our resistance here is achieving.'

'And meanwhile you will be suffering incalculable casualties.'

'You keep using the word "you", Major, whereas I thought you wanted to use the word "we".'

'You wish General Mihailovic to come to your aid?'

'I would have supposed it was his duty to do so, if the attack *is* directed at Uzice. Just as we would come to his aid were the attack to be made on him.'

'Hm.' Curtis finished his wine, and Sandrine topped him up. 'He would have to be in overall command.'

'I think we would need to have a meeting, as quickly as possible, to decide our strategy,' Tony said.

'Hm. Yes. I will see if I can arrange it. Will your man come?'

'Certainly.'

'Yes. Well . . .' He wiped his mouth with his napkin. 'That was a splendid meal, Mademoiselle Fouquet. Now I must be getting along. It's been a long couple of days, trekking through these mountains.'

'You're not starting back tonight? You're welcome to sleep here.'

'That's very kind of you. But I prefer to travel by night. It's safer. And my guides know the mountains very well.' He stood up, and put on his cap. 'Until our next meeting.'

Tony saw him to the door, then returned to help Sandrine with the washing-up. 'I do not like that man,' she said.

'I would say the poor chap has been pitchforked into a situation, and a world, which is totally outside his experience. He obviously doesn't trust us enough to spend the night here, in comparative comfort, as against bivouacking on an empty hillside in the rain.'

She snorted. 'And do you think he is really going to report you guilty of murder?'

'I think he is going to do his duty as he sees it, when the time comes. We'll just have to wait and see.'

Moonlight flitted through the trees, casting long and sudden shadows which seemed to be accentuated by the night wind. Wassermann stamped his feet and slapped his gloved hands together. Not that he was cold. But meetings like this always made him nervous. However much he might be backed up. He looked over his shoulder, caught the reassuring glimpse of metal amidst the trees. But the fact was that, although anyone who tried to attack him would be instantly cut down, he would still receive the first shot.

'They are here,' Ulrich said.

The man seems to have eyes like a cat, Wassermann thought. But now he could himself make out the shadowy figures emerging out of the gloom.

'Major!'

'Heil Hitler!'

'Heil,' the Cetnik agreed.

Wassermann peered at him. He was a young man, short and stocky. Like all the Cetniks, his hair was long and he had a straggly beard. He wore a somewhat drab and untidy khaki uniform, in strong contrast to the German's immaculate black one. 'Matovic! You have something for me?'

'Your plans are known to the Partisans,' Matovic said.

'How?'

Matovic shrugged. 'One of your people must have talked too loudly.'

'But not one of yours.'

'Not one of mine,' Matovic said, choosing his words carefully. 'I am risking a great deal in coming here.'

'Why?'

'We have received a British liaison officer. A Major Curtis.'

'How?'

'He came by parachute.'

'From where?'

'Alexandria.'

'That is a long way. You knew he was coming?'

'We were informed.'

'But you did not inform us.'

'I am sure you appreciate, Herr Major, that it is necessary that General Mihailovic maintains good relations with Britain, and, through them, with our government-in-exile in London, and remains utterly trusted by them.'

'You are saying that the general did not authorise this meeting?'

'He does not know of it.'

'So why are you here? What would happen if he were to find out about it?'

'I would probably be shot, sir. I am here in fulfilment of our bargain.'

'That your parents would be safeguarded as long as you cooperate. I understand, Captain. What does this Englishman want?'

'As I said, he has come to liaise between his government and

General Mihailovic. But he also wishes to bring the Partisans and the Cetniks together.'

'Will he succeed?'

'I doubt that. Much will depend on what you mean to do.'

'You have just said that our plans are known.'

'Only that you are moving a large force of men and materiel into Yugoslavia. It is very necessary that I know how you intend to use this force.'

'So that you can tell this British officer?'

'Of course not. But it will be necessary to put General Mihailovic in the picture. If you intend to drive into the mountains, well, he will need time to make adequate dispositions.'

'How can you do that if he does not know we are meeting each other?'

'I will tell him I have obtained the information from our agents in Belgrade.' He gave a brief smile. 'As I have, have I not?'

The two men glared at each other, then Wassermann said, 'I will tell you what dispositions your general will need to make. It is our intention to liquidate the Partisans. We intend to attack and recapture Uzice. Will they attempt to defend the town?'

'I cannot say. Would you like the general to command them to evacuate it?'

'Would they take any notice of his command?'

'Probably not. They have invited us to support them.'

'Well, make them think that you will, without actually giving them orders either to stand or to flee. As you say, they are unlikely to obey your orders anyway. Now, if they stand, we shall blast them out of existence. If they evacuate the town, they must be stopped from escaping into the mountains. This will be your business.'

Matovic gulped.

'Stragglers can be arrested and turned over to my people. Large bodies must be checked and held while you report their position and enable my people to come up.'

'But . . . that will be open civil war.'

'Did your general not forbid the Partisans to occupy Uzice in the first place?'

'Yes, he did.'

'But they went ahead anyway. That was in fact an act of mutiny, in defiance of his orders. Their rash action has brought, or is going to bring, great hardship on his own people. He is entitled to take action against them.'

'But not to hand them over to you, Herr Major.'

'What happens to them after you arrest them is of no consequence, and in any event can be explained. So, you arrest and disarm, say, three hundred men retreating from Uzice. What to do with them would be a problem, would you not agree? While it is still under consideration, you are informed of the approach of a German unit. It will then be your duty to abandon your prisoners, making sure they have no weapons, and escape with your own people. This is standard military procedure.'

'I do not think this Curtis will approve.'

'Who is in command, General Mihailovic or Major Curtis? Anyway, you can always dispose of him. He could always stop a stray bullet.'

'That would make London suspicious.'

'Well, handle it your own way. Just do it. There is one more thing. Should your people capture Tito or his chief aides – I am thinking principally of the Englishman, Davis, or the Frenchwoman, Fouquet – we wish them handed over to us, alive. You know these people?'

'I was there when they first joined our forces.' Matovic gave another smile, this one sinister. 'They refused to accept General Mihailovic's orders. He had them locked up, but they broke out. I tried to stop them, but they hit me on the head. I would very much like to capture them. Especially that woman. She is very beautiful.'

Wassermann snorted. 'Well, Captain Matovic, you will have to restrain yourself. We want them alive and unharmed. Remember that.'

'If my people capture either Davis or Fouquet they will wish to collect this reward you are offering.'

'They will receive it. But we want the principals. Remember, alive. And preferably unhurt.'

'I will remember. When is the attack to take place?'

'There is no need for you to know that. Just keep your men on alert, and when the shooting starts, cover all the escape routes from the town. Do not fail me in this, Captain Matovic. You know the penalty I will exact if you do.'

Matovic looked as if he would have said something more, but changed his mind and rejoined his bodyguard, who had been waiting just out of earshot. Together they faded into the darkness.

'Can we trust him?' Ulrich asked.

'As long as his parents are living in Belgrade, yes,' Wassermann said.

'And do you think he will be able to persuade Mihailovic to cooperate?'

'I think there is every chance. Mihailovic is desperate to regain control of the movement, and to do that he must get rid of this fellow Tito, so I imagine he will play along with us. I see a great victory looming, Ulrich. The end of this Tito.'

'And the capture of Davis and Fouquet.'

'Oh, indeed,' Wassermann agreed. 'Do you know, I sometimes think that is what I want more than anything else.'

After having let them escape in the first place, Ulrich thought, all in pursuit of your tortuous ambitions. But he kept his thoughts to himself.

'What have you got for me?' Tito asked.

Curtis looked apprehensive. 'General Mihailovic has asked me to tell you that it must be your decision as to whether or not you defend Uzice. Regretfully, he is not in a position to render you any positive assistance at this time.' Tito glanced at Tony, who was standing beside his desk. Tony shrugged. 'However,' Curtis went on, 'General Mihailovic told me to inform you that, should you determine to retreat, or should the anticipated battle go against you and force you to pull out, if you make your withdrawal to the mountains to the north-west, he and his people will render you all the assistance in their power.'

'That is very reassuring,' Tito said. 'Thank you, Major. And thank General Mihailovic for me.'

Curtis hesitated. 'What reply do I take to General Mihailovic?'

'That I have not yet finalised my plans. These will depend on how and when and in what strength the Germans move. He will know of them in good time.'

Curtis looked at Tony, but received no encouragement there. 'Very good, sir. I should tell you that we have information that the German corps has crossed the frontier, and will be in Belgrade tomorrow. We anticipate that they will commence the operation as soon as their people have regrouped and a plan of attack has been formulated.'

'That is exactly in line with our own appreciation of the situation. Again, thank you.'

Another hesitation, then Curtis saluted, and left the room.

'Well,' Tito said, 'at least we know where we stand.' He went to the table on which a map of the region was spread. His staff officers crowded round. 'Now,' he said, 'the sensible thing for us to do, as we know that the Germans intend to move against us, would be to get out now. But to do that would be to admit defeat without firing a shot, and the Germans will trumpet it as a great victory, which it will have been, certainly in propaganda terms. Our people support us, and in time the world will support us, because we have proved our determination to fight, and that determination must be displayed time and again.'

He looked round at their faces. 'I do not wish anyone to be under any false illusions about this. We are going to lose this battle, simply because they will come at us in overwhelming strength. We are going to have to retreat. But before we do that, we are going to give the Nazis what our English friends' – he smiled at Tony – 'will call as bloody a nose as we can. And to do this, we are aided by everything we know of the German war machine, based on their manoeuvres in France and in Russia; this indicates that they will seek to envelop us in their well-known pincers. They will bomb us first, here in Uzice. Immediately after that, they will launch a frontal attack, but only on a limited scale, to pin us down. When we are committed, their two flanks will seek to fall upon our rear. This is classic military history, eh? Hannibal used these tactics against the Romans at Cannae. The Zulu impis did the same. However, each situation is slightly different, as is ours now.' He pointed at the map. 'Belgrade is north-east of us, and it is from there that the Germans will advance, using the one good road between the two towns for their wheeled transport. Their pincers will therefore have to move left and right of that line, which is to say that their right-hand pincer will come at us from the north. But that is broken, hilly country, interspersed with streams. This right-hand swing will travel more slowly than the other, and it is not good country for panzers. The left-hand pincer will have a much easier time of it, for the country down there is reasonably flat, and there is at least one good road, which comes to us by way of Kragujevac. That is therefore the more dangerous swing.

'Now, as you know, I have had our people prepare a defensive line behind the town, and it is to this line that our main body will withdraw as soon as the bombardment starts. Again, I wish you to make no mistake: this is only a temporary measure. We cannot hope to stop this force, much less defeat it, with our limited weaponry and ammunition supplies. But we must inflict as many casualties as is possible before, during and after our retreat. So, Colonel Asztalos, you will take your regiment into the hills to the north. You will harass the enemy right-wing pincer, but do not get drawn into a full-scale engagement. You, Colonel Davis, will take five hundred men down to the town of Kragujevac, here.' The town was south-east of Uzice. 'That is ideal panzer country, if only because they will be able to use the road. However, there are also streams and ravines. I am thinking especially of the one outside Kragujevac, which is crossed by a bridge. That bridge is essential for the panzers to make any quick progress. If it is blown, they will be held up for a considerable time.' He gave a quick grin. 'If it could be blown with a tank or two actually on it, that would be even better. In any event, you will harass and delay the enemy advance as far as you are able, but again without being sucked into battle. Hit them hard, and then retreat quickly. Both of your forces will withdraw as necessary back to Uzice. Then our entire force will evacuate south-west into Bosnia, and let the Germans attack an empty town.'

'Are we not going to link up with the Cetniks?' Asztalos asked. 'Is not their main strength concentrated in northern Bosnia?'

'Yes,' Tito said. 'Mihailovic's headquarters is situated on and around Mount Ravna. That is, north of Sarajevo. We will not go in that direction.' Another look around at their faces. 'Because that is what we have been invited to do.'

'You think they would betray us?'

'I do not wish to find out.'

'But,' Tony said, 'that means you think Curtis is a traitor.'

'No, I do not,' Tito said. 'But I am sorry to say that I think he is a dupe. He was sent here to liaise between Mihailovic and the Allies, but also to try to bring about a rapprochement between Mihailovic and myself. He is carrying out his allotted task to the best of his ability. He has no idea – because the idea has never been presented to him – that Mihailovic would like to see us destroyed every bit as much as the Germans. We shall have to see what develops. If the Cetniks come down from their mountains to engage the Germans, then we will change our plans. If they do not – and frankly I do not expect them to – then we will operate on our own. Our retreat will be south-west, as I say, into southern Bosnia. Our rendezvous will be Foca. Here.' He touched the map. 'I have been in contact with the people there, and they will welcome us.'

'You do not suppose the Cetniks would attack *us*?' someone asked.

'I think it would be best if we did not put temptation in their way. In fact, I think it would be wise for you to treat any Cetnik units with whom you come into contact as hostile until they prove to be otherwise. This applies especially to you, Colonel Davis, as you will have the furthest to go to rejoin us.' Tony nodded. 'Now, are there any questions?' Tito asked.

'What of the inhabitants of Uzice when the bombers come?' someone asked.

'I have spoken with the mayor. I have told him that evacuation would be the best course, but that such evacuation must not in any way hinder our operations, and would therefore have to take place to the north-west. However, he has told me that most of his people would rather remain, and take their chances in their cellars.'

'Does he realize that they will be at considerable risk, less from bombs, perhaps, than from reprisals?'

'He understands this, but the decision is his and his council's. Thank you, gentlemen. Time is running very short. Colonel Davis, a word.'

Tony remained as the other men filed from the room. 'You said I must take a regiment of *men* to Kragujevac.'

'I am replacing your regiment, yes,' Tito said.

'My girls won't be happy about that, sir.'

'Do you think they are ready for close combat?'

'They think they are, and they are desperate to engage the enemy.'

'Do they have any idea what it is like to be hit by a bullet? Or perhaps more importantly, to see a comrade, maybe a close friend, hit by a bullet?'

'Not as yet, sir. But it has to happen some time.'

'And do they have any idea what will happen to them if they are taken prisoner?'

'Sandrine holds seminars on that subject.'

'And she should know. Very well. I wish you fortune. Get rid of that fellow Curtis as quickly as you can.'

'Then you really don't trust him.'

'I trust him as an officer and a gentleman, Tony. But for that very reason he will feel duty-bound to report to Mihailovic everything he has seen and heard here, and I do not wish Mihailovic to know anything of our plans. Both you and

Asztalos must move out by dawn tomorrow, and Curtis must be gone long before that.'

Tony saluted.

Curtis had waited for him. 'You realize this is pure suicide.'

'All war is pure suicide, Major.'

'But you will go along with this.'

'Of course I will. Wouldn't you go along with it, if these were British soldiers?'

'Yes I would. The point is—'

'That these are not British soldiers? They are fighting for us.'

'Are you sure of that? Can you be sure they are not fighting for some sinister plan of General Tito's?'

'From where you are standing, Major, that comes very close to treason.'

'Why?'

'I have already explained that Tito is concerned with the present rather than the future. The present is the business of fighting Nazi Germany. As long as he is doing that, with all his might, I am going to support him, with all my might. Now, Major, may I suggest that you have something to eat, catch a couple of hours' sleep, and then leave.'

Curtis's brows drew together. 'Am I being expelled?'

'You are being requested to leave Uzice. We have a great deal to do . . .'

'And you do not wish me to see you doing it. I get the message.' Curtis turned his somewhat sour gaze upon Sandrine, who had joined them. 'And you will follow blindly, mademoiselle.'

'I will follow, Major.'

'Then I will wish you good fortune, and hope to see you again.' As there was obviously not going to be another invitation to dinner, he summoned his guides, and walked into the gathering gloom.

'Is he right?' Sandrine asked.

'Surely,' Tony said. 'But we have survived a few suicides in the past. Get your people together.'

One of the things that always disturbed Tony was the youth of his command – and even his various commanders. Obviously, to fight in the guerilla army, even more than in a regular force, fitness was a high priority, and this was thin on the ground where ordinary Yugoslav women were concerned. Apart from the city chic, they were educated to be beasts of burden and mothers, and by the time they were thirty were invariably overweight and permanently overtired. Thus recruiting a female fighting force meant aiming at young girls and women, either unmarried or only recently so.

The remarkable thing was the numbers who had come forward. Partly, Tony supposed, this was peer rivalry – if you can have a gun, why can't I? But there was also a genuine desire to fight; almost every member of his regiment had seen her home and family destroyed or broken up. And equally he needed to remember that Yugoslavia itself had only a very thin veneer of civilised behaviour spread across centuries of viciously brutal dominance by, and resistance to, the Turks; thus there was not a member of his command who did not have a relative, often only a couple of generations back, who had been executed or forced into a Turkish harem. He could not help but wonder how English womanhood, and more especially maidenhood, would respond to such a situation, which presumably could still happen. He remembered reading a comment by some foreign visitor to the effect that English women had the innocence of belonging to a country that had not been invaded for nearly a thousand years.

There was no innocence in the faces of his company commanders as they assembled before him, even if not one of them was older than Sandrine – and at least two of them were very nearly as handsome as the Frenchwoman. But their faces were at once strong, and hard, and enthusiastic. They handled their weapons exactly as did Sandrine, with loving anticipation of using them, and there was quite an assortment. Most possessed a variety of somewhat ancient rifles, but several had tommy-guns, and quite a few sported revolvers or automatic pistols, either holstered round their waists or slung over their shoulders nearly all were also armed with frightening-looking knives. He was glad they would be fighting for him, and not against him.

'This is going to be your first action,' he told them. 'I know you will do your best, and hit the enemy where it hurts. Now alert your people, and then get some rest. We move out at three.'

There was a little rustle, and the women exchanged glances. 'Do we take prisoners?' asked Sasha Janitz. She was one of the handsome ones, tall and strongly built, with aquiline features and long black hair, which, unusually but sensibly, she wore tucked inside the collar of her jacket. He had a sudden insight that to be captured by Sasha Janitz would be the most horribly exciting way to die.

'No,' he said. She gave a charming little pout. 'Just kill them.'

'What of our own casualties?' asked Anja Wroch.

'You will not have the time to bury your dead. They must be left. But any wounded who can move must be brought out.'

'And those who cannot move?' Sasha asked.

'Must be left. I am sorry, but there it is. They will be given a grenade and advised to blow themselves up rather than be captured.'

Again the women exchanged glances, but they still had the confidence of inexperience, that perhaps that situation would not arise. 'And our dispositions?' asked Draga Disilivic. She was a blunt-faced, heavy-set young woman, with large hips and breasts and powerful legs. Having seen her training, Tony reckoned she was as strong as any man.

'I will make those on the ground,' Tony said, 'when we have reconnoitred the situation. Dismissed.'

They left, muttering to each other.

'They are looking forward to it,' Sandrine said. 'Killing the enemy.'

'Are you?'

'Oh, yes,' she said. 'Oh, yes.'

Five

Ambush

'A ren't they a splendid sight?' Angela von Blintoft clung to Fritz Wassermann's arm as they stood at the gates of the palace complex and watched the tanks roll by on the street outside. In every cupola there was a figure standing to attention, right arm thrown out in the Nazi salute. Behind the panzers came the infantry, a glitter of green helmets and uniforms and black boots, marching beneath their banners in perfect unison, battalion after battalion.

The street, which was overhung with flags of red, white and black, was crowded with spectators. The people were quiet, however. Although they were unable to resist the dramatic appeal of a military parade, they yet understood that these men were their masters rather than their friends.

'Do they hate us?' Angela asked.

'Oh, undoubtedly,' Wassermann said. 'But then, the conquered always hate their conquerors. With time, however, they usually grow to accept the situation. And after this campaign is completed, they will have no further reason to resist us.'

She squeezed his arm; she no longer made any secret of the fact that they were lovers. Papa had never enquired as to whether they had been to bed together, had accepted, as Angela was a lady and Wassermann a German officer, that if they had, or were contemplating it, they were also contemplating marriage. And although she knew that he did not actually care for the idea of his police chief as his son-in-law – because of both the age difference and Wassermann's lack of an upper-class background, as exemplified by the absence of a

102

'von' before his name – he could not doubt that the major's constant attention had done wonders in helping his daughter to overcome the trauma of her mother's death. Neither he nor anyone else had the slightest idea of the games they played in private, even if some of the clerks at Gestapo headquarters might wonder at the number of times the major took the general's daughter into the downstairs office late at night. 'I wish you didn't have to go,' she said.

'I am looking forward to it. I have waited a long time for the opportunity to really deal with those thugs.'

'But if you were to be hit . . .'

'There is no chance of that. I am not going to be in the front line. My business is cleaning up after the soldiers have destroyed them.'

'Then let me come with you.'

'Your papa would never agree. Listen, you can join me after the battle.'

'Promise?'

'Promise. I will arrange it. You will miss nothing, really.'

'Oh, you darling. Papa!'

Blintoft had watched the parade surrounded by his senior officers. Now he approached them. 'Come, Wassermann,' he said benevolently. 'Leave her alone for five minutes. We have plans to make.'

The general stood above the map on the huge table in his office. 'Now then, gentlemen,' he told the lesser generals and colonels who stood about him, 'the first thing I have to say to you is that our business is to entirely wipe out this group calling itself the Partisans. Now, let us consider what we have to do. Our information, gathered so diligently by Major Wassermann' – he allowed his gaze to flicker up and over his prospective son-in-law – 'is that the Partisans are grouped in and around Uzice' – he prodded the map – 'in the number of roughly three thousand men. That is a sizeable force. We also know that they have established a defensive perimeter behind the town, to which they will withdraw once our aerial bombardment commences. Bearing this in mind, I have determined that we shall not carry out the proposed aerial attack.'

He raised his head to look at the faces around him, daring anyone to question his decision. 'As I have said, our objective is total destruction of the enemy, much as we have achieved in Russia. We had to use aircraft there, both to destroy the enemy air force and to destroy his transport infrastructure to prevent him moving his people about, either in support or withdrawal. None of those factors applies here. The Partisans have no air force, and they have no reserves, either of men or munitions, on which they can call. And it has been proved that aerial bombardment, while it has on occasion been very destructive of retreating troops and civilian morale, does not necessarily have that effect on entrenched and determined personnel, and we must anticipate that these Partisans will be determined. I am also of the opinion that it would be counter-productive for us to destroy the town – and the civilian population. We need these people working for us, not lying in their graves. Also, the wanton destruction of the civilian population would alienate international opinion. So what we need to do is drive Tito's people into the open, in disorganised retreat, and *then* loose our air force on them.

'Now, I personally will command the main assault force, which will consist of the entire First Division and one brigade of the Second Division. We will move out of Belgrade at dawn the day after tomorrow, and advance straight on Uzice. I may say that the enemy has no artillery to speak of either, and thus no means of preventing our advance. There is a good road from Belgrade to Uzice, and I estimate that we will be in position to begin the assault by five o'clock, that is, one hour before dusk. The assault will begin at that time, the moment our infantry have disembarked from their trucks. My estimate is that the enemy will be anticipating that an aerial attack will precede one on the ground, and thus will be taken by surprise if we move straight into action. Now, he may elect to fight for the town, or he may choose to withdraw to his second line. If he does the latter, he is playing into our hands; we will occupy the town, and then bombard his position without fear of civilian casualties. If he fights where he is, well, that is where our pincer movements come in. These will commence their advance at dawn tomorrow, that is, twenty-four hours before the main body. The right will sweep to the north, the left to the south, using the Kragujevac road.' He looked at the respective brigadiers. 'You will establish your positions to the right and left rear of Uzice by midday on day two, that is, five hours before our arrival in front of the town. You will wait there, not engaging the enemy, until the frontal assault commences, following which you will destroy any and all enemy units attempting to retreat. Of course, when I say that you will not engage the enemy until the frontal assault commences, should he discover your position and attack you, you will defend yourself with all possible vigour, informing us of the situation by radio. Unless this happens, or unless you encounter unforeseen delays, radio silence will be maintained. Understood? Very good. Any questions?'

'If he stays and fights in the town, what of the civilian population?'

'They will have to take their chances. But we will not deliberately be targeting them.' He gave a brief smile. 'As I intend to call on the Partisans to surrender before beginning our attack, if there are civilian casualties the enemy will be blamed for involving them unnecessarily. Yes?' He pointed.

'Are we to anticipate any resistance from the Cetniks, Herr General?'

'Major Wassermann?'

'No, sir. The Cetniks will not interfere.'

'But when the Partisans retreat – as we must suppose they will at some stage – will they not move back on to Cetnik-held territory, seeking support?'

'It is our assumption, and our intention, that they will do so, Herr Colonel. But they will receive no assistance, and indeed, where it is practical, the Cetniks will block the Partisan retreat to enable us to overtake them.'

'You are saying they intend to fight for us?'

'No, sir. I am saying that they will welcome the destruction of the Partisans. I believe their leaders feel that, with the Partisans out of the way, it may be possible for them to come to some agreement with us.'

Heads turned to look at Blintoft. 'Let us dispose of the Partisans first, gentlemen, with or without Cetnik assistance, and then reassess the situation. Anything else?'

'Will you be using the Ustase in any capacity, Herr General?'

'Yes. But strictly to clean up any pockets of resistance which may remain after our assault. They will be under the command of Major Wassermann. Very good, gentlemen. To your posts. Operation Weiss commences at dawn tomorrow. Major Wassermann . . .'

Wassermann stood to attention while the other officers left the room. Then he closed the door.

'You know what I want, Fritz,' Blintoft said.

'You wish Tito, Davis and Fouquet alive, if that is possible.'

'At least one of them. Please do not suppose that this is on account of any personal hatred I may feel for them. I am of the opinion that a show trial of them, or any one of them, for the murder of my wife, followed by their public execution, will do our cause the greatest possible good, not only here in Yugoslavia but throughout the world, to show the world that we mean to uphold the rule of law.'

Hypocrite, Wassermann thought. Your real desire is to hear them shriek for mercy as I torture them. But he nodded, gravely. 'You will have them, Herr General. If they survive the battle, you will have them.'

'Good. I am assuming that you have the witnesses – the Brolics and that man Kostic – in a fit condition to appear in court?'

'They will be, Herr General.'

'Well then, let us go home and have a drink, and toast our victory.'

*   *   *

The young woman panted, 'They are coming!'

'What did you see?' Tony asked. He, and his unusual command, were breakfasting in the low hills to the west of the town of Kragujevac, just over a mile away; beneath them the road, at a similar distance, wound to their left into the hills surrounding Uzice. They had arrived the previous evening after a forced march, and had been resting up, but at dawn Tony had sent out a patrol of a dozen of the youngest and therefore fittest of the women to proceed beyond the town and reconnoitre.

Now they had hurried back, their corporal flushed with excitement. 'Truckloads of infantry, sir,' she said. 'With tanks in front.'

'Distance?'

'Five miles.'

Tony stood up and levelled his binoculars. The road stretched out of sight beyond the town, but now he could see dust in the distance. 'Right,' he said. 'A and B Companies, you will enter Kragujevac, and form a perimeter on the north-east. Captain Janitz, you will get hold of the mayor, and tell him to have all his people stay indoors and out of sight, as there will be shooting. You will remain concealed until the bridge is blown, then you will open fire and hold your position until I fire a rocket, when you will withdraw to this position.' Sasha Janitz nodded, her face determined. 'C and D Companies,' Tony said, 'will cross the road and take cover on the north side. You also will not reveal yourselves until after the bridge is blown, then you will fire into the enemy column, maintaining your attack as long as possible. As soon as the enemy has regrouped, I will fire a second rocket, and you also will then retire in good order, returning to Uzice by the best possible route.' Draga Dissilivic saluted, and went to assemble her women. 'E Company will take up their position this side of the road,' Tony said, 'with the same orders, except that you will be under my personal command.' Anja Wroch, tall, thin and hatchet-faced, also saluted, and went off.

Tony took another sweep of the still empty horizon, and then of the sky. It was a November sky with complete cloud cover, and the clouds were low and black, promising imminent rain. But for the moment it was dry. Rain would not be welcome, because if the ground softened, their withdrawal would leave fairly obvious tracks; on the other hand, the Germans would in any event know they would retreat to Uzice, so it would not matter all that much, except for making the journey more uncomfortable.

'Should we not see the aircraft by now?' Sandrine asked.

Tony shook his head. 'The main body will be some hours back. The bombing won't commence until they are in position.' He grinned. 'If the cloud cover allows them to see us at all. Let's check these explosives.'

Sandrine opened the haversack, and very carefully took out the sticks of gelignite. 'It is ridiculous that the commanding officer should have to lay the explosives himself,' she complained.

'I'm the only one trained to do it,' he pointed out, examining each stick for any signs of sweating. 'Seems all right. Let's go.'

They made their way down the tumbled hillside to the ravine, passing as they did so the various members of E Company, lying amidst the boulders and bushes, their rifles thrust forward, while a cluster assembled their machine gun. They all wore the Partisan uniform of blouse and pants and sidecap, and looked surprisingly military, but as their training was of a very recent variety – and they were women – they could not resist the desire to chatter amongst themselves; hopefully they would be in action before the Germans would hear their voices.

And then? Not one of them had the slightest idea what to expect. But then, neither did he. Over the past few years he had seen sufficient action, both in Flanders, before his first wound, and here, since the start of this local war. He had seen enough people killed or maimed, and he had even watched women being slaughtered, as in Divitsar. But that had been cold-blooded murder; none of those women had been armed, or even attempted to resist the Ustase.

The only woman he had ever seen die, gun in hand, had been Elena Kostic. That memory haunted him. He had tried to tell himself that was because she had been his mistress. But by the time Elena had died their romance was long over, as they had both known.

The truth was that, as he had reflected earlier, for all his experiences he retained that absurdly romantic English notion that women were there to be protected, not carelessly killed, or even more carelessly offered to be killed. To which could be added his concern – a concern already voiced by Tito himself – as to how his girls would react to seeing their comrades torn apart by bullets. Would they utter a collective shriek, and run away? Or would they continue to obey orders, and stay in being as a fighting force? Well, he thought, he was about to find out.

The ravine was some ten yards wide, very deep, and with steep sides. It was as effective a tank trap as anyone could have devised. The bridge itself did not look terribly strong, and would thus be the easier to blow. Carefully Tony climbed into the underneath of the structure, and placed the dynamite inside the joists, increasingly aware of the growing if still distant rumble of sound. Sandrine stood patiently beneath him, handing up each stick as he beckoned for it. For all her characteristic complaining – which she maintained about food, lodging, clothes and weather – she was utterly reliable, because she had such complete faith in him.

'Good enough.' He attached the wires and climbed down, and they retreated along the ravine and up the bank some fifty feet away, slowly paying out the cable. Sandrine's job was now to brush stones and pebbles over the wire to conceal it, at least from the casual gaze. Then they returned to the control box, which was in the shelter of a thick clump of bushes some distance away from where E Company was positioned.

Now the grind of the approaching motors was quite loud. Sandrine blew him a kiss. 'I feel just as I did in that attic, listening to the train coming,' she said.

'Let's hope this one turns out better,' he said, pushing the first large cartridge into his Verey pistol chamber, and reflecting that any one of his inexperienced command could fire prematurely and give their position away, but at least on this occasion when the enemy replied they would not be shooting at defenceless women.

It was now nearly noon and surprisingly warm, but, with the sun still absent, he felt he could use his glasses without the risk of some sharp-eyed Nazi officer spotting the glint amidst the supposedly empty hillside.

Sandrine lay on her back with her eyes closed. 'It is so peaceful,' she said. 'Why do men have to fight?'

'Because they always want something that belongs to somebody else,' he suggested, and made out the first truck. 'Damnation.'

She sat up, pushing hair from her eyes. 'They are here?'

'But not in the right order.'

'Let me see.'

He gave her the glasses. 'There are tanks,' she said.

'But preceded by a truck. They are suspicious, possibly of minefields, and certainly of any traps. That means they will inspect the bridge before they allow the tanks to use it.'

'Shit!'

'It isn't a catastrophe. It means we won't be able to take any of the panzers in the explosion. But we can still hold them up.' Anja Wroch had joined them to watch the approaching enemy. 'Tell your people to stand by,' Tony said. She nodded, and crawled away.

Slowly the enemy column approached. First they saw the isolated truck, well out in front. This was followed by a line of six tanks, in single file on the narrow road. Behind them was an even longer line of closed trucks, each no doubt filled with men. They were certainly not anticipating any ambushes, their only concern apparently being possible booby traps or minefields on the road itself.

The top of the column drew abreast of the little town, which was entered by a slip road, and Tony held his breath; he knew that A and B Companies were in position along that road, and here again a single overexcited shot would ruin his dispositions. But there was none, and the column rumbled forward until the advance truck reached the bridge. Here it stopped, and it seemed to Tony as if the whole world was holding its breath.

Two men got down from the truck, and walked on to the bridge. Tony glanced at Sandrine, and watched her fingers tighten on the butt of her tommy-gun. To the right he heard the click of Anja's machine gun being made ready; it sounded deafening, but did not apparently reach the men on the bridge. They turned, as if to walk back to the waiting truck, and Tony's heartbeat quickened. If they were not going to investigate more closely . . .

But then one of the men stopped, and turned again, and his companion stopped also. There was a brief discussion, and the first man left the bridge and began to climb down the embankment. Once he got under the bridge he would clearly see the explosives. Tony glanced at Sandrine, and waggled his eyebrows. She responded by doing the same, showing she understood.

The man was now standing beneath the bridge, hands on hips, looking up. He said something to his companion, who was standing above him. The upper man turned to look back down the column, and raised his arm to signal . . . and Tony pressed the plunger.

The bridge went up first, carrying the two men with it, and spewing wreckage over the truck, which caught fire and then itself exploded, its other occupants tumbling across the road. Then all of Tony's command opened fire, the chattering of the machine guns being interspersed with the louder cracks of the rifles and the gentler patter of the tommies. The men escaping the exploding truck were cut down in moments, and several of the tank captains, standing confidently in their cupolas, were also hit, although no damage was done to the tanks themselves. Further back, the lead infantry trucks were caught in the fire from A and B Companies. In several cases the drivers were hit in their cabs, and the trucks went out of control, some careering down the embankment beside the road, others crashing into those in front of them, while the men hastily disembarking were also chopped down by the wall of fire arising from the slip road.

For some ten minutes all was confusion and glorious mayhem, then whistles blew and men began to take cover and form into ranks, while the tank cupolas turned from left to right and their cannon opened up on the hillside, sending shells thudding and exploding into the trees above the women.

'Let's go,' Tony said, and fired his Verey pistol, at the same time grabbing Sandrine's arm and dragging her away from their original position. And a moment later a shell burst exactly where they had been crouching.

From their new position higher up the hill he surveyed the scene beneath him. The remains of the advance truck still burned, surrounded by its dead occupants. The panzers had definitely been halted; at the moment they had nowhere to go, although they continued to fire left and right into the low hills to either side. In several places the trees and bushes had been set alight, and smoke was drifting across the morning. The infantry trucks were still unloading their men; there were corpses and wounded scattered on and around the road, but the German officers had their men under control, and were advancing on Kragujevac behind a series of volleys.

Tony fired his second Verey cartridge, and then again dragged Sandrine away, as he had again revealed their position. From his next point of view, he could see A and B Companies withdrawing out of the town; there were a reassuringly large number of them. On the far side of the road, Draga and her people were already lost to view amidst the trees and scrub of the hillsides. Anja and her company were all round him, also retreating in haste. Gratifyingly, they were bringing their dismantled machine gun with them.

Sandrine remained at his side. 'Go with Anja,' he said. 'Take command.'

'And you?'

'I have to make sure Sasha's people get clear. I'll be right behind you, as soon as they come out.'

'If anything were to happen to you . . .'

'Nothing is going to happen to me. Now go.'

A last hesitation, then she crawled away to join the women. Tony waited for her to be out of sight, then ran along the hillside, bent double. The Germans were still keeping up a considerable fire, but from a distance. The odd shot crashed through the underbrush, but did very little damage, apart from setting up more fires. Now, indeed, he heard the whistles calling for a ceasefire, as it was clear that the Partisans were out of range, at least for the moment.

A few minutes later he came upon the retreating members of A and B Companies, chattering amongst themselves as always, wildly exhilarated, and the more so at the sight of their commanding officer. 'We killed them,' one of the girls shouted. 'Oh, we killed them!'

'Well done,' he said. He passed them and saw Sasha, who was commanding the rearguard, looking as neat as always; even her hair was still in place.

She came up to him and saluted. 'Sir!'

'Well done,' he said again. 'Casualties?' He had observed that she was not as ebullient as her girls, just as he had seen that, of the twenty-odd bringing up the rear with her, most were bleeding from hastily tied bandages.

'What you see. There are seven dead. And . . .' She hesitated.

'Yes?'

'Three too badly wounded to move.'

'You made sure they knew what to do?'

She hung her head. 'I could not do this. One of them came from my own village. We have been friends since we were girls.'

'Shit,' he muttered. 'What did you do with them?'

'I left them with the mayor. He promised they would be looked after.'

'Well, it's done. Let's find the others.'

113

'I have disobeyed orders. You are angry with me.'

'I'm just sorry for your friends.'

'Will you shoot me?'

'Our business is shooting Germans. Not each other.'

'And you?' she asked, falling in beside him.

'We did better. You had the post of honour.'

'Sandrine?'

'Up ahead with E Company. We'll catch them up.'

'Was it a victory, Colonel?'

'Depends how you interpret the word. We did what we were told to do, and disrupted their movement. Now let's get out of here.'

The end of an engagement, when the adrenaline had stopped pumping and the excitement had faded, always left Tony feeling rather flat. And this time there was not even the compulsion of being pursued to keep the emotions stirred.

The Germans had clearly been shaken by the ambush. They would in any event have to repair the bridge before they could get their tanks forward, and were no doubt using every man available to accomplish that, in order to try to keep to whatever was their schedule.

Thus a general air of mental and physical exhaustion had set in, and Tony and Sasha had a lot to do to prevent straggling. The women had marched all night, and a good deal of their stamina had dwindled along with the exhilaration of combat; soon they began to remember those they had left behind, whether dead or seriously wounded. Meanwhile the less seriously wounded now became a problem, as two of them found they could no longer walk and had to be carried on improvised stretchers – after what had happened at Kragujevac, he did not suppose the women would obey a command to abandon them – and the others groaned or wailed continuously.

Sasha was a tower of strength as she roamed around her command, chivvying, bullying, on occasion even slapping faces to keep people moving. But she was as glad as anyone when, at dusk, they found themselves at one of the many streams which coursed down from the hills, and Tony, sure they had gained a sufficient lead to escape any pursuit, and equally that they would be back in Uzice and in position long before the left-hand pincer could come up, called a halt for the night. 'May we light a fire?' she asked.

'Yes, but control it.'

He watched most of the women stripping off to plunge into the water. Sasha's expression was quizzical. 'Does this disturb you?'

'They're a handsome bunch.'

'Am I allowed to go in also?'

'That would just about make my day. But that water must be pretty cold.' The little valley was filled with shrieks and squeals.

'Won't you join us?'

'You mean I wouldn't be gang-raped?'

'I'd protect you.' She seemed to be perfectly serious.

'Maybe later. I need to have a look around.' He left her, and climbed higher up the hillside to the best available vantage point. Once there he unslung his binoculars, and looked back along the way he had come. He could not resist a quick inspection of the bathing women, and particularly Sasha, her body somewhat ruddy – so unlike Sandrine's in that respect – but equally voluptuous, with large, low-slung breasts and huge nipples, gleaming as she waded into the water.

Her invitation had been fairly obvious. There was no way of knowing whether that was personal attraction, a desire to get close to her CO, or the sheer animal sexuality created by having been in combat. That was common to most men, so there was no reason for it not to be similarly common to most women.

He remembered how, when they had been on the run together, Elena Kostic and Sandrine had shared his favours, Elena with perfect contentment, but Sandrine always searching for possession. He did not doubt that Sasha Janitz would willingly take on the Elena role – one of the big problems of war, and more especially this war, so nearly a civil conflict, was the utter breakdown in morality it engendered. Nor did he doubt that she would be just as exciting in bed as the big Croat woman.

But Sandrine would never go for it. She might like to consider herself a child of the Left Bank, but in many ways she had the viewpoints of a middle-class matron. And he had no intention of doing anything to upset Sandrine. If she was a one-man woman, he was the man for her. He wondered where she was. Only a few miles further on, he reckoned.

His main business was with what might be happening behind him. It was now quite dark, and there was nothing to see. Kragujevac was long out of sight – even the hillside fires seemed to have burned out – and if he could just make out the road, there was nothing on it. In any event he did not suppose the Germans would continue in the dark – even if they had managed to repair the bridge – given the obvious possibility of another Partisan ambush. He wondered if, the advance of their pincers having been disrupted, they would modify, or even call off, their plan. But that was wishful thinking. The damage he had caused had been only a pinprick.

He returned to the encampment, where a fire was glowing and food was being prepared. The November night air was chill, and the women were all dressed again – to his relief. 'Is all well?' Sasha asked, handing him a tin plate of roast sausage and beans, and sitting beside him with her own.

'Seems they're nursing their wounds. Probably literally.'

'Do you think my girls will be all right?' He preferred not to reply. 'I know,' she said. 'If they are taken they will be shot, no matter how badly wounded they are.'

'I'm afraid that's likely. It's what may have happened to them before that which bothers me.'

'What was I to do?'

'You did what you had to do,' Tony told her. 'When you command men, or women, your first duty is to the task in hand. Once you have done that to the best of your ability, your second duty is to the people under you, to see to the well-being and safety of the majority. No one can ask anything more of you, and this is what you have done.'

She shivered. 'Would you have left them?'

'Yes. But I would have advised them to shoot themselves before allowing themselves to be taken prisoner. Now, I'm afraid the lives of the mayor and his family may be in danger.'

'Fuck, fuck, fuck,' she said. 'I have fucked everything up. Why don't you shoot me?'

'I happen to prefer you alive.'

She digested this for several minutes, then she said, 'I wanted to fight in this war. I wanted to kill Germans, for violating our fatherland. I did not expect—'

'No one does,' he said, wondering what her nationality was. He had deliberately adopted Tito's point of view, never inquiring into the backgrounds of any of his people, determinedly regarding them all as Yugoslavs, and as patriots rather than either Communists or monarchists. But suddenly he was curious about this so attractive young woman, who, like them all, had found herself in a situation she could not have envisaged in her wildest nightmares only a year ago. 'Is Belgrade your home?' he asked.

'No, no. I am from Sarajevo.'

'You mean you are a Bosnian.'

'Is that important?'

'Not in the least,' he said, not altogether truthfully; he could not help but remember that it had been a shot fired by a Bosnian schoolboy that had started the First World War, of which this was surely only the second round.

She took their empty plates to the stream to rinse them, and returned with two cups of strong black coffee. 'Listen,' she said, kneeling beside him. 'Let me sleep with you tonight.'

He turned his head to look at her.

'I want to be held in your arms,' she said. 'I want to feel you in me.'

'Me? Or any man?'

'You. I am so afraid.'

'You are not afraid.'

'I am afraid,' she said. 'Not of what may happen to me. I am afraid of what I have done. Condemning those three girls to death. Please help me, Colonel.'

Not for the first time in the past six months he realized that this war contained situations never envisaged at Sandhurst. 'You can sleep in my arms,' he said. 'But we'll keep our clothes on.'

'Because of Sandrine?'

'It's a cold night,' he pointed out.

'Wassermann!' General von Blintoft marched into the major's office. 'I have just received a radio message from Brigadier General Leesing. He has encountered strong enemy resistance at the village of Kragujevac.'

Wassermann frowned. It was late afternoon, and he had spent the entire day assembling his people and making sure they knew what he wanted of them. Now he was thinking only of a hot bath and an early night, after a last dinner with Angela; he did not even intend to bed her tonight. He knew the next few days were going to be exhausting.

'Apparently there has also been enemy activity in the north,' Blintoft went on. 'This has been brushed aside. It is in the south that the situation is serious. Leesing estimates that he will be at least six hours late in arriving at his rendezvous. How did they know he was coming? There has been treason.'

'It is possible, sir, that the Partisans worked out how we would attack them. The plan was, after all, fairly, ah . . . It has been used before,' he said, in preference to the word 'hackneyed'.

Blintoft glared at him. 'Are you criticising my dispositions, Herr Major?'

'No, sir,' Wassermann lied. 'Not at all. The plan has proved eminently successful in the past, and against a variety of opponents.'

'Then you are suggesting that this man Tito is some kind of military genius.'

'Not at all, sir,' Wassermann said again, less convincingly. 'He has been lucky in that he has made counter-dispositions that have turned out successfully. Will this delay cause any change in your plans?'

'I have been considering this, and I do not feel a change is necessary. Leesing claims that he was opposed by overwhelming force. Well, he had five thousand men. You told me that Tito only commands three thousand.'

'I would say that Brigadier General Leesing is exaggerating, sir.'

'Well, he was certainly attacked. Even if by only a few hundred men. But he claims that the dead Partisans, and the few that were taken prisoner, are all women. Can you believe that?'

'Perhaps another exaggeration, sir.' Wassermann was beginning to wonder if General Leesing had gone mad.

'Well, in any event, whoever composes the Partisan force, its very existence means that those people, male or female, cannot at the same time be with Tito in Uzice. He will be weaker by that number. And even if Leesing is six hours late, he should still arrive in time to cut off the Partisan retreat. No, no, we will carry out our plan. However, there are two things I require of you. The first is that, as it appears certain that Leesing *will* be late reaching his rendezvous behind the Partisan lines, Mihailovic will have to take a more active role. Contact him by radio, and tell him to move some of his people up to the south-west of Uzice, just in case the Partisans try to escape through there. He will hold that position, and if necessary check them until Leesing comes up.'

Wassermann pulled his nose. 'He won't like it.'

'Are we supposed to worry about his likes and dislikes?'

'He will not like it to be publicly known that he is obeying our orders.'

'Oh, come now. This will not be public. Just see that it is done.'

'Yes, Herr General.'

'Then I wish you to get down to Kragujevac and sort things

out. Find out who betrayed us. See that they are made an example of.'

'Yes, Herr General. May I have that command in writing?' Blintoft raised his eyebrows. 'It is a formality, sir. I may have to shoot one or two civilians – or people who will claim they are civilians, at any rate.'

'Oh, very well. You shall have your instructions in writing.'

'Thank you, sir. I may also need additional forces.'

'Use Leesing's people. He is still there. I can spare you no one else. We commence our advance at dawn.'

As you have told me a dozen times, Wassermann thought. He was gaining a distinct impression that the general was nervous. He summoned Ulrich. 'We are moving out,' he said. 'Have everyone ready to go in an hour.'

'Trouble?'

'Nothing we can't handle.'

Ulrich saluted and left. Wassermann gazed at the radio transmitter in the corner of the room. He could not give any instructions to Mihailovic, because he had never actually given any orders to Mihailovic, only to those of his subordinates he could control. That was a mistaken assumption on the part of the general which he had never corrected; the suggestion that he had the Cetnik commander in his pocket had enhanced his standing. He did not know if Mihailovic was aware of the liaison between one of his captains and the Germans; Matovic had never given any indication that he was acting other than on his own, and it was not a relationship Wassermann intended to expose. He could contact Matovic, he supposed, but someone like Matovic would hardly be able to influence events at this stage. After all, he reflected, it is not always that easy to make radio contact; sometimes it is impossible. So perhaps a few of Tito's people would escape and join the Cetniks. He reckoned that would quickly involve sufficient internecine squabbling to be self-destructive, especially if the Partisans felt they had not properly been supported.

Meanwhile, when he had dealt with Kragujevac, there would

be even more dissent between Tito's people and the Cetniks. See that they are made an example of, the general had said. That was an order he had been waiting to receive for six months.

He left headquarters, and was driven in his command car to the residence. Guards saluted, servants bowed as he strode through the various halls to the governor-general's apartment.

'Fritz!' Angela hurried out of her room, wearing a dressing gown and smelling of bath salts. 'I did not expect you so soon.'

'I came to say goodbye.'

'Now? You are not staying to dinner?'

'I am sorry. I have to leave now.'

She frowned. 'There is trouble? You said you would not be leaving until after the attack.'

'There is some trouble,' he acknowledged. 'But nothing I cannot handle.' He took her in his arms. 'I shall be gone a few days. Maybe a week.'

'Oh, Fritz.' She clung to him. 'Do take care.'

'I always do.' He kissed her, hugged her body against his, allowed his hands to roam over her shoulders and down her back to squeeze her buttocks. 'Keep thinking of who I may bring back with me.'

Six

Capture

Wassermann and his escort drove all night, passing on their way a small convoy of ambulances going the other way, and reached Kragujevac just after dawn.

He was appalled to see that the left-wing pincer did not appear to have moved at all. There were sappers working on the bridge, but the tanks remained parked along the road, and the men were bivouacking; it still had not rained, although the clouds continued to be low and heavy.

A sergeant directed him to where Brigadier General Leesing was seated with his officers, breakfasting. 'Ah, Wassermann,' Leesing said. 'Come and have a cup of coffee. Your information was not so accurate, eh?'

Wassermann accepted a cup. 'My information?'

'You did not know about these women, eh? Women! Shooting at my men. *Shooting* my men.'

'They are from the town?'

'I have no idea. Seven of them are dead. The other three were badly wounded. They were in such pain I had them drugged with morphine. They need surgery. You can take them back to Belgrade with you.'

Wassermann handed his empty cup to an orderly. 'With respect, Herr General, captured guerillas have never been considered prisoners of war.'

'These are women, Wassermann.'

'Taken in arms against the Reich. They are still not covered by the Geneva Convention. Where are they?'

Leesing waved his hand. 'Show the major, Bruno.'

'May I ask when you intend to move on, Herr General?'

'I am informed that the bridge will not be ready before ten o'clock this morning. We shall resume our advance as soon as it is safe.'

'The main body has already left Belgrade, Herr General. General von Blintoft expects you to be in position by this afternoon at the latest.'

'I have informed General von Blintoft that we will be late. He accepts this.'

Wassermann was tempted to make a further comment, but decided it would be a waste of time. 'You were going to show me these prisoners, Captain.'

The captain led Wassermann away from the road to a clump of trees, where the seven bodies were stretched out, uniforms bloodstained, faces coldly indifferent to what might now happen to them. But he was interested to note that they *were* all wearing a uniform of sorts.

'And the wounded?'

The three women looked as dead as their comrades, except for the fact that their eyes were shut and they were breathing. Their uniforms also were bloodied. 'They are badly wounded,' the captain said. 'They must be got back to Belgrade as quickly as possible. We supposed you would bring an ambulance with you. One was requested. All of our vehicles have been required to transport our own casualties.'

'I passed them on the road. Were they severe?'

'Yes. Twenty-seven dead and forty-three wounded, all in a matter of ten minutes. We were taken entirely by surprise. Now you will have to send these women back in one of your cars.'

'I have no intention of doing that,' Wassermann told him. 'These women were taken in arms against the Reich. They will be shot, if they do not simply die.'

'But . . .' The captain was clearly appalled, and tried a different tack. 'They actually weren't taken in arms, Herr Major. We found them in the house of the mayor.'

'He was giving them shelter?'

123

'Well, I suppose you could say that, sir. They had been placed in his house by the retreating guerillas.'

'That is what he told you. But you were fired upon from the town.'

'We were fired upon by people from along that slip road over there.'

'Who have now just disappeared.'

'Who *retreated*, Herr Major. We saw some of them in the trees further up that slope.'

'Some of them,' Wassermann observed. 'Very good, Captain. I want you to select a hundred of your best marksmen, and assemble them on the slip road.'

'I do not think there is any chance of overtaking the guerillas now, sir.'

'We do not have to overtake them, Captain. They are right here, waiting for us. Assemble your men.' He blew his whistle, and Ulrich hurried up. 'Bring your people and the Ustase squad into the town with me,' he said.

'Ah . . . will we not be totally exposed, Herr Major?'

'They will hardly attempt any overt action against us under the guns of a tank squadron and a brigade of infantry,' Wassermann pointed out.

Ulrich was clearly considering that these people, or at least their compatriots, had only recently opened fire on this same imposing array, but decided against saying so. The command cars were summoned, and the little cavalcade drove into the town while Captain Ubert assembled his men, having checked with General Leesing that it was in order to obey the major. 'I assume he intends to make some arrests,' Leesing said. 'We must give the police their head, Ubert. Up to a point, anyway.'

The town hall was in the square, and here Wassermann found the mayor and several other dignitaries waiting for him. As, it seemed, was most of the town, very nearly ten thousand people, relieved that their houses had been left undamaged by the fighting. 'Herr Major.' The mayor was a short, stout man, but he wore his chain of office with great dignity. 'May I assist you?'

'Yes,' Wassermann said, stepping down from his car. 'I am here to arrest all of your people who fired upon our column this morning.'

'None of my people took part in the battle, Herr Major. The guerillas were from Uzice.'

'Did your people make any attempt to prevent this cowardly ambush?'

'How could we, Herr Major? They were heavily armed. We have no weapons.'

'But you willingly gave shelter to their wounded.'

'Well, they were women. And they were badly hurt. They could have died.'

'Did you not know they were going to die anyway? Those taken in arms against the Reich, or assisting anyone in arms against the Reich, in Reich-occupied territory, are by definition traitors to the Reich and will be treated as such. This entire town is condemned as guilty.' The mayor goggled at him. 'However,' Wassermann said, 'I am disposed to be generous. I will not trouble your women and children. Well, not more than is necessary. But you will assemble every adult male in your community. I define adult as anyone over the age of fifteen. And that includes you.'

The mayor gulped. 'We are to be imprisoned? All of us?'

Wassermann smiled at him. 'No, no, Herr Major. You are going to be shot. All of you. I will allow you time to say farewell to your loved ones.'

Sandrine kept E Company going all night; they had suffered no casualties, and were perfectly fresh. They regained Uzice just before dawn, and she dismissed them and went to bed herself, exhausted. She expected to be joined by Tony, but when she awakened a few hours later she was still alone. And oddly disoriented. All around her was the bustle of the town preparing to defend itself against the anticipated attack, but there was no sound of aircraft overhead, as had been expected. She dressed herself and went out, but no one had the slightest idea of what had happened to A and B Companies, although the other two had come in. 'They must have been delayed,' Anja said. 'And they had the furthest to travel.'

'I must go and look for them,' Sandrine insisted.

'You cannot leave the town without permission,' Anja objected. 'Not when we are expecting an attack.'

'Show me this attack. And tell me who is in command of this regiment in Tony's absence?'

'Well, you are.'

'Right. I am giving myself permission to look for them. Until I return, or Tony arrives, you will be in charge.'

Anja looked doubtful. 'Do you wish to take some of us with you?'

Sandrine shook her head. 'I will do better on my own.' She knew she ought to report to Tito, and obtain his permission to go and search for the missing women, but she had an idea that he wouldn't give that permission. Instead, she filled her water bottle, packed some rations, reloaded her tommy-gun, and walked out of the town.

As she was well known to everyone, no one attempted to question where she was going or tried to stop her. She took the direct route that they had used the night before last, increasingly disturbed that there was no sign of the returning women – or their commander. She walked for a good two hours, fording the odd shallow stream, sticking to the valleys between the low hills but staying off the road, until she realized that Tony was not coming this way; indeed, when she sat down for a drink of water and something to eat – it was now past noon – she thought she could hear the grind of engines in the distance. That could only mean that the Germans had repaired the bridge, and were advancing again. Up this valley!

Hastily she repacked her haversack, slung her tommy-gun, and climbed the hillside beside her. Tony had either been caught and overrun – which she refused to accept – or he had taken a more westerly route, so as to be out of the path of the German advance. Of course that was what he had done.

At the top of the hill she paused for breath, and looked about her. Real visibility was limited by the other hills that rose all around her; she could see neither Kragujevac nor the road beyond it. But she could see into the next valley, and wanted to scream for joy when she saw movement down there, flitting in and out of the trees with sufficient stealth to indicate that they were not Germans. They surely had to be Tony's women.

She ran down the hill as quickly as she could; she could not risk attracting attention by firing her gun. She arrived at the foot of the slope in a rush of pebbles and dust, and looked left and right. She seemed to be alone, but a moment later she heard movement, and saw people coming through the trees towards her. But these were men, not women, and unlike the Partisans had their hair long, and most of them had beards. 'Shit!' she muttered, and then reminded herself that they were all on the same side. But what were Cetniks doing in Partisan-controlled territory?

'Greetings,' she said. 'Did you know there are Germans coming this way?'

'You are a Partisan,' one of the Cetniks accused.

'Sandrine!'

Sandrine's head jerked. 'You!'

'I thought you were dead,' Maric said. 'How did you escape from the sewers?'

'You bastard,' Sandrine said. 'You betrayed us. You knew the Germans were waiting at the fifth exit!'

'I knew we could not all escape as long as they were looking for us. But once they had you, I knew they would stop looking for me. As they did. Only they didn't have you.' He grinned. 'But now they can have you, and we will get the money.'

For a moment Sandrine was too furious to understand what he had just said. 'You are both a traitor and a deserter!'

'Not at all. I have simply decided to serve General Mihailovic instead of General Tito.'

Sandrine released the catch on her tommy-gun, while understanding that she was far too outnumbered to hope to survive. But then she gave a sigh of relief as she recognised the man coming through the trees towards her. 'Captain Matovic!'

'I am Major Matovic now, mademoiselle.'

'I congratulate you. And it is good to see you again.' Which was a lie. She remembered too well his antagonism when she, and Tony and Elena, had been in the Cetnik camp; this man had been responsible for Elena's arrest. But she had to talk her way out of the mess she had got herself into.

'As it is to see you, mademoiselle.' He looked up the hillside behind her. 'Where are the rest of your people?'

'Around,' Sandrine said cautiously.

'And what are you doing here?'

'I . . . We are scouting. I should ask, what are *you* doing here.'

'Scouting,' he said. 'I do not think you have any companions. You said "I" just now. Anyway, we would have heard them.' He drew his pistol, and thrust it forward before she could react. 'Lay down your weapon. You are under arrest.'

'How can you arrest me? How can you dare to do so?'

'Because you are a wanted woman, and because there is only one of you and twenty of us. And because we are old friends, are we not? The last time I saw you was a moment before your English paramour hit me on the head.'

'It was Ivkov the bath-keeper who hit you on the head.'

'At Davis's order. Where is the bath-keeper?'

'He is dead.'

'Well, if you do not wish to join him, lay down your gun.'

Sandrine hesitated, then laid her tommy-gun on the ground. 'Then what is going to happen to me?'

'There are so many things I would like to have happen to you, mademoiselle. So many things I would like to do to you myself.' Matovic sighed. 'But my duty calls. I must hand you over to the Germans.'

Sandrine stared at him for a moment in utter consternation. Then she dropped to her knees to regain her tommy-gun, but before she could do so her arms were seized by two of the Cetniks. 'You are a treacherous bastard!' Sandrine spat at him. 'A dog!'

'And you are a victim of the fortunes of war, mademoiselle.'

'May we play with her, Captain?' Maric asked. 'Just for a little while. I have long wanted to have this woman.'

Matovic considered. 'Well,' he said, 'I promised to hand her over unharmed. So there must not be any serious injuries. But I am sure a woman like the famous Sandrine Fouquet would resist arrest. Or attempt to do so.'

Tony and Sasha got their people moving at dawn. They sat up together, and looked at each other, Sasha's cheeks pink as she smoothed her hair. They had not had intercourse, but she had unbuttoned her pants and put his hand inside, closing her thighs on him and moving sufficiently to satisfy herself while she had kissed him almost savagely. He had not attempted to withdraw. He did not consider that he was being unfaithful to Sandrine in restoring Sasha's morale; he reckoned she was his most able subordinate – after Sandrine, of course. But now the secrets of the night had to remain secrets.

She brought him breakfast and coffee. 'What do you want us to do?' she asked.

'Rejoin our people,' he said.

'And Sandrine.'

'Yes,' he said. 'And Sandrine.'

Although Sasha's nerves – and more – had been restored by the night's rest, their problems had increased. Now seven of the wounded were no longer capable of walking, and they had no analgesic drugs. 'Make more stretchers,' Tony said. 'We cannot leave them behind.' This slowed their progress even more. He had hoped to regain Uzice by mid-morning – it had taken them less than twenty-four hours to get from the town to their position outside Kragujevac – but it was noon before they saw the rooftops and were challenged.

'Colonel Davis,' said the lieutenant commanding the picquet. 'We have been worried about you.' He looked over the exhausted women.

'We had some problems,' Tony said. 'The rest of my people?'

'They came in this morning.'

129

'And the Germans? We have seen no planes.'

'There have been no planes. We do not understand.'

Tony nodded. 'Sasha, take your women into camp and dismiss them. I will send you medics for the wounded. You must rest for a while, or until the Germans attack.'

Sasha hesitated, looking as if she would have said something, then rejoined her company.

Tony reported to Tito, who was waiting with apparently total confidence and patience in his office. 'That is good work,' the general said. 'How long do you estimate they will take to get moving?'

'A minimum of six hours. Then their advance will be slow, in anticipation of another ambush.'

'Excellent. That means they will hardly have the time to establish their position before our withdrawal commences. How did your women behave?'

'Very well, in battle. A considerable reaction set in after we withdrew. We took some casualties, and we had to leave our more seriously wounded behind.'

'You would have done better to shoot them.'

'I did order that to be done. But my women would not obey.'

'So they are not quite as battle-ready as you supposed. They will learn. What are they doing now?'

'I have dismissed them for a few hours. They are all exhausted.'

Tito nodded. 'I have had a report from our scouts that the main German force has left Belgrade, and is advancing towards us along the road. I estimate they will be here by dusk, so we may anticipate an aerial bombardment at that time or even during the night. I would say the main assault will begin at dawn. So we are going to start moving out as soon as it is dark, back to our secondary defence. But it is essential to force the enemy to commit herself and attack the town. That will mean it will take him several hours to disengage and regroup before he can begin his pursuit. You go and have a sleep, and then get your regiment together and prepare to move out.'

Tony saluted. He was as exhausted as anyone, didn't even want to think of food until he had had a lie-down in Sandrine's arms. But the apartment was empty.

He went to the barracks where Anja and her women were resting. 'Oh, Colonel!' Anja greeted him. Like the others, she was down to her underwear, despite the chilling air, and drinking beer. 'Sandrine found you, then. She was very worried about you.'

An icy hand seemed to clasp Tony's heart. 'What do you mean, found me?'

'Well . . .' Anja looked puzzled. 'When you did not come in this morning, she became worried, as I said. She said she would go and find you.'

'Who went with her?'

'No one. She just went off.'

Tony left the barracks and stood on the street, utterly at a loss. All around him people were preparing for the battle, boarding up their windows, filling sandbags – as if either sandbags or a few sheets of plywood would keep out an aircraft bomb or a tank shell.

He went to headquarters, where Tito regarded him somewhat wearily. 'There is a problem?' Tony told him. 'She is very fond of you,' Tito agreed. 'We must hope that she has not got herself into trouble.'

'I wish permission to take a squad and go after her, sir.'

'I cannot permit that.'

'With respect, sir . . .'

'With respect, Colonel Davis. I know this woman is very important to you. But I have to consider her as just a single unit of all the many whom I, and you, command. It was very foolish of her to go wandering off by herself. She is actually guilty of desertion, and so close to the enemy.' He held up his finger as Tony would have spoken. 'We must hope that, having failed to find you, she will return, at which time you will no doubt discipline her. If she has come to some harm, there is nothing any of us can do about it now. I certainly cannot permit one of my senior officers to go wandering off at such a time as this. You have a regiment to command, Tony. Five hundred women, for whom you have as much responsibility collectively as for any one of them individually.'

'She could have fallen and hurt herself, be lying helpless in some ravine.'

'That would be unfortunate, but she is an experienced guerilla. She will know how to survive, and how to get back to us.'

'She is out there looking for me. She will expect me, in turn, to go looking for her.'

'I am sure she has more sense than to expect that at this time. I have said that I am sorry. And, I have to tell you, disappointed. I thought that she was reliable, a soldier first and a woman after. Now it appears that I was wrong. Dismissed, Colonel. And I expect to see you at the head of your regiment when we pull out.'

Tony saluted, and left the office. He knew Tito was absolutely right. Sandrine had broken every rule in the book. The trouble was, Sandrine did not believe that any of the rules in the book – or any book – applied to her. As far as she was concerned, there was only her, and him. And now . . .

Of course, he told himself, nothing could have happened to her. The Germans had been several hours behind them, and even if she had returned to the neighbourhood of Kragujevac, she would hear them long before they could have any idea she was in the vicinity. While if she had fallen and hurt herself, Tito was right in expecting that she was sufficiently experienced to cope with any injury. Besides, she knew this country so well, had traversed it so often, there was very little risk of that.

He just wished she would come back.

Brigadier General Leesing stood up in his command car, and gazed at the scene before him in utter consternation. The bridge having been reported repaired, he had just given the order to move out when he and his staff had been alerted by the firing. They had ignored the first couple of volleys, but when they had become continuous and unceasing they had to be investigated.

Now he gazed at two rows of men, one of them lying dead on the ground, the other still alive and shuffling forward under the muzzles of the German rifles. He listened to the wails and screams of the women and children, who had been herded into the other side of the square, again kept under subjection by the pointed rifle barrels. He watched several of his men staggering past the command car, heads drooping, rifles trailing, unable to manage even a salute; to his horror he saw that one or two were in tears. German soldiers? 'What in the name of God . . . ?'

An officer clicked his heels. 'I am sorry, Herr General, but they cannot stand it. After the second or third volley their hands start to shake. They are young, you see, and inexperienced . . .'

'Who ordered this?'

The captain licked his lips. 'The SS major, Herr General.'

'Wassermann? Where is he? Have him brought to me immediately. And stop this murder.' The captain hurried off, and Leesing sat down to take off his cap and wipe his brow with his handkerchief. His aides followed his example. But the rifle firing and the chain of shuffling men continued.

'You wished to see me, Herr General?' Wassermann appeared beside the car. Even he was looking a little pale.

'I wish to know what the devil you are doing, committing mass murder like this. Why hasn't the firing stopped? I commanded it to be stopped.'

'I am acting under orders, Herr General.'

'Orders? Orders? Whose orders? I have given no such orders.'

'An order was given by General von Blintoft personally, Herr General.'

'Do you expect me to believe that?' Wassermann unbuttoned his breast pocket, and handed him the written order. Leesing gazed at it in consternation. 'This is an open order. It does not authorise anything like this.'

133

'It instructs me to make an example of the people who attacked you, Herr General. This I am doing.'

'These were not the people who attacked us. They were guerillas. Partisans.'

'And do you suppose these people are *not* Partisans, simply because they have hidden their weapons?'

Leesing glared at him, but Wassermann would not lower his eyes. 'And my men? Some of them are in tears. They are in no condition to fight a battle.'

'I agree with you, sir. I am very disappointed in them. Hopefully they will improve with experience. I would recommend that no disciplinary action be taken against them.'

Leesing looked as if he might burst a blood vessel. Then he said, 'I will make a full report of this incident, Major.'

'Of course, Herr General. May I have my order back?'

Leesing looked very inclined to tear the paper up. But it had been signed by the commanding general, and he did not doubt there was a copy at headquarters. He handed Wassermann the paper. 'Let us leave this place,' he told his driver.

The bridge was crossed, but very slowly. As there was at least a twelve-hour march beyond it, there was no possible hope of Leesing arriving at Uzice before well into the night at the earliest, by which time the attack would be in full swing, and if the Partisans decided to pull out there would be nothing to stop them, at least on the south-west. Leesing would be in for a reprimand, which should occupy him for a while, Wassermann reflected. Not that he was the least concerned for the future. His orders had been explicit, and while Blintoft might very well feel that he had been overzealous, he would have to accept the situation.

He withdrew his men from the town when the last male had been killed. 'You may bury your dead,' he told the women, who appeared to be in a state of collective shock. 'Although I would say it makes more sense to burn them.' The unit then moved along the road some two miles, and there pitched camp. 'Double sentries,' Wassermann told Ulrich.

'You think they will seek revenge? Women?'

'It was women who attacked the brigade,' Wassermann pointed out.

'Uncanny,' Ulrich commented. 'How long must we remain here?' He was obviously anxious to be away.

'Until the assault on Uzice has been completed. We will hear the firing. Then we will move out to clean up the pieces. So we may have a restful day. Join me for lunch. Albrecht is a very good cook.'

'I am not hungry, Herr Major. And I am very tired. If you will excuse me . . .'

Wassermann waved his hand. The poor fool was another would-be critic. He had, in fact, turned quite green during the mass execution. He was a faithful subordinate, but he would never be anything more than a subordinate; he lacked the stomach for command, for taking the necessary and often ruthless decisions that went with responsibility. Neither he nor Leesing could see that on this day the guerillas had been dealt a blow from which they would never recover.

He had small faith in a German triumph tonight. Oh, it would be trumpeted as a victory, as the Partisans would undoubtedly have to abandon Uzice and withdraw into the mountains. He did not doubt that some of them would accomplish that, even if they had to fight their way through the Cetniks. But no matter where they went, where they now sought shelter, people would think twice about helping them. Because they would remember Kragujevac.

His servant had pitched his tent, and placed a folding chair and table in front of it. Wassermann sipped his lukewarm wine – what he would give for a bottle of good, cold hock – and watched five people approaching. Two walked in front. One was a lieutenant carrying a drawn pistol; the other wore a khaki uniform and was unarmed. They came quite close before he could recognise the guerilla. Then he said, 'Good God!'

'This man came to us under a flag of truce, Herr Major,' the lieutenant said. 'He says he has something of the greatest importance to tell you. He has been searched.'

'Thank you, Dittring. You may leave us.'

'Ah . . .' Dittring looked apprehensive.

'I assure you, Dittring, this man is not going to attack me. Are you, Matovic?'

'No, Herr Major.'

'So you may leave us, Dittring.' Wassermann waited for the lieutenant to withdraw. 'What have you got for me?'

'What would you like, Herr Major, more than anything else in the world at this moment?'

Wassermann gazed at him for several seconds, then looked past him to where the other three people had remained standing. They were still some distance away, but they were close enough for him to see that only two of them wore German uniform. The other . . . 'You are not claiming to have Davis?'

'The next best thing, Herr Major.'

Wassermann stood up. 'Approach!' The soldiers marched Sandrine forward. Her wrists were bound behind her back, and she had lost her cap. Her hair was untidy, and her clothes were dishevelled and torn; several buttons were missing from her blouse, and the blouse itself was out of her pants, flopping open to expose her breasts – she wore no brassiere. But otherwise he was looking at perhaps the most beautiful woman he had ever seen, a woman who made a schoolgirl like Angela look just like . . . a schoolgirl.

'She is quite unharmed,' Matovic assured him. 'The bruises are superficial. She attempted to resist when she was informed that she was going to be handed over to you.'

Wassermann gazed at Sandrine's face for several seconds; she returned his stare without a blink, her expression coldly impassive. Then he slowly looked up and down her body. 'How did you do it?'

'I must confess, Herr Major, that she walked into our arms, literally.'

'Can she not speak?'

'Is there anything to say?' Sandrine asked in a low voice.

'I think there is, Fräulein. I think there is a lot you will have to say. Has she been searched?'

136

'Yes, I have been searched,' Sandrine snapped.

'But I think I will do it again. One cannot be too careful. Thank you, Matovic. You have done very well.'

'There is the reward . . .' Matovic reminded him.

'Of course. But I do not carry ten thousand Deutschmarks about in my pocket. You will receive the reward; I will contact you when it is suitable for us to meet again. In the meantime . . . Sergeant, this man has safe conduct out of our camp.'

The sergeant clicked his heels. Matovic looked at Sandrine. 'I will wish you good fortune, mademoiselle.'

'I hope God will have mercy on your soul,' Sandrine said. 'Because I will have none.' Matovic hesitated for a moment, then walked away.

'I think you would do better to consider your own soul, mademoiselle,' Wassermann said. 'But do you mind if I call you Sandrine? We are going to get to know each other so very well, you see.'

Not for the first time that day, Sandrine had to resist a strong temptation to scream. In fact, for all her tendency to give little shrieks when surprised, she was not given to screaming, or to extreme fear. For the past six months she had lived in the shadow of imminent death, as had all the Partisans, and, indeed, most of the inhabitants of Yugoslavia – and that included the Germans. Her awareness of being alive had centred entirely upon Tony, on his survival and his well-being. Thus even at this extreme moment she could feel relief that he was clearly safe; were he not, either Matovic or the Germans would know of it. But while she had known she was living on borrowed time, and accepted it, she had always assumed that she would go out in a blaze of gunfire, like Elena Kostic, shouting defiance and shooting at the enemy to the last, vitally aware of being *alive* until the fatal bullet swept her into oblivion. Just to walk into the arms of the enemy because she had assumed they were friends was not only stupid, but criminal.

Thus she had had to endure. Although they had not actually raped her, in the dictionary definition of the word, they had stripped her naked and amused themselves with her body. She had only been able to reflect that she had been in this position before, when she had been captured by the Ustase, and she had survived, and been able to avenge her mistreatment. But then she had had Tony and Elena at her side. Now she would have to endure this man, and she had a suspicion that he was going to be a tougher proposition than even Ante Pavelic.

She had never met Wassermann, had never even seen him before – apart from that brief glimpse of him at the railway station the day Frau von Blintoft had been shot – but she had heard of him, of what he was capable of, and on their way here they had passed close to Kragujevac, and heard the moans and the wails of the women burying their dead. She had to conclude that the people of the town had been presumed guilty of assisting the Partisans, if only by not attempting to prevent them from laying the ambush, but there was really nothing they could have done to stop it, and to shoot every male adult in revenge . . . The man who could have carried out such a crime against humanity had to be a monster. Who was now smiling at her.

'Do you not wish to call me Fritz?'

'I will call you anything you wish, Herr Major,' Sandrine said. 'If I can also call you anything *I* wish.'

'Then we have a deal. I enjoy it when women call me names. It inspires me to do things to them. And you . . . Do you know that you are far better-looking than I had expected, or hoped? That photograph does not do you justice. Dismissed,' he told the waiting sentry; the sergeant had gone off with Matovic. The sentry saluted, and left. 'Come over here,' Wassermann invited. Sandrine, her wrists still tied behind her back, approached him and stood next to the table, on which Albrecht had placed a fresh bottle of wine.

'Another chair,' Wassermann commanded. 'But first . . .' He stepped up to Sandrine, put his hands inside her blouse, grasping each breast in turn to give it a gentle squeeze, then stooped to do the same to her thighs and between her legs, caressing her buttocks. Sandrine stayed still, and kept her breathing under control. 'Very good,' Wassermann said. 'Now, I am going to release your hands. You will like that, eh? When I have done that, you will sit down and lunch with me. We shall be very civilised. But I must warn you that should you attempt to use your combat skills – I am sure you have many combat skills – I will hurt you very badly. I have combat skills as well, you see. More than you, I would say. And I also have the support of Albrecht.'

Sandrine waited while her wrists were freed, and she massaged them as the blood flowed back into her hands with exquisite pins and needles. Wassermann gestured her to a chair, and she sat down, for the first time realising how tired she was. As for what was happening, and what was going to happen, he was clearly enjoying himself, living out some fantasy which had happily, for him, come true. Her only business was surviving for as long as possible, in the hopes that Tony would eventually rescue her. That could not be a hope – it had to be a certainty.

Albrecht had produced another glass. Wassermann sat beside her, and poured. 'What shall we drink to?'

'Your damnation, and that of all your friends,' she suggested.

He chuckled. 'I think it would be better to drink to us. Our relationship.'

'Are we going to have a relationship?'

'Oh, indeed, I have said this.'

'You mean I am not to be shot, or hanged, immediately?'

'Good heavens, no. I would not dream of it.' He waited while Albrecht served the meal. 'We will first of all establish the relationship of which I spoke. You will then be handed over to the Gestapo for interrogation. But as I both command and control the Gestapo in Yugoslavia, this will only serve to further our relationship. You will then be required to confess to the murder of Frau von Blintoft, as well as quite a few other crimes against the Reich that you are known to have committed . . .'

'I did not murder Frau von Blintoft.'

'Oh, I know you did not pull the trigger. But you were there. You were part of the murder squad. You are as guilty as anyone. But no doubt you will tell us the name of the man who actually fired the shot.' He paused, and Sandrine stared at him. 'Oh, well, as it happens, we know it already. But when we have questioned you for a while, you will be put on trial with various accomplices of yours who are in our possession already. I'm afraid it will have to be a show trial, with camera recordings and all that sort of nonsense. This is what General von Blintoft wants, and what he will have. And then, when you have been found guilty, you will be hanged in the public square in Belgrade. Sadly, there will not be a trap. You will be hoisted by a rope, slowly. Your hands will be bound, but not your legs. You will be able to kick.'

Sandrine finished her wine. She felt physically sick, but she was not going to let him see that. 'And suppose I am found not guilty?'

He gazed at her for several seconds, then burst out laughing. 'I do adore women with a sense of humour. You are not eating.'

'I really am not hungry.'

'Ah, well. In that case, let us begin our relationship. In there.' Sandrine got up, and went into the tent. Her legs were trembling, but he could not see them inside her trousers. Wassermann followed her, ducking his head. 'Take off your clothes. Face me.' Sandrine obeyed, bending to unlace her boots, pulling off her socks, letting her trousers drop around her ankles, and then taking off her blouse. Then she let her drawers follow her trousers to the ground. She was in a position where she could only suspend reality to the best of her ability, keep telling herself that what was about to happen to her had no meaning, that she would eventually survive and recover. With Pavelic she had always felt that it would be possible to escape, once he had sated himself. She wondered if this could apply to this man? Somehow she did not think so. But she would not despair.

'So much beauty, unadorned,' Wassermann reflected. 'It is the most delightful of sights.'

'I would be better after I had had a bath,' Sandrine said.

'You are sufficiently delightful now,' he assured her. He moved against her, fondled her breasts and buttocks, her belly and pubes. He did not feel that he was in any way being unfaithful to Angela. Having sex with this woman was not in the slightest degree an act of love. It was an act of conquest, of triumph over the enemy, which would at once degrade her, and, he was sure, make her the more vulnerable to the pain he intended to inflict upon her. Besides, the idea of having sex with a woman he intended to torture was compellingly attractive.

But he could feel the suppressed muscular tension beneath his fingers. She made him think of a steel spring, coiling up before unleashing itself with deadly force. And he needed to remember, judging by her record, that the force would indeed be deadly, were she ever to be given the chance to use it. 'However,' he said, 'I think it would be better for both of us, and much safer, if we bound your hands behind your back again. I intend to take you from behind, anyway.' He turned her round, and secured her wrists. She made no protest. 'Aren't you going to say anything?' he asked. 'You were going to call me names.'

'I can be patient,' she said. 'There will be time enough to call you names when you are lying at my feet, waiting to die.'

He glared at her, then swung his hand. It crashed into her cheek, and she fell to the ground. Unable to break her fall, she could not resist a little moan of pain. Wassermann stood above her, breathing heavily, having to resist the temptation to kick her, again and again. He wanted her, so very badly. But suddenly he realized that at this moment he could not have her, no matter how hard he tried. He could not account for it, had to assume he was overtired; he would never admit it might be his still looming memory of the massacre he had commanded, the hundreds of men being shot down in cold blood. Perhaps, if he continued to feel her up . . . But then, he also wanted to hurt her, so very badly, and he knew that if he tried to have sex with her, and could not erect, much less ejaculate, he *would* hurt her, very badly, and even visibly. And that was not part of his plan – at least not in the first instance.

She would keep. She would still be at his mercy when this brief campaign was over, and he had nothing more to do than enjoy himself. But until then . . . He knelt beside her, rolled her to and fro for some minutes while he savaged her, slapping her buttocks, squeezing her breasts, putting his hands between her legs to squeeze her there too, pulling her hair, both on her head and at her pubes. Sandrine gasped, and uttered one or two moans. But she would not cry out. Another few minutes, he thought, and I will kill her.

He stood up, leaving her lying there, and stepped outside. 'Albrecht! Summon Captain Ulrich.' Albrecht scurried off. Wassermann returned inside the tent, where Sandrine was struggling to rise to her knees. He knelt beside her and freed her wrists, and she looked at him in surprise. 'Get up,' he commanded. 'And get dressed.' She hesitated, suspecting that he was playing some game, then cautiously picked up her drawers.

'Sir?' Ulrich stood in the tent opening, looking bewildered.

'Come in, Ulrich.' Ulrich entered the tent, cautiously, and did a double take when he saw Sandrine pulling up her pants. 'You haven't met,' Wassermann said. 'This is Mademoiselle Sandrine Fouquet, of whom I know you have heard.'

'Sandrine Fou . . . ?'

'Oh, indeed. Everything comes to him who waits, eh? Sandrine, this is my aide, Captain Hermann Ulrich.' Sandrine buttoned her blouse as best she could; there were only two buttons left. 'Would you not agree that she is twice as handsome as we thought?'

'Ah . . . indeed, Herr Major.' Ulrich had got his breath back. 'But how . . .'

'Our good friend Matovic delivered her into our hands. Now, Ulrich, I am placing her in your hands.'

'Sir?' Ulrich looked extremely apprehensive.

142

'She is a most important prisoner,' Wassermann reminded him. 'I wish you to take her back to Belgrade, and lock her up. Now listen to me very carefully. I do not wish her harmed in any way, and I wish her to be kept incommunicado until I return. No one is to know of her arrest.'

'Yes, Herr Major.'

'And Ulrich, do remember that she has a sting which can be fatal. You will take four men with you, and make sure that she is handcuffed until she is in her cell. Then you should take every precaution to make sure that she cannot commit suicide.'

Ulrich clicked his heels, and gazed at Sandrine. Who gazed back, her face expressionless.

'In Belgrade you will place her in the care of Anke,' Wassermann said. 'But be very sure that that harpy does not harm her in any way. Nor do I wish her raped. Do you understand?'

Ulrich's face was stiff. 'I am not in the habit of raping women, Herr Major.'

'I was not thinking of you, you dolt. I was thinking of Anke.'

Ulrich gulped.

'Well then,' Wassermann said, 'off you go.' He chucked Sandrine under the chin. 'Amuse yourself until I can come to you. Then we will resume our unfinished business.'

Seven

Retreat

I t was late afternoon before the dust could be seen across the plain below Uzice. Having had a short but intense sleep before carrying out a brief and fruitless reconnaissance south-east of the town, Tony was with Tito and the other officers on the north-eastern outskirts to watch the approach of the panzers followed by the truckloads of infantry.

It had been a dreadful day. At every sound behind him he had spun round, hoping against hope that it might be Sandrine, standing there with that slightly quizzical expression of hers . . . but it never had been. He had inspected his women, sat for some time with the seven badly wounded, who had been tended by the army doctors and given painkilling tablets, but even in their drowsy state they had understood his anguish; it was shared by the entire regiment. 'If there is anything we can do . . .' Draga told him. Sasha stood aside, watching him with brooding eyes.

But now at last there was the prospect of a fight, although they were puzzled about the German tactics. 'There are no aircraft,' someone observed once Tito had called a meeting of his commanding officers to discuss their own tactics.

'Then they will not attack until dawn,' suggested someone else.

'I think he means to outsmart us,' Tito said. 'I think he will just keep on coming. So we may expect the attack this evening, without air support.'

'In the dark, sir?'

'In the dark. He does not care who gets killed. I imagine

144

he has told his men to shoot everything or anyone that moves, and burn any structure they do not like the look of. Well, we certainly wish them to engage. Captain Ivanovic, your regiment will defend the town for half an hour following the initial attack, then you will withdraw. This manoeuvre will have to be carried out as rapidly as possible, but order must be maintained. You will be covered by the main force.' Ivanovic, young and eager, saluted. 'The rest of you will begin your withdrawal to the prepared position now,' Tito went on. 'What is the latest report from the north-east sector, Colonel Asztalos?'

'The right-hand pincer is in position, sir, in the woods four miles from the town.'

'Very good. Colonel Davis?'

Tony's reconnaissance, with Sasha and a squad of her girls, had been at least partly able to mount a search for Sandrine without disobeying Tito's orders. They had not found her, but . . . 'There is no sign of the left-hand pincer as yet, sir. But there is evidence that there have been people in the area. I would say they were Cetniks.'

Tito was frowning. 'In what strength, would you say, Colonel?'

'Not great. Perhaps twenty men.'

'Then they must have been a reconnaissance only. In that case, their main body must have been close behind. Well, gentlemen, we always assumed it was possible that Mihailovic might attempt to cut off our retreat, which is why it was never my intention to withdraw towards him. We are going to the south-west. This will take us away from the right-hand pincer, but it must still be prevented from moving towards us. Colonel Asztalos, you will take your men back to the north-west. This is to mask our retreat. Do not make contact with the enemy until either they attack you or you receive my command. The order will be the word "go". When that is received, you will launch a holding attack, and then withdraw to the south-west to link up with the main force. Understood?' Astzalos saluted. 'The rest of you,' Tito said, 'will withdraw in regiments to the prepared position. Once there you will dispose yourselves in your allotted sections as indicated on the map, and await assault. But you will also await the order to withdraw. When this comes, you will do so, leaving your positions in order of deployment. You also will move south-west into Bosnia. We will retreat as separate units to lessen the risk of heavy casualties to air attack, as we must expect the enemy to harass us in every way possible, but we will keep in touch and reunite as soon as it is practical. As I have said, our ultimate destination is the town of Foca. This is situated on the River Drina, about sixty kilometres south-east of Sarajevo on the eastern slopes of Mount Lilija. This means that it is defensible not only in a tactical sense but in a strategic one as well, while its proximity to Sarajevo will enable us both to keep in touch with what is happening and to obtain supplies. I know there are German forces in the city, but they will find Foca a harder nut to crack than Uzice.'

'Can we expect any local support?' someone asked.

'I believe we will be well received by the locals, and those hills will provide good concealment. Now there is one thing I need to make clear. The Germans are coming here to destroy us. It is our business, our duty, to remain in being as an army, in order that one day – hopefully one day soon – we may be able to counter-attack and avenge ourselves. Thus we cannot, under any circumstances, allow ourselves to be destroyed. By that I mean there can be no delays, or gallant last-minute stands, to assist our wounded. The orders I gave earlier still stand. Those who can walk will be taken along. Those who cannot must be abandoned to fend for themselves, with sufficient food and water and ammunition for survival, if possible. You should advise them against allowing themselves to be taken prisoner.' The assembled officers listened, stony-faced. 'I know this will be an intensely difficult decision to take, both for you and for them. But they must understand that if they are captured they will in any event be shot by the Germans. After being tortured to reveal our whereabouts and dispositions. As I have just said, the preservation of the army is paramount. Any questions?'

'What is our response if we are not well received by the Bosnians, General?'

'It must be as low-key as possible. Bear in mind an old Chinese saying: a guerilla force is like the fishes in a river; the river can exist without the fish, but the fish cannot exist without the river. We want no clashes with the local population. We want their support. You have all been issued with money, both paper and gold. Pay for what you have to obtain. And there are to be no reprisals. Dismissed. Colonel Davis.' Tony waited as the other officers left the room. 'I have placed your regiment in the rear of the army. That means you will be the first to pull out.'

'Do you not suppose my women have proved themselves in combat?'

'Indeed they have. By their action at Kragujevac they have bought us the time we need.'

'Then are they not worthy of a fighting role?'

'I have given you the most important part of all to play. No matter how well Asztalos carries out his task, you will still be the first across the front of the right-hand pincer, therefore you will be taking the most risk. When the retreat begins, you will no longer be the rear of the army, but the advance guard. You will also be self-contained; there can be no doubt that to have your women integrated in the midst of our men would have a bad effect on their fighting ability – the men's, at any rate. Your girls have proved their ability to sustain casualties, and remain in being as a fighting force; I do not know if my men could maintain the same resolve when a handsome young woman is shot down at their side. Even more do I doubt the resolve of my men to abandon a wounded woman to the mercy of the enemy. Therefore I am sending you on a more northerly route than the rest. This means not only that you will have further to travel, but also that you, together with Asztalos's regiment, will in effect be the right wing of the retiring army. But he will still be a march behind you.'

'What of the severely wounded we brought in with us?'

'They will have to remain here. Place them with local families. Make sure they have no weapons and no uniforms to give them away, and that they understand that their survival will depend on how well they can act their roles.'

'And their wounds?'

'Will have been suffered in the German attack. There will be civilian casualties, after all. But there is another, and even more important, reason for your women to lead the retreat. That woman, Sasha Janitz, is a Bosnian. Her father is actually mayor of a village there. I do not remember which one, but she will tell you. She will therefore be returning to friends, and she will pave the way for our acceptance.'

'Do you think she will do this?'

Tito grinned. 'Persuade her, Tony. Make her your adjutant, in place of Sandrine.'

Tito had raised the subject. 'And Sandrine?'

Tito sighed. 'If she has not yet come in, we must assume that she is dead.'

'Or taken by the enemy.'

'I do not believe that someone as capable, and as realistic, as Sandrine would allow herself to be captured. Do you?'

'No,' Tony had to admit. 'She would never allow herself to be captured.'

'So she is dead. We will remember her, and we must hope that she took as many of the bastards with her as she could. But Tony, all of us, and you and Sandrine more than anyone, have been living on borrowed time for the past six months. If any of us survive this war we will count ourselves fortunate beyond belief. But that is not going to stop us from fighting for as long as we can. Now go about your duty. And kill Germans.'

Tony rejoined the women, who were sitting or lying around their barracks waiting anxiously for their orders; the sound of the approaching panzers was now clearly audible. 'We pull out at dusk,' he told them, and looked at his watch. 'That is, in one hour from now. You will draw rations for one week, and make sure your canteens are full, although there should be no shortage of water. There will be an issue of a hundred rounds per woman. Questions?'

'Why are we leaving instead of fighting the Germans?' someone asked.

'The entire army will be retreating,' Tony told her, 'as soon as we can no longer be overseen from the air. We are the advance guard.'

'Can we take our wounded?'

'Anyone who can walk and bear arms. The others will be taken care of.' They exchanged glances, rightly not believing him. 'Get to it,' he said. 'Time is passing. Captain Janitz.' Sasha came to him. 'As of now, you are my adjutant,' he told her.

Her mouth made a delightful O. 'You mean . . .'

'I mean that Sandrine is regarded as dead.'

For a moment she gazed at him. Then she said, 'I am very sorry.'

'Are you?'

Her nostrils flared. 'I will replace her as best I can.'

'Thank you. I have every confidence in you. Our first business is to get to Bosnia. Are you happy about that?'

'Does it mean the war will be carried into Bosnia?'

'There already is a Nazi occupying force in Bosnia, as I am sure you know. But this war will now certainly spill over.'

'Then I cannot be happy about that.'

'But you will do your duty.'

'Yes,' she said. 'I will do my duty.'

'Which, in your case, will include persuading your people to help us.'

'Even if it means their deaths?'

'This is war, Sasha, to the death. Or all Yugoslavia will die. I am particularly thinking of your father. Which village is he mayor of?'

'Wicz.'

'Is it on our line of march from here to the Bosnian mountains?'

She nodded. 'Virtually. You are asking me to sacrifice my own family.'

'Hopefully not. But we will need their help.'

Her eyes glowed at him. 'What do I get in return?'

'What do you wish?'

'To replace Sandrine.'

'I have just appointed you to her rank.'

'I wish everything she had.' They gazed at each other. But he had known it would come to this. She was still excited by yesterday and last night. And he, not to mention the entire army, needed her. And Sandrine? Sandrine was dead, dead, dead, all of that exquisite femininity lying in a crumpled, bloody mess, no doubt already being attacked by ants. All he had left was vengeance. And to accomplish that successfully, he needed the total support of the people he had been appointed to lead. 'All right,' he said. 'You will have everything Sandrine had.'

She stepped against him. 'That makes me very happy. And I will make you very happy too.'

He caught her wrists. 'If you can do that, Sasha, you'll be a miracle-worker. And it'll have to keep until we can spare the time. Right now we have a lot to do.'

They placed the wounded women on stretchers, and distributed them amongst those of the townsfolk who were prepared to have them. It was a heart-rending business, and more so for Sasha than himself, Tony reckoned, because these were members of her own company, who knew they were unlikely ever to see their comrades again. They clung to Sasha's hands, and implored her to come back to them.

'As soon as I can,' she promised, and looked at Tony with anguished eyes.

Then it was time to move out. The advancing Germans were clearly visible now, at a distance of hardly more than a mile, the tanks lined up, the infantry disembarking from their trucks and deploying to left and right. On the town perimeter, Ivanovic's men were dug in and waiting; they had some machine guns and a couple of mortars, but they were not firing as yet, saving their ammunition for when the attack commenced. Behind them, the town was shuttered and quiet; even the cats and dogs had withdrawn from the streets in anticipation of the coming battle. The various other regiments were assembling to pull out, making way for the women who filed through them. There were exchanges of jests and quips, given and received in high spirits and good humour. Tito was there with his people, and shook hands with both Tony and Sasha. 'Good fortune,' he said. 'We will meet in Foca.'

Tony took his place at the head of the column, Sasha immediately behind him, and Draga and Anja leading the other officers. As they left the houses, they heard a stir of noise behind them. A German command car had rolled forward under a flag of truce. Tony could not hear what was being said, but presumably the Germans were calling for the surrender of both the town and the Partisans. And clearly the demand was refused. The women had left the town some half a mile behind them when the tanks opened fire.

Shells screamed into and over the town, exploding with gushes of sound, often accompanied by equal gushes of flame and smoke. The rearguard immediately returned fire, and the gathering dusk was turned into kaleidoscopic cacophony. 'Keep going,' Tony told his women, not that they needed much encouragement. None of the shells had been thrown behind the town as yet, and they moved in perfect safety, reaching the prepared trenches and earthworks without loss. By then it was becoming quite dark, and Tony studied his plan with his flashlight, Sasha at his shoulder. They located their allotted position quite easily, and settled down to wait, the radio being set up so that they could listen for the word of command.

Now they could look back at the town. They could see little of the battle because of the gloom, but there were already numerous fires, and the noise continued to be tremendous. Tony and Sasha moved up and down the ranks, encouraging the women and reminding them that they had a long night ahead of them. But soon they saw another regiment picking its way towards them, and then another, and a few minutes later there came the signal, 'Go!' Immediately firing broke out to the north as Asztalos went into action. 'Pack up that gear,' Tony commanded. 'Move it!'

He sent Sasha up to the head of the column while he remained behind to make sure everyone was coming out. Anja stayed with him, and once everyone was moving he left her in charge of the rearguard while he returned to the front. 'Look there,' Sasha said. Now they could see the flashes to the right, and they could hear the various tones of the different weapons being used. 'I feel it is bad,' she said, 'that we should be moving in such safety while all around us there is fighting.'

'We're obeying orders,' he reminded her. They marched into the darkness, Tony using his compass to keep them heading steadily just south of west, as instructed by Tito. The firing remained heavy both behind them and on their right, but began gradually to fade. After an hour Tony allowed them a ten-minute rest, and this pattern he maintained throughout the night; the women were very fit and full of spirit, and only a handful fell asleep and had to be slapped into wakefulness. They were following a rough track, which had once been a road, but now, although a useful aid to direction, was an uneven, potholed switchback. Progress was very slow in the dark, as people constantly fell into holes or tripped and sprawled on the earth, handicapped as they were by the bandoliers and cartridge belts slung around their necks and over their shoulders. No one complained about either the bruises they suffered from their falls or the weight they had to carry – they were all too afraid of being left behind.

Eventually the sounds of battle were only a dim rumble, and because of the hills they could no longer even see the glow of the burning town. It was past midnight when there was a challenge from out of the darkness. 'Who comes?'

'Deploy,' Tony muttered, and the women spread out; the night suddenly filled with the rustle and clicks of their weapons being made ready for use. 'Identify yourself,' he commanded.

Bearded men emerged out of the gloom; behind them Tony could discern the outlines of a rough barricade across the road. 'We serve General Mihailovic,' someone said.

'And we serve General Tito,' Tony replied.

Sasha stood at his elbow. 'They will have a machine gun,' she muttered. Tony squeezed her arm.

'You are fleeing Uzice?' the Cetnik officer asked.

'We are taking up a new position,' Tony countered.

The officer was now only a few feet away, and thus he could make out the flutter of Sasha's hair; on the march it had emerged from its normal hiding place down her collar. Equally he could discern that the people immediately about her were also women. 'You are the women's regiment,' he remarked. 'We have heard of this. And you are fleeing.'

'Yes, this is the women's regiment,' Tony told him. 'And as I have said, we are changing positions. Move your people, and let us through.'

'My orders are to permit no one to pass along this road,' the Cetnik said.

'And my orders are to move along this road,' Tony said. 'Which is what I intend to do. I have five hundred women at my back, every one armed.'

'Women,' the captain sneered.

'You have five minutes to clear the way,' Tony told him, and levelled his tommy-gun. The Cetnik stared at him for several seconds, attempting to decide how determined he was. 'Four,' Tony said. The officer turned, and ran back to the barricade. 'Charge!' Tony shouted. 'Open fire!' The women ran forward, tommy-guns chattering and rifles cracking. The Cetnik captain was struck in the back, and fell to the ground, the women trampling on him. The machine gun fired a single burst, and was rewarded with several shrieks of pain. In no time at all they reached the barricade, still firing, scattering men left and right. The brief battle lasted no more than a few minutes before the Cetniks had faded into the darkness, leaving a good dozen men dead, and three taken prisoner.

'Casualties!' Tony called.

Anja reported a few minutes later. 'We have three dead and five wounded, sir.'

'You may bury the dead. Can the wounded walk?'

153

'Three can. The other two have been hit in the leg.'

Tony sighed, and went to the wounded women. One of them was very young, hardly more than sixteen, he thought, her face twisted with pain. The other was both older and calmer, although that she was in pain could not be doubted. He knelt beside them. 'You know we must leave you.' They stared at him with enormous eyes. 'You will have a full canteen each, and a week's rations,' he said. 'Here is some morphine, but keep it as long as the pain is bearable. You have your side arms, and enough ammunition to protect yourselves from robbers.' He forced a grin. 'Or itinerant Cetniks. We must take your rifles. But here is a string of grenades. If your situation becomes unbearable, or if the Germans come up to you, use them. Do not let yourselves be captured. Do you understand this?'

They made brave attempts to smile. Tony straightened, and looked at Anja, whose company they were part of. 'I will just say goodbye,' Anja said.

Tony nodded, and returned to where Sasha was standing over the prisoners, who were all quite young and very frightened, sitting on the ground with their hands on their heads. 'What do I do with these?' she asked.

'We cannot take prisoners.'

'I know this.' She licked her lips.

'But we're not in the murder business, Sasha. Not of our own people. Not right now, anyway. They were only obeying Mihailovic's orders. Turn them loose.'

'They killed some of my girls.'

'As we killed some of them. I'll not have them murdered in cold blood, Sasha.'

She pouted, then smiled wickedly. 'Has it not occurred to you that they may know of Sandrine?' Tony frowned. He hadn't thought of that. And it was extremely unlikely. 'I will ask them.' She knelt beside the youngest of the three, a boy in his teens, who positively blanched as she ran her finger down the faint fuzz on his jaw. 'You know the name Sandrine Fouquet?'

He licked his lips. 'I have heard it.'

'She is worth a lot of money. Thousands of dinars. Do you know this?'

Another lick of the lips. 'There was a poster . . .'

'Yes,' Sasha said. 'You have seen the poster. Now tell me what you know of her.'

'I? I know nothing of this woman. I have never seen her.'

'You did not see her yesterday morning?'

'No. How could I see her? She is . . .' His eyes rolled over the women, who were gathering to look at him.

'Were there not Cetniks south-east of Uzice yesterday?'

'I do not know.'

'I think you do,' Sasha said. 'Do you know what I am going to do if you do not tell me the truth?' From the sheath on her belt she drew her knife. 'I am going to pull down your pants, and then I am going to cut off your balls, one after the other. Then I am going to slice your prick, right up the middle. That is what I am going to do.'

The boy gasped. 'I do not know what happened in the south,' he gabbled. 'We have been in position here for two days.'

'Remember, you have brought this on yourself,' Sasha said, and unbuckled his belt.

The boy screamed in terror and anticipated shame. 'Enough,' Tony said. Sasha turned her head to look up at him; her handsome face was distorted with passion. 'Let him go,' Tony said. 'Let them all go.'

'Why?'

'Because he is telling the truth. He does not know what happened in the south, and thus what happened to Sandrine. Let them go. That is an order.' Reluctantly, Sasha sheathed her knife and stood up. 'Get up,' Tony said. The three men scrambled to their feet. 'Get back to Mihailovic. Tell him we now regard him as an enemy, and that he will pay for this treachery. Get out.'

The Cetniks faded into the darkness.

The women marched all night, again with a ten-minute rest in every hour. Sasha no longer walked beside Tony, but with one of the other companies. He gathered that she was angry at the way he had overruled her, but he didn't expect it to last.

By dawn they were quite exhausted, but they were also close to a stream. 'We'll take a two-hour break,' Tony said. 'Then we start again.'

Predictably, quite a few of the women stripped off and went for a bath. Tony had a drink of water, refilled his canteen, and sat down some distance away from the rest, eating some smoked chicken. And five minutes later watched Sasha walking towards him. She had been bathing, and was naked, water still dripping from her hair; her uniform was slung over her shoulder, together with her belts and weapons and haversack. She made an entrancing, if – remembering the events of the night – somewhat terrifying sight. But she was smiling. 'So, I am forgiven,' he suggested.

She dumped her gear on the ground, knelt, and spread her blanket beside his. 'You are my commanding officer,' she pointed out. 'I obey your orders.' She lay down beside him.

'And now you have come to claim your rights.'

'Do you not wish me to do this? Do you not find me attractive?'

'I find you very attractive.'

'Well then . . .' She took his hand, and placed it on her breast, stroking it up and down the hardened nipple. 'I am yours.'

'Would you really have tortured that boy?' he asked.

'I wanted to. Then. I can be very passionate.'

'I'm sure.'

'Have you never felt that destructive urge? The urge to inflict pain, to hear somebody scream in agony, to know that he is at your mercy? Or perhaps you would prefer it to be a woman?'

'I have never felt that urge.'

'But you are a soldier. A famous soldier. How many men have you killed?'

'I have no idea. But however many, it has always been in combat. Him or me. Never in cold blood.'

'You killed that German woman in cold blood.'

'I did not. I admit that I was going to shoot the general. I did not like it, but like you, I obey orders. It turned out badly.'

'You mean it turned out exactly as Tito wanted. He has his full-scale war. And we are being killed for it.'

'Do you believe in what he is doing?'

'I believe in fighting for the federation, yes.'

'By that do you mean Yugoslavia?'

'Yes. As things are at present.'

'Don't tell me you would like to see an independent Bosnia?'

'Why should I not? Is not England independent?'

'England has been independent throughout its history, give or take the odd foreign conquest. Has Bosnia ever been independent? If it wasn't ruled by the old Serbs, it was ruled by the Turks. And if it wasn't ruled by the Turks, it was ruled by the Austrians.'

'And now it is ruled by the Nazis. It is time we were given a chance.' She rolled across him, straddling him with her legs. 'I did not come to you for a political argument. I came to make love. I am sorry you do not approve of my behaviour last night. I got worked up. I have been worked up ever since we ambushed the German column. I need you inside me.'

'Because I'm the only man around?'

'Because I am your woman now.' She reared up to rest on her haunches while she unbuckled his belt.

'Well,' he said, looking past her at the rest of the regiment, several of whom were looking at him. 'Let's at least get under the blanket.'

'Message from General von Blintoft, Herr Major,' Albrecht said.

Wassermann sat up, and looked at his watch. It was just after midnight. 'Yes?'

'He has taken Uzice. He says there is work for you.'

'Very good. Wake Captain Rimmer, and tell him we move out in an hour. And bring me a glass of schnapps.' He dressed himself; in anticipation of a sudden summons, he had taken the precaution of shaving before lying down, and was ready to go in fifteen minutes. He drank his schnapps, and listened to the stealthy sound of the camp coming to life, the growl of engines as the various vehicles were started. Albrecht himself drove the command car, and Rimmer was waiting for him.

The two officers sat in the back. 'Was there any word on casualties?' Rimmer asked.

'None,' Wassermann said. 'We will be there in a few hours.' The motorcycle outriders zoomed away in front, and the command car followed, with the column following them in turn. They used their headlights, both because the surface was bad, and because the road they took led round the hills rather than into them. In view of what was happening, or had happened, in Uzice, Wassermann did not suppose there would be Partisans around.

He preferred to think of what he would find when he got back to Belgrade, which, with fortune, could be in a couple of days. There was Angela, certainly. He had everything he could wish from Angela . . . almost. She was a lovely girl, and possessing her body had to be a joy. Except that, sexually, she was utterly boring. She never responded, never attempted to do anything to him or for him. She liked to be manhandled, even violently, and she liked him to pretend to torture her. But even to those fantasies she rarely responded in any wildly demonstrative way, preferring to lie there with her eyes closed, uttering little moans of pleasure. He fully intended to marry her, not only for her looks and the secrets they shared, but because she was Blintoft's daughter. As the general was clearly going places, to be his son-in-law had to be the road to success. But he was already accepting that for really enjoyable sex he would have to look elsewhere.

For this reason, Sandrine Fouquet loomed larger. He did not know what the distant future might hold – that depended to a large extent on the success of this operation, and his part in that success – but the immediate future lay before him with glittering attraction. He did not doubt that beneath that composed exterior Sandrine Fouquet was an emotional bomb;

she had proved that often enough in battle. She was going to respond, in the way he liked. And when he tortured her, there would be no make-believe involved.

The darkness began to fade just as they saw the glow in front of them. So, Wassermann thought, the Partisans had elected to fight for the town after all. How remarkable, and personally satisfying, it would be if Davis had also been taken. Tito would be a bonus.

An hour later, as the sun rose, they reached the city itself. There was a roadblock about half a mile away from the first houses, but the barrier was raised as soon as the swastika flag on the bonnet was seen. Wassermann had Albrecht stop anyway. 'Is there still fighting?' he asked the sergeant.

'One or two snipers, I believe, Herr Major. They are being flushed out.'

Wassermann nodded, and replaced his cap with his steel helmet; he had no intention of being killed by a sniper's bullet. Albrecht drove on, more slowly now. In front of them the town was a shattered wreck, brilliantly illuminated in the bright sunlight: the clouds had for the moment cleared. More than half the houses were damaged, and quite a few were in flames. No attempt was being made to put out the fires, and there were masses of people gathering in the various squares and just outside of the town, many carrying pitiable bundles of food or clothes, or clutching their pets – cats and dogs and caged birds – gazing at what had once been their homes. Albrecht used his horn to clear a path through the people, who gazed at him sullenly. One or two even shook fists, but no one attempted to interfere with the column.

They came to another barrier, this one commanded by a lieutenant. 'The general is at the town hall, Herr Major,' he said.

Now it was necessary to enter the town centre. The passable streets were guarded and indicated by the military police, Wassermann's own men, who saluted their commanding officer smartly. As these streets were obviously the least damaged, and had not yet been reached by the fires, Wassermann studied the windows of the houses beneath which they passed, particularly those on the upper floors; he did not suppose all these buildings had been adequately searched, and thus they could easily contain a sniper, determined on death and glory.

But although the occasional shot could be heard in the distance, none was fired close at hand, and moments later he arrived in the main square. This was crowded, lined round all four sides by armed soldiers, while in the centre there were a number of civilians, lying or sitting on the cobbles. 'Who are these people?' Wassermann asked as he stepped down.

'Prisoners, Herr Major. They are nearly all wounded.'

'And why have they been accumulated here?'

'I think they are waiting for you, Herr Major. To escort them to Belgrade.'

Wassermann looked over the prisoners. There were more than a hundred of them, and many were clearly severely wounded. He went up the steps, returned the salute of the sentries, and was shown to Blintoft, who was surrounded by his staff. 'Well, Wassermann,' Blintoft said boisterously, 'we have gained the day, eh?'

'Indeed, Herr General. Were there many casualties?'

'More than I had anticipated. The enemy fought well for a while, then they ran away.'

'I was speaking of the Partisans, sir.'

Blintoft waved his hand. 'What you saw outside. About twenty dead.'

'And a hundred prisoners? There were three thousand men in the town.'

'That was our information. *Your* information, Wassermann. It would appear to have been an overestimate.'

'Have the defensive lines behind the town been occupied?'

Blintoft was frowning; he did not like being interrogated by a junior officer as if *he* was the junior officer, even if the man was to be his son-in-law. 'Of course they have. Again, resistance was minimal.'

'Then the bulk of the enemy has got away,' Wassermann said. He had supposed a couple of hundred might escape, not a couple of thousand. 'Defending the town was merely a holding action to delay us.'

'A few may have got away,' Blintoft acknowledged. 'But I have sent for the bombers. Now that the bandits are in the open, the Luftwaffe will finish the job.'

'If they can find them,' Wassermann remarked.

'If they do not, it will be because there are not enough left to find. I have received a message from Brigadier General Altman that his right-hand pincer has been attacked, but that he is coping with the situation. It is clearly a last-ditch rearguard action.'

'May I ask in what strength he is being attacked, sir?'

'He cannot say. But he does not think it can be more than a few hundred.'

'And General Leesing?'

'He hasn't even come up yet. I am beginning to doubt his competence. Or his enthusiasm.'

'Then the bulk of the enemy forces may have escaped to the south-west.'

'If they have, they will run into the Cetniks, eh? But in any event, the planes will sort it out. You worry too much, Wassermann. Your business is to convey the prisoners back to Belgrade.'

'For what purpose, sir?'

'Well, to lock them up.'

'Until they can be tried, and shot?'

'Well, we shall leave that decision to Berlin.'

'With respect, sir, I do not think Berlin will appreciate being asked to make decisions at a distance of several hundred miles, and concern themselves with what is, after all, a very small sideshow when compared with the Russian front.' Blintoft glared at him. 'If you would leave the matter in my hands, sir, I will deal with it. And with your permission, I would also like to lead a force in pursuit of the Partisans. You said they had to be destroyed. I will make it my business to see that this is done.'

Blintoft continued to regard him for some seconds, but the

anger was fading from his eyes. 'Very good, Major. But you will wait until our forces have evacuated the town. You will also have to liaise with the Luftwaffe.'

'Very good, sir. I will need written orders.'

'Oh, very well. I will give you carte blanche. But I do not wish to know how you handle it. I wish nothing to be done until the army moves out. That will be at dawn.'

'Of course, sir. But I will also require permission to conduct a search of the town. We do not know how many of these scum are hiding, or being hidden, under our very noses.'

Blintoft nodded. 'You have it.'

'Then finally, sir, I will need to retain the use of a battalion of infantry and a squadron of tanks. To pursue the rebels.'

'Very good, Major.'

Wassermann saluted, and left the room. One of the staff officers said, 'He means to kill them all. The wounded, I mean.'

Blintoft sighed. 'You may be right.'

'But, sir, that is against all the rules of war.'

'I have been instructed to treat these people, these guerillas, exactly as we are treating the guerillas in Russia. Do you know, Klepmann, I came here hoping to turn Yugoslavia into a useful and contented province of the Reich. And the first thing that happens is they murder my wife. Thus I have come to agree with Berlin; these people cannot be treated as human beings. They must be liquidated. I would say that we are lucky to have a man like Wassermann to take care of it for us.' Major Klepmann made a remark under his breath. 'What was that, Herr Major?'

'I was praying, sir, that God may have mercy on our souls.'

Blintoft gave a grim smile. 'What you mean, Major, is that God give us victory in this war. There will be no mercy for the losers.'

Tony's brain told him he should not be doing this, because Sasha could never be his kind of woman: she took too much pleasure in killing. He did not suppose Sandrine was any less ruthless when it came to taking life, but in Sandrine's case it was all passion. In Sasha's case, the passion was too closely mixed with pleasure.

Equally, his heart told him that he should not be doing it. That was simply because he knew he should be mourning Sandrine's death. Which he did, even if the true fact of it had not yet sunk in. Yet an even truer fact was that while Sandrine had been everything to him, and he had allowed himself to dream of a shared future after the war, he had known the chances of that ever coming about, of one of them, much less both, ever surviving this conflict, had been so remote as to be almost non-existent. As Tito had said, they had been living on borrowed time for six months.

But the feeling of utter nihilism which kept creeping over him was reinforced by the demands of his groin, which in turn was accentuated by the amount of femininity with which he was surrounded – especially when he held so much throbbing woman in his arms. Sasha, with her tumbling black hair, her full breasts, her narrow thighs, and her long, strong legs, the whole driven by her quite primordial passion, had to be the sexiest woman he had ever known, or had even been able to imagine. She was not only the present, she was the future, when he would fight as ruthlessly as her, seeking only vengeance. Perhaps he should have let her torture that unfortunate boy after all.

Her hands roamed over his body, and she followed them with her lips. The blanket was discarded, but most of the women were asleep, and she did not seem to feel the chill in the air. Neither did he, as he sought the secrets of her body with his hands in turn. She was delicious, as hard muscle slipped into soft flesh, and she began to moan and toss in the ecstasy of orgasm.

She exhausted him, and herself, more than once, then they both fell into a deep sleep in each other's arms – to awaken to the huge *crump* of an exploding bomb.

PART THREE

COUP

> *The attempt and not the deed,*
> *Confounds us.*

William Shakespeare

Eight

Pursuit

It was after dark before Ulrich regained Belgrade. There were still considerable troops, reserves, logistical trucks, ambulances, and food supply vehicles moving up behind the assault force, and the narrow roads were clogged.

He sat in the back of the command car, Sandrine beside him. He was acutely aware of her femininity as well as her attractiveness, although, while he could not get the image of her standing naked in Wassermann's tent out of his mind – with all the erotic suggestiveness of what might just have happened to her, and even more, what was going to happen to her in the near future – he hastily rejected any erotic ideas of his own. His wife, in their house in Hamburg, might not be able to compare with the Frenchwoman as regarded looks, but theirs was a totally happy marriage – and Helga had never committed an act of violence in her life.

As instructed by Wassermann, he had handcuffed her, but he could not stop himself from feeling sorry for the beautiful little blonde. 'If you were to give me your parole, I would release your arms,' he suggested.

'If you release my arms I will kill you,' she said.

Ulrich let it go. But after they had been on the road for a couple of hours, he uncorked his water bottle, and held it to her lips. She drank greedily. 'You know,' he said, 'it might be a good idea for you to commit suicide.' Sandrine turned her head, sharply. 'Well,' he said, 'we will have to torture you. Even if you admit to every crime of which you are accused, answer every question that is put to you, Wassermann will still

167

insist upon it; he is a sadist. And then there will be only the rope, in public.'

'Wassermann has explained this to me.'

'Well, do you really want to endure all of that?' Sandrine continued to look at him. 'If,' he said, 'when we reach Belgrade and you are put in a cell, a loaded revolver was left in the cell with you, you could do the job.'

'You would do this? What would happen to you?'

'Oh, I would be reprimanded, of course. But only for a simple confusion of orders. What I have just suggested is standard procedure for prisoners whom we do not wish to bring to trial. Now, it is certainly the intention of my superiors to bring you to trial. But it is possible for the orders to be confused, and your guards to be under the impression that you are to be, shall I say, disposed of, secretly.'

'Why should you do this for me? Wassermann specifically warned you against allowing me to take my own life.'

'I know. As I said, I would be reprimanded. But . . . I suppose I have a weakness for pretty women. Besides, I know you are innocent of Frau von Blintoft's death.'

'How do you know this?'

'We have the murder weapon. And therefore the finger-prints of the murderer. Svetovar Kostic. So will you accept my offer?'

'When I am tortured, will you be there?'

'Yes.'

'Will you enjoy that?'

He sighed. 'Sadly, I am as gross as any of them when it comes down to it. But I will hate myself afterwards.'

'Well then, you will have to hate yourself.'

'You understand that it will be absolutely horrible for you? And you also understand that I will not be able to repeat this offer? Once I have delivered you, I must return to the front. And when I come back, it will be with Major Wassermann. Please consider my suggestion.'

'I will thank you for making it, Herr Captain.'

'But why? Why undergo all of that, to no purpose?'

'I shall undergo all of that, as you put it, Herr Captain, because I hope to stay alive long enough to see you and all of your people destroyed.'

They finished the drive in silence, and reached the Gestapo courtyard just after eight. Ulrich opened the door for Sandrine, then escorted her along the passageways and down the stairs to the cell section. 'Who is on duty?' he asked the sergeant. 'Ah, Anke,' he said as the woman emerged from the corridor. 'I have a prisoner for you.' Anke looked at Sandrine; if she immediately guessed who she had to be, she did not let it show in her face. She had a placidly pretty face, which matched her somewhat overweight but still statuesque figure, but her eyes were like drops of blue ice. 'Now listen very carefully,' Ulrich said. 'I wish her placed in a good cell, with furniture. You will feed her properly. She is not to be ill-treated. Her handcuffs will be removed, but you are not to enter the cell unaccompanied. She is a very dangerous woman.'

Anke continued to gaze at Sandrine; as she was twice the size of the Frenchwoman, she obviously did not take the suggestion seriously. Besides, as she allowed her gaze to drift down Sandrine's body, past the half-open blouse, it was apparent that she had other things on her mind. 'She will need to be bathed.'

'Then you will escort her to the showers, and give her a piece of soap. You may watch, but you may not touch. She belongs to Major Wassermann, and must be in perfect condition, mentally and physically, when he returns.'

Anke turned away. 'Come,' she said.

'Again, thank you, Herr Captain,' Sandrine said. She followed Anke down the corridor.

Ulrich watched them go. He was a romantic, and could dream of how different things could be . . . but those were dreams. He was a soldier as well as a policeman. But he could still follow a private path.

He got back into the command car, and was driven to the palace. Guards presented arms, and he was shown into the dining room. Curious as to what he would find there, he was taken aback at once by the size and splendour of the room – he had not been here before – and by the young woman, exquisite in a low-cut black evening gown, seated alone at the head of a vast table, surrounded by servants who were waiting on her every move. 'Forgive this intrusion, Fräulein,' Ulrich said.

'You have come from Major Wassermann?' Angela asked. 'And my father? Has the campaign gone well?'

'I have not come from the general, Fräulein, but I understand everything is going according to plan.'

'Have you eaten?'

'Well, no, Fräulein.'

'Then sit down. Serve the captain,' she instructed the footmen. 'And pour some wine. Now tell me, Captain, the major sent you all the way back here to see me? He isn't hurt?' She asked the question almost casually.

'No, no, Fräulein.' Ulrich took a long drink of wine, and had his glass immediately refilled. 'Major Wassermann is fine, and is doing his duty as always.' Now he had a strong temptation to tell her about the massacre at Kragujevac, but that was too risky. But he could still impress her. 'I was actually sent back to convey a prisoner to our cells. As I was returning to Belgrade in any event, the major asked me to bring you up to date with events.'

'You have captured a prisoner so important he had to be brought here by you? It's not General Tito?'

'Sadly, no. But almost the next best thing.'

'Not the man Davis?'

'Again, sadly, no.'

Angela regarded him for several seconds, then she snapped her fingers. 'Fouquet. You have the woman Fouquet!' She looked past him, almost as if she expected to see Sandrine standing in the hall. 'Where is she?'

'She is in our cells. But her capture is a secret, and must remain so.'

'Why? What have you done to her?'

'Absolutely nothing. This is Major Wassermann's command. He wishes to interrogate her personally, and until then he wishes no one to know of her capture.'

'But you have told me.'

'Well, I'm sure that the major has no secrets from you.'

Angela drank some wine, slowly. 'Is she as beautiful as they say?'

'She is a very handsome woman,' Ulrich said cautiously.

'I should like to see her. When you have finished your meal, Herr Captain.'

Ulrich could have kicked himself. He had not wanted her to come down to the cells in the first instance the previous month, and now he had practically invited her there himself. He had been an utter fool to tell her about Sandrine. He had succumbed to the desire to appear important in her eyes. But what did her impression of him matter? She, like Sandrine, belonged to Wassermann.

Angela watched him finish his food and drink the last of his wine. 'I'll get my coat,' she said. As he had expected, it was a sable fur, but in fact it was now quite cold.

She sat beside him as they drove to the headquarters. He inhaled her perfume, and thought that Wassermann was a lucky man. But he was growing increasingly nervous.

'Does she speak German?' she asked.

'I doubt it. But you speak Serbo-Croat, don't you, Fräulein?'

'A few words.'

If only he could gain some inkling of what she sought, what she intended. She was a teenage girl, and could know nothing of hatred and violence. But she had watched her mother being killed before her eyes, and she had watched Svetovar Kostic being tortured with obvious relish. 'I should say, Fräulein, that Major Wassermann has given orders that she is not to be harmed. And in any event, she did not kill your mother.'

Angela had been staring ahead, along the line of the headlamps. Now she turned her head. 'She was there, Herr Captain.? And she shouted to her lover to shoot.'

'Ah . . . that is what Kostic says, yes. We have not heard her side of the story yet.'

'But we will, no doubt.'

'When the major returns, Fräulein.'

Another glance. 'I can assure you, Herr Captain, that the major and I think with one mind.' His nervousness grew. He was entering totally uncharted waters.

They drove beneath the arched entry to the Gestapo court-yard, and the car stopped. The guards stood to attention, eyes rolling as they recognised the governor-general's daughter. Only the night staff were on duty inside the building, but these also sprang to attention as Angela swept past them with a rustle of taffeta and descended the stairs, almost as if she were in her own home. However used they were to seeing her in this building, she had never before come here except in the company of Wassermann. A snap from the sergeant, and the people in the tram hastily stood to attention. Angela ignored them, and turned down the corridor, Ulrich scurrying at her heels. 'Which number?' she asked over her shoulder.

'Thirty-one. Anke has the key.' The wardress was hurrying towards them at that moment, keys jangling. She asked no questions, but raised her eyebrows at Ulrich. 'Open it,' he said. 'But stay with us.'

The door swung in, and Angela stepped through, Ulrich and Anke close behind. The light was on in the cell, and Sandrine was seated at a table against the wall, eating her supper. She looked up at the sudden entry, but kept her face expressionless while swallowing her mouthful and wiping her lips with a napkin.

'Why is she being treated like this?' Angela demanded, speaking German. 'Why has she not been stripped?'

'These are Major Wassermann's orders, Fräulein.'

Angela stared at Sandrine, and Sandrine returned the look, her face remaining expressionless. 'Why is she not afraid?'

'I do not think she knows the meaning of the word, Fräulein,' Ulrich said.

Angela stared at Sandrine for a few more seconds, and

172

Sandrine took another mouthful of food. Then Angela turned and left the cell.

Sasha had been lying on Tony's chest. He rolled her off, and sat up to watch the aircraft wheeling above him, and listen to the chorus of excited alarm as the women also awoke from their exhausted slumber. But there were also cries of pain. The first stick of bombs had been dropped at the far end of the bivouac. Now there were more explosions through the length of the shallow valley as each of the six planes discharged its load.

Tony dragged on his pants as he reached his feet. 'Scatter!' he bawled. 'Scatter and take cover. Lie down.' Screaming and chattering, the women obeyed, some naked, others only half dressed, some carrying a weapon, others too terrified to do anything except run and then throw themselves headlong into the shelter of the first bush they could reach.

Hitherto, in their very limited experience, they had been in control. Because Tony had been in control. This was the unexpected. Which he *should* have expected, because Tito had warned of its likelihood. Though he did not suppose, even had he posted sentries, that it would have done much good; even if the women had managed to stay awake, they would not have seen the aircraft coming in low over the hilltops in time to sound the alarm before the first bombs fell.

He ran towards the stream, and came across the craters and the scattered, lifeless bodies, the more disturbing because several of these were naked. He turned to find Sasha beside him. 'What must we do?' she asked.

'There is nothing we can do,' he told her. 'Except shelter ourselves.'

As he spoke, they heard the roar of the engines as the fighter-bombers came back for another run. They fell together, lying on their stomachs beside a clump of bushes, listening to the chatter of machine guns rising above the sound of the engines; having expended their bombs, the aircraft were coming low to strafe their victims. Again there was a chorus of screams and shrieks. Tony raised his head, and to his horror

173

saw Anja rise to her feet, holding a tommy-gun, and spray the approaching planes with bullets. He did not suppose any of her shots reached them. Instead she seemed to explode as she was struck a dozen times. She flew back into the bushes, arms flung wide, tommy-gun flying through the air. Then the aircraft were gone, vanished behind the hills.

Sasha sat up. 'Will they come again?'

'Probably.' He ran to where Anja had fallen, looked down on her shattered body. At least she had died instantly. Others had not been so fortunate. They lay dead or dying in grotesque postures, or they sat or knelt hugging their bleedings arms and legs and bodies. Many of those who had not been hit were weeping, some even wailing out loud. 'Have them get dressed and collect their weapons,' he said. 'Then dig a grave.'

'That is all they do,' she complained. 'Dig their own graves. How many graves do you wish?' She was close to hysterics.

Tony held her shoulders, and shook her. 'Pull yourself together. They will dig just the one grave. A big one. We do not have the time for anything better.'

Her eyes filled with tears, and she looked as if she would have said more, but instead she turned and went amongst the women, chivvying them to their feet, making them move. Tony followed, in order to discover just what the situation was. The casualties were surprisingly light, because the women had bivouacked over a wide area, but there were still five dead and a score wounded. Four of these were quite serious, and two were bleeding from their legs. He set a squad to work binding them up, giving them sips of morphine where necessary. 'Do we abandon these?' Sasha asked. 'Like the others?'

Everyone stopped work to await his decision. He knew that morale was at its lowest, that there was no guarantee his command was not going to just melt away; a good number of them, including Sasha herself, were Bosnians, and were thus about to re-enter their homeland, where they would be sure of a welcome from their families. Against that there were Tito's orders. But if ever there was a time to disobey orders, this was it. 'No,' he said. 'We carry them with us.'

*   *   *

It was desperately hard work, and progress was very slow, while in the middle of the afternoon the planes were back, re-armed and searching for them. But Tony had expected this, and got them into shelter in time. Now they turned away from the direct route to Foca, heading more to the west, in the direction of Wicz.

Next day they were overtaken by the remnants of Asztalos's regiment, some three hundred men. The men and women fell on each other's necks while Asztalos and Tony embraced. 'We may have a problem,' Tony suggested, looking at the fraternising that was going on.

'Oh, let them enjoy themselves,' Asztalos said. 'With what time they have left.'

'And when half of my people are pregnant?'

'The problem is several months away, my friend. Do you suppose many of them will be alive in three months' time?' Tony couldn't really rebuke him for his pessimism; the facts were obvious. Apart from the aircraft, the German ground forces were also pushing hard, and the Partisans were handicapped by having to carry their wounded.

The next day they suddenly discovered a squadron of tanks and several truckloads of troops only a mile behind them. The pursuit was reported by the rearguard, and Tony and Asztalos went back to inspect the situation from a convenient hillside. 'We are going to have to take them on,' Tony said.

'We are done,' Asztalos said.

'For God's sake,' Tony said. 'We have more than six hundred men and women, every one armed. There cannot be more than a battalion of troops down there; I make that not more than a thousand men, probably less.'

'That is still nearly double our strength. They will have machine guns; we have rifles. And they have those tanks. And they will be able to call up air support.'

'So we must act quickly, give them a bloody nose, and get out again.'

'But why must we fight them? Our business is to get away.'

'We must fight them, old fellow, because we are on foot and they are motorised. That is why they have caught us up in the first place. If we can hit them hard, they will check long enough for us to get ahead of them again. And while we are, hopefully, moving into friendly territory, that territory becomes unfriendlier to them with every mile.' He hoped.

Asztalos chewed his lip, but his men were spoiling for a fight, and the women even more so. All grumbling stopped, exhaustion was thrown away, and morale visibly climbed. Tony and Sasha had their wounded placed together at a hopefully safe distance from the coming fighting, and deployed their people amidst the trees and rocks to either side of the road.

'No one shoots until I fire my Verey pistol,' Tony told them.

Sasha crouched beside him. 'Are we going to win?'

'Yes,' he told her. 'Just like the last time.'

A moment later two motorcyclists came into view, riding slowly. The roar of the trucks could clearly be heard. And then someone fired. One of the cyclists fell, his machine crashing down the slight parapet beside the road. 'Shit!' Tony said.

'I will coat her cunt with pepper,' Sasha said. But Tony was quite sure it had not been one of the women; they were far better disciplined than the men.

The other motorcyclist wheeled his bike, and raced back down the road; no one fired after him. Asztalos crawled through the bushes. 'We must retreat. The element of surprise is gone.'

'It has not. A single shot was fired. They can have no idea of our strength.'

'I will pull my men out.'

'Do that, and I will have you shot,' Tony told him. Asztalos looked as if he would have argued, but changed his mind, and crawled away again.

'He is a coward,' Sasha growled.

'I don't think so,' Tony said. 'Just a pessimist.'

* * *

Wassermann was lounging, half asleep, in his command car when he heard the sound of the shot. He sat bolt upright, as did Ulrich, who had finally caught up with him the previous day.

Wassermann had asked him if Sandrine had been safely delivered, and he had said yes. Wassermann had then asked him if he had seen Angela, and Ulrich again had said yes. 'And did she give you a message for me?'

'She sent you her love,' Ulrich said. Angela hadn't, though. She had been too preoccupied, and perhaps upset, he thought, at actually having come face to face with the famous Fouquet. But he knew that was what his boss wanted to hear.

So Wassermann had dozed contentedly, until being so rudely awakened. Now Captain Rimmer came running back to the car. 'One of the scouts has been hit, Herr Major. There must be guerillas up ahead.'

'But only one shot was fired.'

'That is correct, Herr Major.'

'Therefore there cannot be more than a few of them. We will drive through them,' Wassermann said. 'But prepare your men for action.'

'They may shoot out our tyres . . .'

'Then we will disembark, and clear them. Go.' Rimmer saluted, and hurried off. 'You will follow the trucks,' Wassermann told Albrecht.

'Yes, Herr Major,' the orderly said. But he was looking anxious; even at the rear of the column the command car was exposed.

The squadron of tanks rolled forward. 'Sweep the slopes to either side,' Wassermann said into his radio, and put on his steel helmet.

'Tanks!' Sasha said.

'Tell your people to let them through,' Tony said. 'We cannot stop them. It is the infantry we must beat. There is to be no firing until my signal goes up.' She nodded, and hurried away. 'That goes for your people as well,' Tony told

Asztalos, who had rejoined them, and seemed content to leave the command of the operation to the Englishman.

Slowly the tanks clanked up the road. As each vehicle reached the abandoned motorcycle, its cupola traversed either left or right, and a shot was sent screaming into the trees, exploding to scatter twigs and foliage in every direction, as well as shrapnel, and invariably starting little fires, as they had done outside Kragujevac. Tony had no doubt that some of his people were hit, but with superb discipline they kept their heads down and obeyed his orders not to return fire. The tanks moved on.

'No enemy activity observed,' the radio said.

'What did I tell you?' Wassermann told Ulrich. 'That was some cowardly sniper who has made himself scarce. Proceed, Major Reustaffel,' he said into his mike.

The trucks – whose canvas walls were rolled back from the rear to expose their machine guns – rolled forward, emerging from the hills into the valley, looking up the roadway to where the last of the tanks were still visible. The sound of the engines drowned all other noise, but both Wassermann and Ulrich swept the hillsides with their binoculars. They had travelled for half a mile along the valley when Ulrich said, 'I see metal.'

'Where?' As Wassermann turned, a rocket soared into the air above them, and all hell broke loose. They were assailed by several hundred bullets, all fired at once. Men screamed and shouted as the flying lead slashed through the remaining canvas and into the machine-gunners. Tyres exploded and vehicles slewed to and fro, several coming right off the road, their discomfort accompanied by cheers from the Partisans.

'It is Kragujevac all over again!' Sasha shouted, rising to her feet in her exuberance. Tony grabbed her belt, and pulled her down again. For the Germans were disembarking from their vehicles, firing as they did so, and the dead and wounded machine-gunners were being replaced, and were sending streams of metal into the trees. Some of the cheers turned to shrieks. This was a much more serious conflict than

Kragujevac. And now the tanks were turning to come back into the fray. Tony drew his Verey pistol, and fired another rocket, sending the bright light soaring above the brief battle.

'We can kill them all,' Sasha objected.

'How many cartridges do you have left?'

'Well, a dozen rounds.'

'So we get out. We can't stop the tanks. Go, go, go. Be sure to take your wounded.'

'And you?'

'I will be right behind you.' But he waited to make sure everyone had seen his signal, and watched German officers running up and down the line of trucks, shouting orders, directing fire. And frowned. Two of the men wore black uniforms, and seemed to be in general command. And one of them had the insignia of a major. It had to be. He holstered the glasses, and picked up the rifle by his side. It was payback time for Sandrine's death.

'Deploy!' Wassermann shouted as he ran along the road, pistol in hand. 'Into the trees. Kill the bastards. Into the—'

He found himself lying by the side of the road. He had no idea how he had got there, only that he was curiously breathless, as if he had just run half a mile. And that his helmet had come off, and thus he was improperly dressed.

He looked at Ulrich, who was kneeling above him, face contorted. Ulrich was speaking, but Wassermann could not hear him. And now, without warning, he was struck by a searing pain which seemed to have taken hold of his entire body. Before he could stop himself he had screamed in agony, at once to his embarrassment and shame. Now there were other people crowding round, and medics were tearing at his uniform, seeking to bandage him. Someone held something to his mouth, and he swallowed the liquid before he knew what he was doing. It tasted foul, and he wanted to vomit. But he could do nothing save lie there, and a few minutes later the valley began to rotate about his head. His eyes drooped shut.

Rimmer joined Ulrich. 'They are retreating. Do we follow?

My God!' He noticed Wassermann for the first time. 'Is he dead?'

'Not yet. We must get him back to Belgrade.'

'But . . . what are we to do here? We have them on the run.'

'Until the next time they ambush us,' Ulrich said grimly. 'We will ask Belgrade for instructions. Meanwhile, we will camp here, and hold our ground. See what prisoners you can take. But only in this neighbourhood. Ah, Major Reustaffel.' He stood up as the tank commander approached. 'Major Wassermann has been hit.'

Reustaffel looked at Wassermann, who was being loaded on to a stretcher; both his uniform and the ground where he had fallen were a mass of blood. 'He's not dead?'

'No, sir. But he is very badly hurt. I consider it of the greatest importance to get him back to Belgrade. And the other wounded, of course. You will have to take command.'

Reustaffel pulled his rather long nose. He was a tactical tank officer, and had never commanded any large body of men. 'What do you consider we should do?'

'I have already called in my men, sir. I consider we should halt here until we receive orders from Belgrade on how to proceed.'

'Yes. Yes, that is a sound idea. You don't suppose those Partisans will come back?'

'If they do, sir, and attempt to attack us in an estab-lished defensive position, I think we should be able to deal with them.'

'Yes. Yes, you are right. I will see to it. Will you call Belgrade?' He was obviously in a very nervous state.

'Yes, Herr Major,' Ulrich said. 'And then I must see about evacuating Major Wassermann.'

Nine

Women

There was less immediate reaction to this battle than after Kragujevac. Casualties had actually been higher, but no one had any doubt that they had inflicted more on the Germans, and they had certainly checked the pursuit; even the wounded were reasonably happy. But Tony was well aware that there were troubles ahead, even if he could feel a personal sense of satisfaction that it had been his shot that had both halted the pursuit and avenged Sandrine – if the SS officer had indeed been Wassermann.

Foca, their rendezvous, was only just over a hundred miles south-west of Uzice, but it was a long hundred miles as they climbed into the high country, with peaks of several thousand feet to either side, carrying their wounded. Moreover, it was now well into November and the temperature was dropping sharply at night, with frequent snowfalls.

They were now almost out of both ammunition and food, although thanks to the ever-present mountain streams, and the now fairly incessant rain, they had no shortage of water, even if on more than one occasion it was necessary to break a thin layer of ice to get at it. But as they climbed out of the valleys, the increasing cold went hard on empty bellies. Yet for the first couple of days after the battle, spirits stayed high. This was principally the work of Sasha. 'Now we are across the border,' she told them. 'We are in Bosnia. And my village, Wicz, is only a few miles away. There we will find food and shelter. And medicines for the wounded.' They were all out of morphine.

*   *   *

181

They reached Wicz the following afternoon. The villagers turned out to stare at the six hundred-odd ragged guerillas, who marched with no discipline but who were expecting an enthusiastic welcome.

This was not evident. The people watched in silence as the column reached the town hall, where the mayor waited for them, surrounded by his wife and several teenage children, all obviously close relatives of Sasha. Who ran up the steps to embrace them. 'Papa! Mama!' Tony and Asztalos waited at the foot of the steps while their people gathered behind them.

Mayor Janitz accepted Sasha's hug with some reluctance. 'Why have you come here? With these people? Who are they?'

'They are my friends. They are my comrades.'

'You mean they are Communists.'

'No, Papa, we are not Communists – at least, not all of us. We are Partisans. We have just fought against the Germans, and won. But some of us are wounded. They need medicine and care. And we are short of food. And we are very tired.'

'You have fought the Germans,' her father said. 'Belgrade Radio has warned that anyone giving shelter to guerillas will be shot. Have you not heard what happened at Kragujevac?'

'I was there.'

'You? You caused that to happen?'

'I was fighting the Germans. With my comrades.' She threw out her arm to encompass all of them.

'They shot all the men in the town. You knew this?' Sasha stared at him with her mouth open, then turned to look down the steps at Tony. He couldn't believe it either. 'Your futile resistance is destroying the country,' Janitz said. 'You cannot stay here.'

Sasha's face registered even more disbelief. 'We need aid for the wounded,' she said. 'We need food. You must help us. You must help me. I am your daughter!'

'You abandoned me, you abandoned your *family*, to go off and become a bandit. You have made your own bed. You must

182

learn to lie in it. My responsibility is to my people. I cannot endanger them.'

Sasha turned to look down the steps at Tony, this time seeking guidance, her expression still registering total disbelief.

'We are six hundred armed men and women,' Asztalos said. 'Let us take over the town, and take what we wish.'

Tony recollected Tito's warning; that was one command he was not prepared to disobey. 'There may be another way,' he said, and went up the steps.

'This is our commanding officer,' Sasha said. 'Colonel Tony Davis.'

'I have heard of you,' Janitz said. 'You are wanted for murder. I have seen the poster.'

'Quite a good likeness, don't you think?' Tony asked. 'I understand your problem, Your Worship. My people and I will happily move on. But surely your people will not object to selling us what they can spare?'

Janitz frowned at him. 'You have money?'

'Yes.'

'How much?'

'How much do you have to sell?'

'I will have to consult my people.'

'Do that. But while you are doing that, I wish *my* people to be fed.'

'I have always heard that the English are a nation of shopkeepers,' Sasha confided. 'Do you think it would help if I told Papa that we are to be married?'

'Ah . . . at this moment, no.'

The villagers turned out to have a good deal to sell, once they had a look at the gold coins possessed by Tony and Asztalos. They were less impressed by the paper dinars offered by the rank and file, but eventually accepted even these; because of the war and the consequent restrictions upon movement, they had quite an accumulation of food and goods they had been unable to offer in any sizeable market. Asztalos was still reluctant to part with his money when they could so easily have taken what they wanted by force, but Tony reminded him of Tito's instructions, and he grudgingly obeyed.

When they moved out the next day, they were well fed and their wounded were properly bandaged, although a dozen still needed to be carried on stretchers. But they had not been able to buy more than twenty-four hours' supply of food for so many people, and this was gone by the next day. And of course there had been no munitions available.

The following day their troubles began again. It was now raining almost all the time, interspersed with snow showers, and was intensely cold, while their hunger grew with every step. As a result of their discomfort and their appetite, both of which led to increasing exhaustion, straggling became a serious problem. Tony and Sasha and Draga roamed up and down the steadily lengthening column, exhorting, chivvying, on occasion even striking people to get them moving; Asztalos preferred to march in gloomy silence. The only good thing about their situation was that the unbroken low cloud protected them from air strikes.

'Nasturtium soup,' Sasha explained, handing Tony a steaming mug, and sitting beside him with her own. 'I made it myself. It is quite spicy.'

'But tasty,' he said. 'My congratulations.'

'Do you think I am a good cook?'

'You are an excellent cook.'

'Do you think we will survive, and reach Foca?'

'Yes. Most of us.'

'I hope we do. Because after the fighting has stopped . . .' She changed her mind about what she was going to say.

Tony squeezed her hand. 'I am sorry about your parents.'

'*You* are sorry. I am ashamed. They are traitors.'

'They want to survive. You cannot blame them for that. They'll forgive you, when the shooting stops.'

'It is a matter of whether I will forgive them.'

'They're your family.'

'I do not wish them to be my family any more. You are

184

my family now. Will you take me to England after the war?
I should like to live in England.'

As with Elena Kostic, he found it quite impossible to
imagine this girl living in a Somerset village, having tea with
the vicar's wife . . . being his wife. Oh, Sandrine, Sandrine!
'Let's get to the end of the shooting first,' he suggested. 'And
then make our plans – if we are still around to make plans.'

Three days later they reached Foca.

'Tony!' Tito embraced him. 'We had given you up for lost. It
is good to see you.'

'And to see you, General. My people need food and rest.'

'And they shall have both. We have heard how you fought
a German column, and came off best.'

'It was more like a draw.'

'An English term. As you prevented them from achieving
their objective, you were the victor. Now, tell me, what do
you think of Foca?'

'I think it is ideal,' Tony said. The little town, perched on
the slopes of a mountain and possessing a fast-flowing moat
in the River Drina, was certainly defensible. It could only be
approached from one direction, and the mountain looming
above it made it difficult to bomb with any accuracy. 'All
we need is some logistical help.'

Tito grinned. 'We have had that. While you were, as usual,
covering yourself in glory, we were also having our success,
admittedly with the aid of a little luck. It so happened that we
entered the town of Bradina by surprise, and came upon a train
just pulling out of the station. We halted it, and captured its
contents. You will not believe this, Tony, but it was a German
supply train. It was loaded with arms and ammunition. And not
only that, with goodies as well. Here, have one of these.' He
pushed a box across the table. Tony opened it, and surveyed
the rows of liqueur chocolates. 'There were dozens of those,
and special cheeses, as well as a lot of good quality liquor.'

Tony chose one and munched. 'Delicious. Have you any
plans?'

'A great many,' Tito said. 'The enemy are claiming that we have been destroyed. Well, I expected this.'

'How many effectives have we got?'

'Now that you have brought in your people, as well as Asztalos's . . . How is he, by the way?'

'Not in very good shape. I am speaking of his mental condition.'

'Well, we must bring him back to health, and confidence. And of your six hundred . . . ?'

'I have about fifty carrying wounds of one sort or another – physical ones, that is. Almost everyone is bruised in some way or other from the terrain. I also have a dozen cases of frostbite.'

'They will be attended to.'

'And morale, I'm afraid, is generally very low.'

'Even after your victory?'

'It was costly. We lost seventeen people, six men and eleven women.'

Tito frowned. 'Why that proportion?'

'I would say it is because the women are more enthusiastic when the shooting begins, and are more inclined to show themselves as they look for a better target.'

'Hm. You have got our medics to work?'

'On the physically wounded, yes.'

'Well, we shall have to restore their morale. Anyway, as I was saying, even if you have only five hundred effectives, we muster some two thousand. And we are already recruiting – both sexes. I think that in a few months we shall again have a sizeable army.'

'Will we be allowed a few months, General?'

'I think so. Winter is now upon us, and the Germans reckon we are beaten. We will lie low during the cold months, and plan an offensive for the spring. Though I intend to demonstrate that we are still in being as a military force before then.'

'And Mihailovic?'

'I have that gentleman very much in mind, Tony. It will be interesting to see what sort of relations he maintains with

Belgrade during that time. Obviously, I am very reluctant to inspire a civil war on our domestic front as well as having to fight the Germans, but equally obviously we can never again place any trust in his cooperation. Now, we have managed to bring out some radio equipment. This is being set up now. What I want you to do is make contact with Alexandria, and persuade them not to believe anything the Germans, or the Cetniks, may be telling them about our collapse, and equally persuade them that we are the people they should be supporting. Despite what we managed to pick up from the German supply train, we still lack the requisite ammunition to mount any kind of serious offensive. If they will arm us, we can again be a most effective fighting force.'

'Judging by what Curtis had to say, I'm not exactly flavour of the month with my superiors,' Tony reminded him.

'Nevertheless you must try.'

Tony nodded. 'I'll do my best. May I take a box of these chocolates for my captains?'

'Of course.' Tito grinned. 'Must keep the ladies happy, eh?'

Hermann Ulrich stood to attention in front of General von Blintoft's desk. 'I congratulate you,' the general said. 'You say you have chased the bandits into the Bosnian mountains? Well, let them stay there and freeze. How many escaped?'

'I do not think it can be more than a few hundred, Herr General.'

'That is good. That is very good. Now, what is the report on Major Wassermann?'

'I'm afraid it is very bad, sir. He underwent emergency surgery at the scene, to remove the bullet. Fortunately, it did not penetrate the lungs, but several ribs were broken, and his stomach is damaged. He also lost a great deal of blood.' He paused; he was surprised that the general had not been to visit his prospective son-in-law.

'So, is he going to die?' Blintoft asked.

'The surgeons think they can save his life, Herr General,

at least for the time being. He has been given a massive blood transfusion, and is at present stable. But he is going to need several more operations, and they are unhappy about his prospects here in Belgrade. They feel they lack the proper equipment for such complicated surgery.'

'So they wish him sent back to Germany.' Blintoft snorted. 'Well, I suppose he will have to go. When?'

'That is another complication, Herr General. The surgeons feel it would be dangerous to move him before he has regained some strength. They say it may take a few weeks for him to do this.'

'And they can keep him alive for that time?'

'They seem confident of this. Although, because of his internal injuries, he will have to be kept under sedation.'

'Well, I am sure they will do all they can. Now, Ulrich, about this other matter . . .'

'With respect, sir, may I ask how Fräulein Angela is taking the news?'

'She does not know of it yet.'

'But . . . is she not engaged to the major?'

'Yes,' Blintoft said sadly. 'But I feel that for her to be told of his condition, while the memory of the death of her mother is so fresh, might have a depressing effect.'

'But has she not asked about the campaign? About the major's part in it?'

'I have told her that he is commanding the force that is chasing the bandits, and that he will continue to do so for a few weeks yet. If I were to tell her the truth about his part in the campaign . . . You were there, Ulrich. You were at Kragujevac. Is what Brigadier General Leesing put in his report true?'

'I have not seen General Leesing's report, Herr General,' Ulrich said cautiously.

'Well then, is it true that Major Wassermann shot five thousand men and boys before their womenfolk?'

Ulrich sighed. 'I regret to say that is correct, Herr General.'

'Did you not try to stop him?'

'I protested, sir, but there was no way I could stop him. General Leesing tried to stop him, but he did not succeed either. He had an order' – Ulrich cleared his throat – 'signed by you, sir.'

'Yes,' Blintoft said. 'I had no idea he would go so far. And is it true that he massacred the wounded taken at Uzice by driving tanks over them?'

'Yes, sir.'

'The man is a monster.' Ulrich preferred not to reply to that; it was permissible for the general so to describe an inferior, but not for him so to describe his boss. 'So, he executed every prisoner he could lay hands on,' Blintoft mused.

'Will there be repercussions from Berlin, Herr General?'

'If there are, I doubt they will be very stringent. When you think what they are doing to guerillas in Russia, I do not think they are going to bother very much about a few thousand Yugoslavs. That does not make me feel any better. And then, what about the prisoners he was supposed to take? What about this Tito, and the man Davis and his girlfriend, the people who murdered my wife? They have all escaped, eh?'

Proving, Ulrich thought, that the general *had* been more interested in avenging his wife than in destroying the Partisans. But he also realized that he now had to feel his way through a minefield. Ulrich was well aware that the SS was responsible to no one save Heinrich Himmler, and through him, ultimately, the Führer. As far as the army went, it was a state within a state, over which the generals had no jurisdiction. Whatever this moon-faced blithering idiot might report to his superiors could not have the slightest effect, good or bad, on his career. Whereas what Wassermann put in *his* report, whenever he was in any condition to make a report, might make all the difference between promotion and demotion. And whether the major was ever going to be capable of returning to duty or not, he was apparently going to survive, and would undoubtedly remember that he had given Ulrich explicit instructions that Fouquet was to be kept incommunicado.

At the same time, he did not feel he should tell the general a direct lie. So he chose his words with great care. 'Some prisoners were taken, Herr General. I escorted them back to Belgrade myself. They were people Major Wassermann intended to interrogate personally when he returned. Would you care to see them?' He reckoned that if Blintoft went to the prison of his own volition, he was off the hook.

'No, no,' the general said. 'I do not like that place, or the people who work there. Oh, yourself excluded, of course. Will you be interrogating them?'

'Ah . . . when I am sure that the major will be in no condition to do so for some time, sir.'

'Very good. If you do get around to it, and discover anything of interest, you will let me know.'

'Of course, sir.'

'Though I imagine that Davis and Fouquet are either lying unrecognisably dead somewhere, or have escaped into the mountains. Thank you, Ulrich. Dismissed.'

Ulrich stood his ground. He needed to know how Angela, who knew that the prisoner was Fouquet, was going to react to what had happened. 'With respect, sir, I feel that Fräulein von Blintoft should be informed of her fiancé's condition.'

'You may be right. But frankly, I cannot bring myself to do so. I have explained my reasons.'

The cue for which he had been waiting. 'I quite understand, Herr General. I would be prepared to undertake the task for you.'

Blintoft raised his head. 'You?'

'Well, sir, I am Major Wassermann's closest associate. I may be able to tell her in an acceptable way.'

'And will she not feel that I have been neglectful of my duty?'

'I do not think so, sir. If I explain your reasons – that you are reluctant to add to her grief over her mother – I should think she will entirely understand, and be most sympathetic.'

'Hm. Well, very good, Ulrich. I give you permission to tell my daughter.'

'And allow her to see the major?'

'Oh, very well. If that is what she wishes to do.'
Ulrich clicked his heels.

Angela stood at the bedside, and looked down at Wassermann.
Ulrich stood at one shoulder, and the sister at the other, waiting
to catch her if she should fall. The doctor stood on the other side
of the bed, also watching her. As if I would, she thought. I did
not faint when I looked at Mama. Why should I faint now?

In fact, she could see very little of him; as with the last
time she had seen her mother, the sheet was pulled to his
neck, and there was an oxygen mask over his face. His eyes
were closed.

'He is under sedation, you see, Fräulein,' the doctor explained.
'This is because, when conscious, he experiences considerable pain.'

'But you say he will live.'

'I believe so, Fräulein.'

'And be able to live an ordinary life?'

'Ah . . . given time, yes.'

'Thank you.' She bent over the bed, and kissed Wassermann
on the forehead. The sister's eyes filled with tears at such
devotion. Angela straightened. 'When next he wakes up, tell
him I was here, and will come again,' she said, and left the
room, Ulrich hurrying behind her.

'You are being very brave,' Ulrich said.

'Thank you.' Angela did not actually know what she was
being. She was not even sure what she was feeling, or had felt,
since Ulrich had told her that morning. Because for the past few
days she had been aware of the most conflicting emotions, at
once stimulating and disturbing. She could not get the image of
the Frenchwoman out of her mind. She had never expected her
to be so soignée, so beautiful, so calm, when she was a woman
who had killed, mercilessly, and who must know that she was
going to be killed, mercilessly. Sandrine Fouquet had made
her feel inferior, and she did not enjoy that. She had known
the strongest temptation to return to the cells to look at her –
and then to have her taken into the office and strapped to the

chair, and *hurt* her until that lovely mask disintegrated and she shrieked for mercy the way the man Kostic had done. But she had told herself that pleasure could wait on Fritz's return, and be shared with him. It had been a dream, and she had dreamt it every night before falling asleep.

But now Fritz was back, and he was not going to interrogate the woman for a very long time. Nor was he going to hold her in his arms for a very long time. Perhaps for ever, because even if he recovered from his wound, he would always be a shattered wreck of a man. She did not wish to be married to a shattered wreck of a man. Did that mean she had never loved him? She knew she had not. She had fallen in love with his aura of power and omnipotence, and cold cruelty. None of which had any meaning now. Or would ever have any meaning again.

So, as had happened after her mother's death, she was again adrift, and this time there was no one to turn to; she knew her father too well to suppose he could ever be a rock on which to hang her emotions, because he would simply be unable to understand them. But she was not the same girl she had been the moment before her mother had died. She might only be a few weeks older, physically, but her brain had aged a thousand years. Wassermann had done that. At her request, to be sure. He had reached into the dark recesses of her soul as she had revealed them to him, and taken out what was there, exposed it to the air, allowed it to roam free. She did not know if it would ever return to secrecy and subjugation, as required by polite society. She did not know if she wanted that to happen. Because however much she might hate herself from time to time, when she was in the grip of her demonic passion she had known the purest ecstasy. She was in the grip of such a passion now.

'The car will take you home,' Ulrich said.

'Where are you going?'

'I must go to the office. I suspect there is a great deal waiting for me there.'

'Including that woman.'

'Ah . . . yes. You understand, Fräulein, that I have not told your father that we hold her. These were Major Wassermann's instructions, you see, and I would not like to disobey him while he is injured.'

'I quite understand, Captain. And I agree with your decision. I shall not tell Papa either. However, if you are going to Gestapo headquarters, I would like to come with you.'

'May I ask why?'

'I wish to see this woman again.'

'And may I again ask why, Fräulein?'

'For one reason: she is now responsible for the death of my mother *and* the serious injury to my fiancé.'

'Fouquet cannot possibly have had anything to do with the wounding of Major Wassermann, Fräulein. She was already in the cell here in Belgrade when he was hit.'

'She is a Partisan, is she not? And it was a Partisan who shot the major. They are all equally guilty.'

'I think you should go home, Fräulein. I know you are under a severe strain. I would not like you to do something you might regret.'

'You are the one who should be worried about actions you might regret, Captain. I wish to see this woman. If you do not take me to her, I shall be obliged to inform my father that you have been deceiving him.'

Ulrich opened his mouth and closed it again, less from concern at what Blintoft might be able to do to him – which was, as he had reflected earlier, very little – than at the attitude of this apparently innocent girl. At the same time, he did not really wish to become embroiled in a quarrel with the general, at least not until Wassermann was able to support him. Besides, what could another inspection accomplish? He shrugged. 'If you are that desperate, Fräulein.'

They drove to the Gestapo headquarters in silence. It was the middle of the afternoon, and the place was busy. Sentries stood to attention at the sight of the governor-general's daughter, as did the clerks inside. Angela ignored them, and followed Ulrich down the stairs and along the corridor. Anke waited for them, eyebrows arched.

'Fräulein von Blintoft wishes to interview number thirty-one,' Ulrich told her. Anke shifted her gaze to Angela, without visibly changing her expression. 'Be sure you remain with her at all times,' Ulrich said, reflecting that that would restrain Angela from any unacceptable action. 'If you will excuse me, Fräulein. There will be a car waiting for you when you wish to leave.'

'Thank you, Captain.'

Anke led her along the corridor, unlocked the door of cell thirty-one. Sandrine was lying on her back on her bed. Her torn clothes had been replaced by the plain, shapeless, ankle-length blue prison uniform, and her feet were bare. She had clearly been sleeping, for her head turned sharply as the door opened. But she did not move, although her eyes were watchful. 'What have you done to her?' Angela asked, speaking German.

'I have done nothing to her, Fräulein. I was ordered to do nothing to her.'

'You mean she just lies here, all day and every day?'

'She is exercised for an hour every morning. Then she is bathed, and she is fed twice a day. Those are my orders, given to me by Captain Ulrich.'

'You bathe her every day?'

'I escort her to the shower baths,' Anke said. 'I am not permitted to touch her.'

'But you watch.'

'Yes, Fräulein, I watch.'

'When is she bathed?'

'As I have said, every morning after her exercise.'

'I would like her to be bathed again, now.'

Anke frowned. 'She has already been bathed today.'

'It can do her no harm to be bathed twice in a day.'

Anke glanced at the door. 'The captain . . .'

'I am superior to the captain. I am the governor-general's daughter.'

Anke considered briefly. Then she said, 'You wish to watch this?'

'Yes,' Angela said.

'Very good, Fräulein. Get up, thirty-one,' she said in Serbo-Croat.

Sandrine had been listening to the conversation; Angela realized that she understood at least some German. Now her eyes were more watchful than ever. 'What for?' she asked.

'You are going to the showers.'

'I have already been to the showers today.'

'It is the Fräulein's wish.'

Sandrine did her best to keep her face as expressionless as usual, but Angela could guess the various considerations that were passing through her mind while she looked at her, directly, for the first time. Then she threw back the covers, swung her legs out of the bed, and stood up. 'Will she attempt to resist us?' Angela asked.

'I do not think so, unless we touch her.' Anke moved to the door, and jerked her head. Sandrine went to the door, and Angela followed. Her feelings, the emotions bubbling in her brain and in her stomach, were threatening to overwhelm her. But she could wait. She was not yet certain of what she wanted to do to this woman, save that she wanted to see some expression enter that face, those eyes, just as she wanted to hear her scream – even if she knew she could not use electricity, with Ulrich so close.

The three women walked down a side corridor to the showers. They passed one or two other guards, who looked at them curiously, but did not comment. The bath chamber itself was stark, a row of doorless stone cubicles, each about four feet square; the shower heads protruded from the walls, just higher than the average head. On the opposite wall was a bench running the length of the room, and above it, a rail. The baths, at this time of the afternoon, were deserted.

Sandrine removed her dress, and hung it on the rail; she wore no underclothes. Now her flesh was pink. It might have been the chill, which down here penetrated even the heating, or, Angela thought, it might have been her own presence; she must be used to being watched by Anke. 'Does she always blush?' she asked.

'No, Fräulein.'

Then it is my presence, Angela thought. She had achieved at least a minor triumph.

Sandrine stepped into the nearest cubicle, switched on the water, and shuddered as she was struck by the powerful jet. She soaked herself, then switched off the water to use the soap, goose pimples standing out all over her body, enlarging her nipples. Angela gazed at her, then noticed a length of hose lying on the floor. 'What is that for?' she asked. Sandrine switched on the water again, and rinsed urgently.

'We use that for punishment,' Anke explained. 'But it is also useful for interrogation.'

'How?'

'It is the muzzle velocity, Fräulein. I can reduce it to the thinnest of jets, so that it feels like a knife cutting the skin.' She smiled. 'And the beauty of it is that properly used, like the electrical charges, it leaves no mark. But it is even better, because it will not kill – unless the prisoner happens to have a weak heart.' Her smile widened. 'But then death will have been by natural causes.'

Sandrine stepped out of the cubicle, and reached for her towel; now she was shivering with the cold. 'I would like to see it work,' Angela said. Anke raised her eyebrows. 'On her.'

Anke looked at her, and then at Sandrine, who was still towelling herself vigorously to restore some warmth to her body. But she had been listening, and now she stopped rubbing herself and faced them, the towel held protectively in front of her. Anke licked her lips. 'The captain—'

'Said that I was not to be harmed,' Sandrine said in German.

'So you do speak our language,' Angela said. 'Go back into the cubicle.'

Sandrine gazed at her for a few seconds, then glanced at Anke. She was clearly debating whether she could attack them, but while Angela knew *she* would have no chance against her, she also knew the prisoner could not hope to take on the pair of them, especially as Anke was so much the bigger and obviously stronger woman. Sandrine squared her shoulders for the coming ordeal. 'I will report this to the captain,' she said.

'When next you see him,' Angela agreed.

Sandrine hung the towel on the rail, then stepped into the cubicle, and stood with her back to them. 'We may get wet,' Anke said.

'Do you usually get wet when using the hose?'

'Yes, Fräulein. To save my clothes I usually undress myself.'

'Then do so.'

'And you?'

'I will undress also,' Angela said. Again Anke licked her lips. And why not? Angela thought as she took off her fur and hung it on the hook by the door; she was getting two beautiful women at the same time. She kept her back turned as she took off her dress and slip, and then her knickers, before unfastening her suspender belt and stooping to roll down her stockings. Only when they were about her ankles did she remove her shoes, and only then did she remember she was wearing a hat. She took off the fur turban as well, laying it with her other clothes on the bench, and then fluffed out her hair. Then she turned, beginning to shiver in the cold, to discover both of the other women staring at her; Sandrine had turned round. While Anke was also naked, a mountain of a woman. 'Commence,' Angela said.

Anke switched on the hose from a tap in the floor beneath the bench. The water spurted out, and for a third time that day flooded Sandrine's body. Sandrine backed against the wall, holding her breasts with her hands; she knew what to expect. Anke twisted the nozzle, and the jet thinned, and now she directed it against Sandrine's face. Sandrine gasped, and tossed her head, and stepped from side to side, but the jet always followed her, bringing red flushes to the pale skin, which had assumed a blueish tinge from the cold. 'She does not seem to be in any discomfort,' Angela said.

'That is because the jet is still soft.'

'I wish to make her feel. Give it to me.' Angela took the hose from Anke's hands, twisted the nozzle tighter yet, and aimed it at Sandrine's pubes. Sandrine gave a little shriek and turned round, only to have the jet slash into the cleft of her buttocks. She turned again, hands instinctively dropping, and Angela directed the jet against her exposed breasts. Sandrine gave another shriek, and her self-control snapped. She sidestepped the jet, and, before Angela could react, hurled herself forward and out of the cubicle. Her shoulder struck Angela's, and Angela's feet skidded on the wet floor, and she sat down heavily with a splash in more than an inch of water, giving a squeal of her own. Sandrine then turned to face Anke, but she was too late. Anke swung her hand in a karate chop, striking Sandrine on the shoulder; the Frenchwoman went down like a stone. Angela turned on to her knees. 'What have you done?'

'The bitch attacked us,' Anke snarled.

'You have killed her!' Angela wailed, lifting Sandrine's head from the water, which was still flooding the floor. She was aware of an entirely new emotion, but one that was every bit as strong as any she had ever felt before. Here was transcendent beauty, and she had been trying to destroy it, just as she had been trying to destroy transcendent courage and determination. Here was . . . She didn't know, save that she knew she had always wanted to hold this woman in her arms, from the moment of their first meeting. She did so now, hugging her tightly against her breast.

'She won't die,' Anke said. 'She's tough.'

And Sandrine was giving little gasps as she regained consciousness, her lips moving against Angela's breasts. 'Get out,' Angela said.

'And leave you here with her? She'd kill you.'

'Get out!' Angela shouted. 'Out!' Anke hesitated, then retreated to the doorway. 'Right out,' Angela said. Another hesitation, then Anke went through the door, and closed it behind her.

Sandrine gave a little moan, and Angela hugged her some

198

more. 'Listen,' she said. 'Try to sit on the bench, and I will dry you.' Sandrine's head moved back as her eyes focused. 'I am sorry,' Angela said. 'I . . . I meant to hurt you. Now I . . .' She licked her lips as her hand slid up and down Sandrine's arm, and then moved lower to caress her buttocks. 'You must let me help you,' she said. 'Or you will catch pneumonia.' Angela's lips twisted. 'So will I.'

She got to her knees and then her feet, grasped Sandrine's armpits, and with a great effort got her up and seated on the bench. She was actually the taller woman, although she doubted she had more than a fraction of Sandrine's hard-muscled strength. She massaged Sandrine's back and shoulders and breasts with the towel before turning her attention to her legs, kneeling at her feet, tentatively moving up to Sandrine's thighs. Slowly Sandrine's breathing returned to normal; she did not seem to notice what Angela was doing. 'Where is the woman?' she asked.

'Outside.'

'You sent her away?' Sandrine's tone was incredulous.

Angela stood up. 'Dress yourself. Yes, I sent her away.' She began to dry herself.

Sandrine pulled on her dress, then sat down again to dry her feet, lifting them from the wet floor on to the bench. 'Why did you do that?'

Angela began to dress. 'I did not want her here.' She turned to face her.

'And she went? Do you not know—'

'That you could probably kill me? I know that. She went because I told her to do so. I know you can harm me. But if you do not, I can help you.'

Sandrine's lip curled. 'You can save me from Wassermann?'

'Wassermann is close to death. He was shot while pursuing the guerillas.'

Sandrine's lips parted. 'Then . . .'

'I cannot let you go,' Angela said. 'Not now. But I can make sure that you are not harmed, and continue to be well treated, as he commanded. And in time, it may be possible to, well, perhaps exchange you. Or at least make sure you are not executed.'

'Why should you do this? I am your enemy.'

'Can enemies not be friends?' Sandrine stared at her. 'Or even . . .' Angela bit her lip. 'You are shivering. Here . . .' She wrapped her coat round Sandrine's shoulders. Instinctively Sandrine stroked the fur; she had never worn anything like this. And then her fingers touched Angela's. 'I will take you back to your cell now,' Angela said. 'And we will . . . talk.'

Angela sat opposite her father at the dinner table. She had had another bath when she had come in, a very hot bath, with sweetly scented foam and soap. But she still felt cold. And yet wildly exhilarated. She had, suddenly, almost mysteriously, created a relationship, the sort of relationship she had dreamed of all of her life. She had beauty, and a surprising amount of response, literally at her fingertips. She knew that the response was an act, that Sandrine was only concerned with survival, but that did not matter, because she was in control, holding as she did that survival in the palm of her hand. She had never been in control of a relationship before, had always rejected relationships, simply because of that lack of control. Even with Wassermann, while she had wanted him to turn her personality no less than her sexuality inside out, to do that she had had to submit to his own personality, his own aura of omnipotence. Now she had replaced that relationship with something better; now she was the controller instead of the controlled, and she was excited by it . . .

'How did you find Fritz?' Blintoft asked.

Awakened from her thoughts, Angela started. 'He is in a terrible state.'

'So I understand. You know he is to be returned to Germany for treatment?'

'As soon as he can travel, yes.'

'I am told that should be in about a fortnight.'

Angela nodded. 'They told me that too.'

'You will, of course, accompany him.'

200

Angela had been cutting her meat. Now the knife slipped, and a splodge of gravy was deposited on the white tablecloth. One of the footmen hurried forward with a napkin to clean it away. 'Don't you want to?' her father asked.

'I think my place is here, with you.'

'And I think your place is with your fiancé. You do intend to marry him?'

'Well, Papa, it seems unlikely that he is going to be capable of marrying anyone for a long time.'

'You can be married while he is in hospital.'

'But . . . a marriage has to be consummated.'

'Are you trying to tell me that you have not slept with him?'

Angela gave an embarrassed glance at the waiting butler and footmen. 'Now is not the time, Papa.'

'Bah. They are only servants. I would like an answer.'

'Well . . .' Her tongue stole out and circled her lips, and she drank some wine, her hand trembling, causing liquid to spill from the glass. It immediately soaked into the linen, but this time no one moved. 'We were very much in love.'

'*Were?* Have you stopped loving him because he has been wounded?'

'Of course not, Papa. But . . .'

'I am still in love with your mother. And she is dead.'

'Oh, Papa . . .'

'So, you will accompany Wassermann back to Germany, and you will remain at his side until he is well enough to hold your hand, and then you will be married at his bedside.'

Angela stared at him with her mouth open; she simply could not believe what she was hearing. Just when her life had taken a new and exciting turn! 'But why, Papa? I have always felt that you never even liked Wassermann.'

'I have never liked Wassermann,' Blintoft agreed. 'I think he is a murdering thug. It was your idea to take up with him, and I allowed it to happen because I thought a flirtation might help you to get over your mother's death. I had no idea that it would immediately become an affair.'

'I am sorry, Papa. As you say, I was distraught over Mama's death. I know I made a mistake. But now . . . Surely it can be ended without any fuss. No one can expect me to marry a man who may well be a cripple for the rest of his life.'

'I'm afraid there are a great many people who expect you to marry Wassermann,' Blintoft said. 'Including the Führer.'

Once again Angela stared at him with her mouth open. 'The Führer knows of Fritz and me?'

'The Führer knows most things,' Blintoft pointed out. 'I imagine in this case Wassermann confided his good fortune at becoming engaged to you to his superiors, and it got to Himmler, who has the Führer's ear.'

'But why on earth is my engagement to an obscure major of the slightest importance to either Himmler or the Führer?'

'Simply because he is no longer an obscure major. I have this afternoon, only an hour ago, received a communication from Berlin. You understand that following our victory at Uzice I had to make a full account of the events of the campaign. This was largely based on reports received from Wassermann and his man Ulrich. Now it turns out that my initial assessment of our success was an overestimate. According to claims by the British and the Partisans themselves, Tito managed to get a large part of his force into the Bosnian mountains, and is still there, no doubt recruiting and re-arming. So it will all have to be done again, whenever we can get at him, and that cannot be until next spring. Berlin has intimated very strongly that they feel I should have led the pursuit personally, instead of handing it over to a mere major, and giving him an inadequate force with which to carry out the task.'

'Oh, Papa!'

'In addition,' Blintoft went on, 'I felt it necessary to report on the events both at Kragujevac and Uzice, where your fiancé massacred several thousand prisoners in cold blood. To my surprise – and, I am bound to say, my dismay – instead of there being any censure of him for this atrocity, he has been congratulated, by Himmler personally, for his grit and determination to stamp out these vermin. I quote. Again, the implication is that he revealed qualities I lack.' Angela could say nothing; she could see her father's career collapsing in ruins about him. 'And now, in addition, Wassermann has been seriously wounded – while leading the pursuit in my place. My position is very precarious, my dear. And if now, in addition to everything else, my daughter reneges on her engagement simply because this hero – he is to receive the Cross with Leaves – is not at the moment able to bed you, I think that would be the last straw. I hope you understand all this?'

Angela drew a deep breath. 'Yes, Papa.'

'So, as I say, you will accompany him back to Berlin, revealing all the time your extreme grief, and you will remain at his bedside, and you will marry him, and, well, whatever happens after that will depend on how soon he can return to duty. But I imagine they will have to give him a desk job, so you will be able to settle down as a housewife.'

I don't want to settle down as a housewife, with a man I do not love, Angela wanted to scream. I want to be here, with my new lover. But she knew better than to openly oppose her father. For one thing, she was not yet twenty-one. And for another, even if she was, she could never oppose the wishes of Himmler *and* the Führer. 'When will I have to go?' she asked in a low voice.

'As I have said, you will accompany Fritz as soon as he can be moved. We have been told that will be in a fortnight's time. Cheer up. You will be in Berlin for Christmas.'

To be spent with a living corpse, she thought. 'Will I be able to return to Belgrade?'

'Well, I shouldn't think so. Not for a while. I shall miss you. I have enjoyed having you here.'

'Then let me stay, Papa. I feel it is my duty to be with you, to look after you. Fritz will understand, and he will have dozens of doctors and nurses to look after him. You have only me.'

'That is very kind of you, my dear. Very generous. But your duty lies with your future husband. I would prefer not to discuss this again.'

Angela got up, and left the table. She felt if she sat there for a moment longer she would scream. She went to her bedroom, and threw herself face down across the mattress, biting her knuckles. Of all the bad luck! And what would happen to Sandrine in her absence? She would have to give Ulrich some very positive orders. But for how long would he be able to carry them out?

'Fräulein?' Her maid stood by the bed, hovering anxiously. 'Are you all right?'

Angela rolled over, and sat up. 'Of course I am all right,' she said angrily. 'I am to go home to Berlin. Home. What do you think of that, Malic?'

'Oh, Fräulein . . .' Rosa Malic, a small, dark young woman, looked genuinely distressed.

'And you will be out of a job,' Angela said maliciously. 'But you have a fortnight to enjoy your position. I am to go with Major Wassermann.' She got up, went to her dressing table, picked up her silver-backed brush, and hurled it with all her strength at the mirror, shattering it into a thousand pieces.

Ten

Trap

'Come on, come on, come on,' Tony shouted, his breath forming circles of mist as it left his mouth and nostrils. The women were surrounded by the self-made fog. They wore full kit, haversacks and rifles and bandoliers draped over their shoulders as they staggered through the snow. This was the heaviest fall they had had so far this year, and it was not yet the end of November. 'Why must we do this?' Sasha had asked when he had marched them out of their barracks for the exercise. 'There can be no fighting until the spring. The general has said so. That is at least four months away.'

'And by then you are going to be the fittest regiment in the army,' he had replied.

'On a day like this, we should be in bed,' she grumbled. Bed was her favourite place, as long as he was there beside her. Yet despite her grumbling, she was running beside him, keeping up well, panting and puffing but never slackening. By now he knew what strength lay in those slender legs.

They trotted down the last of the slope and into the narrow streets of the town. The people who were out gave them a cheer; they always enjoyed watching the girls working out. Tony brought them to a halt in the town square. 'Dismiss your women, Captain Janitz,' he said. 'I will join you in a moment.'

As he had seen, one of Tito's aides was waiting for him. 'The general would like a word, Colonel.'

Tony followed him to the headquarters building. 'Tony,' Tito said, 'I have someone to see you.'

Tony turned, expecting to see Curtis, although what he might be doing here was difficult to say. But instead he gazed at a little, middle-aged peasant. 'Malic!'

'Colonel.'

'Mr Malic has some news that will be of interest to you,' Tito said, beaming.

'Well?'

'My daughter is personal maid to Fräulein von Blintoft,' Malic said.

'You told me this last month,' Tony reminded him.

'Yes, sir. Well, sir, I have to tell you that Major Wassermann is seriously wounded, and will have to be sent back to Germany for prolonged hospitalisation.'

'Damn,' Tony said. 'I thought I had killed the bugger.'

'Still, he is out of action for a long time,' Tito said. 'But there is more.'

'The major will be accompanied by his fiancée, Fräulein von Blintoft,' Malic said.

'So?'

'Go on, Malic,' Tito invited. 'Tell the colonel how Fräulein von Blintoft and Major Wassermann are returning to Germany.'

'They will take the train up through Vojvodina and Hungary into the Reich.'

'Tell us about this train. It is guarded?'

'There are guards, yes, General. The usual number is a dozen.'

'Will there not be additional guards to protect the major and the general's daughter?'

'No, sir.'

'How can you be sure of this?'

'My daughter heard the general discussing it with his adjutant. The adjutant recommended posting additional guards, but the general did not wish it. He felt that the business should be kept as quiet and unobtrusive as possible. And of course he does not suppose anyone would attack the train, in the dead of winter, just to complete the death of a single man. However, I should say that the guards are in radio contact with Belgrade at all times.'

'Where is this radio mounted?'

'In the front carriage, immediately behind the engine.'

'Very good. And Wassermann and the woman?'

'They will travel in the first-class carriage. This has been reserved exclusively for them and the major's medical team. But it will be guarded.'

'Where is it situated?'

'At the rear of the train, immediately in front of the guard's van.'

'Very good. Now, when does this happen?'

'They leave next Sunday morning at eight o'clock.'

'Five days. Very good. Now what else do you have to tell the colonel?'

Tony had been waiting, in some mystification, to learn how this information affected him personally. 'Well, sir, my daughter, who watches and listens very carefully, has overheard Fräulein von Blintoft speaking with Captain Ulrich, Major Wassermann's aide, who is commanding the Gestapo in Belgrade until a replacement for the major is appointed. When they talk privately, they discuss a prisoner who is being held in the cells, in secret, in the care of a single wardress, incommunicado from any other prisoners or guards. Fräulein von Blintoft visits this prisoner regularly.'

Tony looked at Tito. 'There is something else you have to tell the colonel,' Tito said.

'Ah . . . oh, yes. The Fräulein is teaching herself French, with a phrasebook.'

'My God!' Tony said.

Tito touched his lips with his forefinger. 'Thank you, Malic. Your information is very interesting, and I am sure will be very useful. My adjutant will have something for you.' Malic glanced from one to the other, then touched his cap, and left the room. 'Close the door, Tony.'

Tony did so, and turned to face him. 'Do you think it is possible?'

207

'I think it is not only possible, but probable. Why should the daughter of the governor-general constantly visit Gestapo headquarters? It might make some sense if she was going to visit her fiancé at his office. But her fiancé has been in hospital these last two weeks. And why should she, when she is about to return to Germany, start learning French? Do you know of any French nationals in Yugoslavia at this time who are liable to be in the Gestapo cells, apart from Sandrine?'

'If it could be true . . . Josip, you must give me permission to find out.'

'I will not give you permission to commit suicide, Tony. Since that poster came out, your face is too well known. Set foot in Belgrade, and you will join Sandrine in her cell.'

'If it is Sandrine. I cannot believe it.'

'I have no doubt at all that it is Sandrine. And, like you, I wish to have her back, if only because it would be very bad propaganda were she to be subjected to a public trial and then execution, after having been tortured into confessing to the murder of Frau von Blintoft. This is obviously what they have in mind.'

'You have said that you cannot permit this.'

'Absolutely. But I have a better way of handling the situation, and at the same time reminding the Nazis, and the world, that we are still a fighting force capable of executive action. Your people in Alexandria have not even bothered to acknowledge our attempts to get in touch with them; now we must remind them of our presence. I have in fact been considering how we could hit the enemy this winter. Now we have been given the opportunity. Can you reach a suitable position on the railway line between Belgrade and Novi Sad in four days?'

'You mean to attack the train?'

'You will *destroy* the train. But you will take two prisoners: Wassermann and his girlfriend. You will bring them back here, but the moment you have them, you will send me a single word by radio: success. I will immediately get in touch with Blintoft, and set up an exchange.'

'You think he'll go for it?'

'This girl is his only daughter, and he has just lost his wife. If he does not go for it, he is a monster. But we will have Wassermann as well. The possible execution of an SS officer will make him think a bit. Meanwhile the propaganda value to us of such a coup, and the damage it will do to German morale, demonstrating as it will that the governor-general cannot even protect his own daughter, will be immense.'

'Would you also execute the girl if Blintoft won't play?'

'If he won't play, it means he is determined to execute Sandrine. How would you feel about that?' Tony swallowed. 'Can you do it?'

'I can try. Problem is, I don't know the railway north of Belgrade.'

'There must be somebody in Foca who does. Call for volunteers. How many people will you need?'

'Obviously the fewer the better. What kind of distance are we talking about?'

'From here to the railway? About a hundred and twenty miles, if you travel directly cross-country.'

'In four days. That is practical – just.'

'You could use mules.'

Tony shook his head. 'With all this snow on the ground, their tracks would be too simple to follow. No, we can do it on foot. But as I said, it won't leave me much time for choosing my position.'

'We will find someone who knows the ground. Recruit whoever you wish, and requisition whatever you wish, too. You should leave tonight.'

Tony gave a savage grin. 'I intend to leave this afternoon, General. There is just one thing: this mission has to be secret.'

'Of course.'

'And no one must be allowed to suspect that our end is the return of Sandrine, or even that she is still alive.'

Tito nodded. 'You are thinking of Janitz? Will you take her with you?'

'She's the best person – woman or man – that I have.'

'But you don't think she'll take kindly to Sandrine coming back to your bed.'

'Let's say I'd rather not find out until Sandrine *has* come back to my bed.'

'Your domestic affairs have always been tangled,' Tito said. 'I will leave you to sort them out. But first things first. And that means stopping that train.'

Tony called for volunteers for a special mission. As he had expected, both Sasha and Draga immediately came forward, as did quite a few others, men and women. He accepted his two senior captains, and also three of the men. That made up a party of six. Which he reckoned was the maximum he could take. But then he was surprised by the appearance of Brolic. He had not seen the shopkeeper's son since just before the battle at Uzice, and if he had thought of him at all it had been to suppose him dead.

'You promised to take me with you on your next secret mission, Colonel,' Brolic said.

'Actually, I didn't,' Tony reminded him. 'I said I would bear you in mind.'

'I have been told that you need a man who knows the railway line between Belgrade and Novi Sad. I know this area well. My father had a store in Novi Sad as well as one in Belgrade. I used to take goods up there regularly. I know that railway line like my own back garden.'

Tony considered. If what Brolic said was true, he was the man he needed. And if he could not bring himself entirely to trust the young man's ability to withstand stress, or to keep his hatred of the people who had destroyed his family under control, those weaknesses could only surface after the job had been completed, and could be dealt with then. 'Welcome aboard,' he said.

'So, we go a hundred miles to blow up a railway line,' Sasha said as she packed their haversacks. 'Through the snow.'

'You volunteered,' he pointed out.

'But am I not entitled to ask the reason?'

'General Tito wants us to remind the Germans, and the world, that we are still a fighting force, and capable of carrying out offensive actions.'

'But why this railway line, and on a fixed date so soon?'

'Well, as to your first question, the railway line from Belgrade to the border, and thence through Hungary to Germany, is the only one that matters at this moment. As for the timing, we have information that this particular train, the one leaving Belgrade at eight o'clock on Sunday morning, will be carrying items of great importance to the German command. To deprive them of those items will be a triumph.'

'Items?'

'I am not going to answer any more questions, and you are not to ask them.'

'Well, when I think that we could be sleeping in our warm billet here in Foca, instead of trudging through the snow and getting chilblains, I hope it will be worth it.'

'It will be worth it,' he assured her. Although perhaps not to you, he thought. He was concerned that he might be about to betray her love. But her love was more of an animal instinct, an animal passion, together with a desire to belong to the best, rather than anything of the soul. And she knew he had only taken her, at her invitation, because he had believed Sandrine to be dead. But Sandrine was alive, alive, alive! No matter what the Gestapo had done to her, she was alive. And she would survive, and return to his arms and his future.

He felt so ebulliently happy that what lay ahead of him seemed irrelevant. Until he had to spell it out to his people. 'We have to cover a hundred and twenty miles in four days,' he told them. 'That is, thirty miles a day. If we can maintain two miles an hour for fifteen hours, with a ten-minute break in every hour, we will have nine hours to spare for sleeping and resting. Our meals will be eaten as we walk, except for the evening meal, which we shall endeavour to have hot. Now it follows that to maintain this pace we can have no delays and no distractions. We will go round any obstacles, and we will not engage any enemy, be he German or Cetnik, unless it is absolutely unavoidable. Should any one of us, man or woman, injure himself or become in any way unable to continue the march at the required speed, he or she will have to drop out and return to Foca as best he can. Understood?' They nodded, faces grimly determined. 'Then let's go.'

It was a quarter to three on the afternoon of Wednesday, 26 November 1941.

Most of the army turned out to watch them leave. Tito shook hands with each of them. 'I know you will succeed,' he told them, 'and I look forward to welcoming you back in triumph.' He raised his cap, and the assembled Partisans gave a cheer.

The march was every bit as gruelling as Tony had anticipated. The temperature hovered just above freezing during the day, but plummeted during the night. This was worse than if it had stayed freezing all the time, as an ice-covered road could suddenly turn into ankle-deep slush. In addition it rained, or snowed, every day. This was a valuable aid to concealment – they could occasionally hear aircraft overhead – but did nothing for their comfort. They encountered few people, and those they did meet gave the seven grim faces above the heavily armed bodies – they all had, in addition to their tommy-guns and rifles, strings of cartridges and grenades round their necks – a quick glance and scuttled away. Presumably some were of the traitor mould, and would report what they had seen, but in these conditions there was little chance of any search being mounted even for obvious guerillas. Those German patrols that were about could be heard long before they were seen, and hiding from them was a simple matter.

When they bivouacked for the night, they huddled together in a mass for mutual warmth, too exhausted to do more than gulp their food and drink a mug of steaming weak coffee. That they had hot food at all was a tribute to Sasha and Draga, who every evening lit a small fire and did the cooking, and were ready to go again at dawn the following morning.

Inevitably, not everyone made it. One of the men stumbled and twisted his ankle, and obviously could not keep up. Tony could only show him on his map the way back to Foca and wish him well, and hope that he would have the sense, and the courage, to blow out his brains if he found himself about to be captured, if only so that he would not reveal their destination.

But as they descended into the valleys, it still rained incessantly, however, and the ground was even slushier. Many of the streams that had to be forded were chest-deep even for Tony, who was six feet two inches tall; he had to have ropes slung across the rushing water so that the women could manage. But here, as before, the training he had made them undergo meant that they were far fitter than the men, save for Brolic, who proceeded on his way in brooding silence. 'I do not think he is quite sane,' Sasha confided. 'He never speaks, he never smiles . . .'

'I imagine any truly sane person would condemn us all to the loony bin,' Tony suggested.

There were more people around on the lower slopes, as well as on the more level ground of the plain. Tony changed his order of march, and had them take their nine hours of rest during the day, sheltering in copses or little gullies, and making their way from dusk, which was early, to dawn, which was late, proceeding by way of his compass. Now too they saw more German movements, but in the absence of any recent guerilla activity, these were clearly routine. And just after they had begun to move on Saturday evening, they heard the wail of a train whistle.

'That is the evening train to Novi Sad,' Brolic said. 'We will be at the line by midnight.'

'And you know the best place for the derailment?' Tony shone his torch on the map.

'Here.' Brolic prodded the stiff paper. 'It is a shallow culvert. An explosive charge will not only blow the engine off the tracks, but should bring down the earth to completely block the line.'

'Excellent. Now listen very carefully,' he told them. 'With fortune, we should be able to do this job and have a couple of hours to spare before a pursuit is mounted. We are informed that the German guards are principally at the front of the train, and certainly that is where the radio is situated. So hopefully we will knock that out when we destroy the engine.'

'They will still come after us with everything they have,' someone said.

'I think they will be very careful about that,' Tony said, 'in view of the nature of the goods they are carrying, and which we are here to capture. Now, again according to our information, these goods are contained in the first-class carriage, which is situated at the rear of the train, immediately in front of the guard's van. Obtaining these goods will be the responsibility of Captain Janitz and myself. The rest of you are required to knock out any German resistance remaining after the derailment. There are likely to be civilians on board, but these will almost certainly all be German, and while you should not deliberately target them, do not let them get in the way. When Captain Janitz and I have secured the goods, I shall blow my whistle, and we will retire as rapidly as possible. Understood?'

'With respect, Colonel,' someone said. 'What happens if something happens to you?'

'Captain Janitz will take command.'

'But she will be with you, sir.'

'I take your point. You are thinking that if I go, she goes. In that case, Captain Dissilivic will take command.' Draga looked impressively stern.

'Now will you tell me what we are looking for?' Sasha asked.

'I'll tell you when we get it,' Tony promised.

Anke unlocked the door of cell thirty-one, and Angela stepped inside, blinking because of the brightness of the bulb as compared with the gloom of the corridor. It was early in the evening, and Sandrine sat at her table, reading one of the books Angela had given her. She looked up, but did not speak. 'Thank you, Anke,' Angela said. As always, Anke looked as if there was a great deal she would have liked to say, but after a brief hesitation she withdrew and closed the door.

'She worries,' Angela said, 'that one day you will strangle me.' She crossed the room, and stooped. Sandrine turned up her face, and was kissed on the mouth. 'Would you like to strangle me?' Angela asked.

'One day, perhaps,' Sandrine said.

Angela sat on the bed. For all their intimacy, she was still not sure when the Frenchwoman was joking or when she was deadly serious. 'I should have thought you would be grateful to me,' she said.

'I am.' Sandrine put down her book.

'But you still hate me. Is that because I have made you become my lover?'

'Not at all. I have had a female lover before. Your people shot her.'

'Oh. That is why you hate us.'

'There are other reasons.' Sandrine held Angela's hand. 'But I do not hate you, personally. As you said, I am grateful to you.'

'But you do not love me.'

'We have not known each other long enough for love.'

'I love *you*,' Angela said, almost fiercely. 'I think I fell in love with you when I first saw you. I hated you then. Do you know that it is possible to love and hate someone at the same time?'

'Of course.'

'It is not very nice, I can tell you. But then I stopped hating you.'

'When you saw me in the shower. You fell in love with my body, Geli, not me.'

'It was *you*,' Angela insisted. 'Oh, you have a lovely body, just as you have a lovely face and lovely hair. You are a lovely person. But you also have a loveable personality. I fell in love with your dignity, your confidence, your self-belief. I have none of those things.'

'You will get them, when you have experienced as much as I have.'

'Will I ever?' Angela stood up, suddenly and violently, and took a turn around the cell. 'It is over now.' Sandrine waited, but her eyes had become watchful. 'I am leaving Belgrade tomorrow morning at dawn, to return to Germany,' Angela said. 'I am to accompany Fritz. We are to be married.'

'I thought he was very badly wounded.'

'He is. But I am still to marry him.' Angela's mouth twisted. 'It is the Führer's wish.'

Sandrine looked interested. 'I had no idea you were so well connected.'

'Neither did I. But there it is. Listen, I have left Ulrich orders that you are to be continued in this cell and with this treatment until Fritz is able to return to deal with you.'

'Is he going to return?'

'Not for some time.'

'So, am I to spend the rest of my life in this cell?'

'Would you rather be hanged in public? Listen, I will do what I can for you. Ultimately, it will lie with Papa. I will work at it. But it is too soon after Mama's death to attempt anything now. You must be patient.'

'So it seems.'

'Are you not grateful?'

'Yes,' Sandrine said. 'I am grateful.'

'Then show it!' Angela grasped Sandrine's shoulders, and shook her, violently.

Sandrine took Angela's face between her hands, and kissed her on the mouth. 'I am grateful,' she said.

Angela's burst of anger faded as quickly as it had sprung up. 'Well, I must go now. I would like to think I shall see you again. Would you like that too?'

'Yes,' Sandrine said. 'I think I would enjoy that.'

Angela gazed at her in total frustration for a few moments, then turned and left the cell.

*   *   *

'Careful now, careful.' General von Blintoft stood above the stretcher as it was lifted from the ambulance and carried across the platform into the first-class carriage. This had been entirely reserved for the gubernatorial party, which, in addition to Angela and Wassermann, consisted of a doctor, two nurses, and an armed guard.

The space between two of the rows of seats had been filled in with a mattress-covered trestle, and on this makeshift bed Wassermann was carefully laid, still on his stretcher, while an oxygen mask and bottle were placed on the adjacent seats, ready for use if necessary. He was sedated, and oblivious to his surroundings.

Angela wore black – dress, shoes, stockings, fur coat, and fur hat. As if her fiancé was already dead, Ulrich thought, standing beside the general. Or perhaps it was merely that she knew the colour suited her; she certainly looked quite beautiful.

Blintoft embraced her. 'I know you will take good care of him,' he said. 'Telephone me as soon as you reach Berlin. You will be met there – Himmler has assured me of this – and an apartment has been arranged for you. Though I know you will wish to spend as much time as possible with Fritz.'

'Of course,' Angela said, allowing him to hug her and kiss her on the cheek. Then she looked at Ulrich.

He stepped forward to shake her hand. 'My felicitations, Fräulein.'

She gazed into his eyes, willing him to carry out her instructions regarding Fouquet. But he had already made up his mind about this. His position vis-à-vis the general might be invulnerable, but the Frenchwoman was becoming at once a nuisance and an embarrassment – and a potential risk, in the event that Wassermann never did recover. The moment Angela was gone, he intended to 'discover' the identity of the mysterious prisoner in cell thirty-one, and inform the general. He was sorry to have to let down the Fräulein, but he had his own career to think of, and he did not suppose he would ever see either Angela or Wassermann again.

He stepped back and saluted, and the door was closed.

Angela sat by the window on the far side of the carriage from Wassermann. She wondered if he would survive the journey, which was going to take many hours. If he did not, then there was no reason why she should not return to Belgrade. She would have done her duty. No one could ask anything more of her. And then . . . Why did she bother? Sandrine had never truly shown any attraction to her, however much they might have been able to arouse a mutual passion. It remained a question of ownership. Sandrine was hers! To have so precious a possession ripped from her grasp by men who were only capable of considering the form, the appearance of things, rather than the substance, was infuriating.

She found herself actually considering ways and means of getting rid of the medical people so that she could be alone with the wounded man, just for a few minutes. That was all she would need. But she had to be careful.

'Coffee, Fräulein?' One of the nurses handed her a cup.

'Thank you. How soon will we be in Novi Sad?'

'Another half an hour,' the nurse said brightly. 'It will be necessary to draw the curtains during the stop. We do not wish anyone looking into the carriage.'

'I understand,' Angela said, and used the opportunity to look out of the window. There was not much to see. They had left the last of the houses far behind, and were travelling across a snow-covered landscape, with only one or two distant hamlets to be glimpsed beyond the bare trees. Then the train entered a culvert, the banks of which rose only just above eye level, but sufficiently to blot out the view. Angela turned back to look at Wassermann, and was enveloped in a huge explosion.

Even the first-class carriage, situated at the very rear of the train, bucked and then crashed into the carriage immediately in front of it, being in turn rammed by the guard's van behind it; it hovered for a moment before falling on to its side with a resounding crash. Angela tumbled out of her seat, and fell right across the carriage, landing on Wassermann, who was also thrown forwards and to one side. Dimly she heard the doctor shouting and the nurses screaming, at the same time as she heard a fusillade of shots.

She rose to her knees on the window which was now the floor, aware of pain and a ringing in her ears, and gazed at Wassermann, who lay in a crumpled heap beside her; fresh blood was seeping through his bandages. Then her arm was seized by the soldier. 'You must get out, Fräulein.' He had lost his helmet, and there was blood on his face. Angela blinked at him, but did not object when he pulled her up. 'The back door,' he said.

Angela gazed past him at the doctor and the nurses, just picking themselves up, but they seemed more interested in Wassermann than her. She half-staggered and was half-carried along the various windows. Several cracked under her feet, but the soldier did not stop until they reached the door, which had taken on the aspect of a large hatchway in the rear of the train. Here he let her go, and she sank to her haunches while he tried to get it open, finally drawing his pistol – he had lost his tommy-gun – and firing several shots into the lock.

The noise outside was growing in intensity; there were more shots, joined now by screams and further explosions. Why does he want me to leave? Angela wondered. Will I not be safer in here? The soldier pulled the door down, then turned back to her. 'No,' she said. 'I wish to stay. With them.'

'If they have blown up the train,' he said, 'it is to get at either you or the major. If you remain here you will be killed. Come.' The door, which was opened across the width of the carriage, came to her waist. The soldier held her round the thighs, and lifted her up, grasping her legs to thrust them through the aperture. What insolence, she thought, but she did not resist him. 'Put your legs down, Fräulein,' he panted.

She obeyed him, and gasped. 'There is nothing there.'

He had shifted his grip to her armpits now, and was slowly

lowering her. 'There must be something,' he said. 'You will have to drop.'

He let her go, and her coat snagged on the edge of the door. She listened to the material ripping, and remembered how expensive this coat had been. Then she plummeted down, only a few feet, to land on the snow-covered gravel beside the track with a jar which seemed to travel right up her legs and into her hips. But she was still entirely surrounded by the train. 'I can't get out,' she shouted. 'I can't get out.'

He climbed through the opening himself, and dropped beside her. 'There!' He pointed at a line of daylight. 'You will have to lie down and roll out, Fräulein.' Angela looked down at herself. The front of her fur might be torn, but her expensive dress was so far undamaged. 'You must, Fräulein,' the soldier insisted.

As if to lend emphasis to his words, the sound of shooting was coming closer, as were the screams and the explosions. Angela drew a deep breath and lay flat on the snow, then rolled into the aperture between the side of the train and the parapet on which the track was laid. Her shoulder caught on the metal above, and she gasped and turned back on to her stomach, wriggling sideways. She got her legs through, then her torso, and lastly her head, and, before she could stop herself, went on rolling down the embankment to come to rest in a snow- and water-filled ditch. For a moment she sat there, panting, only slowly feeling the freezing temperature which surrounded her lower half, while she watched the soldier sliding down beside her. He held her arm to drag her to her feet. 'Run!' he shouted.

Angela looked left and right. To her right the train lay in a shattered mess, steam rising from the engine and the first carriages, and now she could see smoke and flashes of flame as fire took hold. Most of the shooting was coming from there. But to her left, beyond the guard's van – also on its side – the track was empty. She turned to run along it, and was checked by a shout from behind her. Instinctively she turned, as did the soldier, drawing his pistol. Instantly there was a shot, and he fell backwards, blood spouting from his tunic to stain the snow. Angela dropped to her knees beside him, but he was already dead. She stared at the blood, and felt sick. This was only the second person she had ever seen shot – but the first had been her mother, hit in almost exactly the same place.

She heard footsteps, and looked up to see a man and a woman. The man had a stubble of beard, and the woman was tall and strong and angry. 'She is a German,' the woman said. 'No Yugoslav would have a coat like that.' She levelled her pistol.

'Wait,' the man said. 'If she is a German . . .' He licked his lips.

Angela lost her head. 'I am Angela von Blintoft,' she said. 'The governor-general is my father. If you spare my life he will reward you.'

The two Partisans gazed at her for a few minutes, then the man's lip curled. 'Blintoft,' he said. 'Your father murdered my parents.'

Angela returned his gaze with her mouth open, realising what he had in mind. 'No,' she said, and tried to stand up. But Brolic seized her shoulder, and threw her to the ground. 'Hold her hands,' he told Draga.

Draga hesitated. 'The colonel may not like it.'

'The colonel is dead,' Brolic said. 'I saw him fall.'

'But Sasha . . .'

'She placed you in command. If I do not take this woman now, I shall be for ever damned.'

Draga considered for a final few moments, then said, 'Make it quick.' Her own parents had been killed in Belgrade by a German bomb.

Angela was again endeavouring to sit up, but Draga held her wrists and pulled her back down, then knelt, pressing Angela's arms into the snow. Angela gasped and tried to kick her legs, but Brolic was kneeling across them as he pushed up her skirt and dragged down her knickers, just as Wassermann had done the first time they had had sex. But that had been a game. This was reality. 'Please,' she begged. 'Don't hurt me, please.'

'I am going to hurt you,' Brolic promised her, taking the

knickers right off and pulling her legs apart to kneel between them while he tugged her coat open and tore at the bodice of her dress, ripping it and her petticoat to reveal her breasts. 'You are going to *scream*,' he told her, dropping his pants and then grasping her breasts to squeeze them as he went down on her.

'You are slow,' Draga said. 'Have you never had a woman before?'

Angela screamed at the pain of his grasp and as she felt him inside her. She made convulsive but unavailing efforts to throw him off, but Brolic was now lying flat on her as he worked away; then he suddenly ceased moving. Angela screamed again, and looked up to see another man standing over her. 'You too?' Draga asked. 'Well, hurry it up.'

'No,' Angela begged. 'Please.'

'She's German,' Draga pointed out. 'That is what she is speaking. German.'

'I have no use for a German slag,' the man said. He kicked Brolic in the backside. 'Let's move. Shoot the bitch, and have done.'

Brolic rose to his knees, allowing Angela to draw up her legs. 'Shooting will be too quick,' he said. 'I am going to crucify the bitch. Then we'll leave her for her father to find. Help me.'

The train whistle uttered a blast as it entered the culvert, and Tony looked down at the plunger beneath his hand; as with the bridge at Kragujevac, he had placed the charges himself, and had to doubt they were going to be successful. He glanced around his small command. None of the men had shaved for four days, and the women were equally unkempt – even Sasha's hair was loose and tangled as it emerged from beneath her woolly hat. They looked a ragged but dangerous bunch. 'You know what you have to do,' he reminded them. They nodded, clutching their tommy-guns and making sure their grenades were easy of access.

The train roared into the culvert. The Partisans were situated on the far side, but they were looking straight down the cut, and when the engine was almost through, and directly over the charges, Tony pressed the plunger. The explosion, and the result, were all that he had been promised by Brolic. The front carriages leapt into the air, and then crashed on to their sides. As they did so, both sides of the culvert collapsed, burying the engine and the first carriage beneath an avalanche of snow-covered earth.

'Move,' he snapped, and leapt to his feet, followed by Sasha, to run along what was left of the top of the culvert towards the rear of the train. Beneath them, Draga and her people went into action, hurling their grenades and firing their tommy-guns. Tony looked down at a scene of utter chaos, as all the remaining carriages had also left the track after cannoning into each other. People were climbing out, looking dazed. Most were in uniform, and all of these carried at least side arms. Tony saw one of the Germans draw his Luger. It never occurred to him that the man might be shooting at him, much less that he could possibly hit him, but a second later he was lying on the ground, for the moment feeling no pain.

'Tony!' Sasha dropped to her knees beside him.

'Fuck it,' he said. 'Listen, get to the last carriage. Get—'

'I must stop the bleeding,' she said.

'I have given you an order.'

'You are hit. I am in command. And I say you come first.' She opened his tunic to look at the seeping blood. And now the pain was too severe to allow him to do more than gasp. 'There is a rib broken, at least one,' she said. 'But I think the bullet has exited.' She unslung her haversack and took out her first-aid kit, expertly applied some antiseptic and then lint to the wound, before pulling his shirt and vest out of his pants to wrap bandages right round his body.

Draga stood above them. 'What has happened? My God! The colonel has been hit.'

'I will care for him. Listen, take command until I can come to you. Are there any other casualties?'

'Not one. But nearly all the Germans are dead. I think there may be some left at the back.'

'Well, go and kill them, and then prepare to pull out. I will need help. Hurry now.' Draga slid down the embankment.

Tony tried to concentrate. 'No,' he said. 'Listen.'

'Sssh,' Sasha said, tying the bandage. 'You should not speak. It will be all right. I am in command.'

'You don't understand. The goods we wish, the reason for this attack, are in the rear carriage.'

Sasha frowned. 'I had forgotten. What are these goods?'

'They are two people. Major Wassermann and Angela von Blintoft. Tito wants them taken prisoner.'

'Blintoft? The governor-general's wife? I thought she was dead.'

'This is his daughter. Listen, she must be captured alive.' As he spoke they heard a scream, and then another. 'Go,' Tony said. 'Go. She must be alive.'

Sasha hesitated, then got up. 'I will be right back,' she said, and slid down the embankment. She ran round the back of the train, and paused in consternation at what she saw. A dark-haired young woman had been stripped naked except for her stockings, and was being thrust against the bottom of the train by two of the Partisans, watched by Draga and a third man. Brolic was standing before her, his knife in his hands, and was preparing to drive it through the palm of Angela's extended hand, while Angela gasped and moaned and shrieked. Sasha ran forward. 'Stop that!'

Brolic turned, his face still contorted with passion. 'This bitch is the governor-general's daughter.'

'And she is what we want. Let her go.' She looked at the torn and scattered clothing spread over the snow. And then at Draga. 'You permitted this?'

'Well,' Draga said, 'if she is the governor-general's daughter . . .'

'The colonel wants her alive.' Sasha picked up the torn fur cot. 'Wrap her in this.'

'She is going to die,' Brolic snarled. 'Do you think a fucking woman is going to stop me?' He lunged forward with his knife.

Sasha's tommy-gun was still hanging round her neck. She levelled it, and shot Brolic through the heart. He went down without a sound, and the other two men backed off. 'I am in command,' Sasha told them. 'Go and make a stretcher for the colonel.'

Angela had slid down the bottom of the carriage, and was sitting at the foot, eyes wide, panting. Draga knelt beside her, and wrapped the fur coat round her shoulders. 'Her tits will be frostbitten.'

Sasha knelt also. 'Well, wrap her up. Use her coat.' She grasped Angela's chin, and moved her head to and fro. 'Do you speak Serbo-Croat?' Angela's eyes rolled as Draga closed the coat across her chest and began massaging her through the thick material. But her response, even if muted, indicated that she understood what had been said to her. 'Listen,' Sasha said. 'We will save your life. But you must help us.'

'That man raped me,' Angela muttered in broken Serbo-Croat.

'You won't die of it,' Sasha told her. 'Now get off your ass, and put on your clothes.'

'My clothes are torn! And . . .' Her face wrinkled with distaste.

'Just do it. They'll keep you warm. Shit!' she muttered as there was a burst of firing from along the train. 'Help her, Draga.'

She clambered back up the embankment, and saw the two men, who had dragged a makeshift stretcher – composed of two coats taken from dead Germans, with rifles thrust through the sleeves – up to where Tony lay. 'What was that firing?'

'Someone moved down there,' Groznic said. 'So we shot him.'

Sasha knelt beside Tony. He was still awake, although clearly groggy. 'Did you get her?' he asked.

'I got her,' Sasha told him, deciding against adding that Angela was not exactly undamaged goods. 'Now we must leave this place.'

'I cannot walk. You must abandon me. You will command. But first, radio Tito. Just the one word: success.'

'I am already in command,' she reminded him. 'And it is my decision that we take you with us.'

'You will not make it, carrying me.'

'We will make it. Put him on the stretcher,' she told Groznic.

'You wish us to carry him all the way back to Foca? That is impossible.'

'You will do it,' she told him,. 'because I have commanded you to do it.' The two men stared at her. They were as well armed as she, and they were each bigger than her. But Sasha's hand was resting on her tommy-gun, and they had seen the ruthlessness with which she had despatched Brolic when he had questioned her command. 'Discard your weapons,' she said.

'We must have our guns.'

'There is no need for them, as you will not be shooting at anyone. Drop them.' The men exchanged glances, then obeyed. 'Now pick up the colonel.' They placed Tony on the stretcher. Sasha knelt beside him, drew his revolver, and placed it in his hand. 'If you have any trouble with them, shoot them. Do you need some more morphine?'

'If you drug me any more I won't be able to shoot anybody. I can bear it. Send that radio message. Then you'd better destroy the set. You can't carry me and it.'

Sasha nodded, and stood up. 'Start moving,' she said. 'I will be back in a few minutes.' She slung the tommy-guns on her shoulder, went to the end of the culvert where the radio had been left, and sent the message. Then she picked up a discarded rifle, and smashed the set into several pieces. Next she went to the rear of the train, where Draga was still helping Angela to dress. The German girl looked like a scarecrow, and she was shivering with the cold; her clothes were still wet. 'You'll warm up when we get moving,' Sasha said. 'Let's go.'

'What is going to happen to me?' Angela asked.

'I really don't know. Keep your fingers crossed.' She grinned. 'And your legs, even if it is a bit late for that.'

'My father would pay much to have me returned, alive and unharmed.'

'I think he is going to have to do that anyway,' Sasha said. 'Move.' Angela looked back at the train. 'There is no time to collect your things,' Sasha said, misunderstanding the look. 'We are in a hurry.'

Eleven

Reunion

Tony managed to stay awake until he was joined by the women, then his pain- and drug-filled brain gave way. His half-conscious mind became a jumble of broken images and uncertain feelings. The pain was ever present, even if dulled by the morphine, just as the constant jolting of the stretcher was also uncomfortable, but his extreme exhaustion, caused by the wound coming on top of the four days' hard slog, meant that he kept drifting off to sleep. Yet his waking images were equally distorted, as he kept seeing Sandrine's face beside Sasha's, while now there was a third face added, quite different from the first two – a hauntingly beautiful face, very young and very frightened, but also containing a strangely attractive element of defiance. It was not a face he had ever seen before, and he could not understand where it had come from.

Then he awoke to complete clarity of mind, to searing pain, combined with an urgent desire to know where he was and what was happening. The stretcher was on the ground, and he was looking up at trees. The air on his face was cold, and now he felt cold on his body as well; he was undressed, and Sasha was bending over his wound. 'He is awake,' a voice said in very uncertain Serbo-Croat.

Tony turned his head and looked at the girl. So she had not been a dream after all. He tried to speak, but could not. The girl held a cup of water to his lips, and he was able to see her more clearly. She wore what had obviously once been very expensive clothes, including a sable fur, although now everything was torn and dirty. Only the matching hat looked undamaged.

Sasha knelt beside him. 'How do you feel?'

'Alive. If somewhat bloody.'

'Are you in pain?'

'Some.'

'I have been saving the morphine. It is going to be some time before we get back. Would you like some?'

'I'll be patient. How far have we come?'

'We have covered just over twenty miles.'

He looked up at the sun streaming through the trees. From its angle he reckoned it was about three in the afternoon. 'But that is splendid time,' he said. 'Twenty miles in six hours?'

'No, no,' Sasha said. 'We took the train two days ago.' He stared at her in consternation. 'We have travelled slowly, partly because of you, but mainly because the country is swarming with soldiers.' She smiled at him. 'But they have not found us yet.'

He considered the situation. 'Are they taking hostages?'

'I do not know. It is likely.'

'And how is Wassermann bearing up?'

'Wassermann?'

'The wounded SS officer. Capturing him was the reason for our raid.'

Sasha bit her lip. 'I do not know. I never saw him. There was so much going on . . .'

Tony turned his head. 'But you got the girl. You are Angela von Blintoft.'

'Yes,' Angela said. 'And you are Davis.'

'Spot on.'

'Your people raped me.'

Tony looked at Sasha, who shrugged. 'It was Brolic. I shot him.'

'I was wondering what had happened to him. Well, Fräulein, these things happen in war. And your people happen to have started this war.'

'Suppose I am pregnant? I will kill myself. And this walking through the snow. My feet hurt, and I am so cold. And there is not enough to eat. Is this the way to treat a lady?'

'Probably not. But we don't classify you as a lady. Tell me about the prisoner your father is holding.'

Angela's nostrils flared. 'The woman Fouquet! Your mistress!'

'That's the one.'

'She will probably be executed in retaliation for this.'

'You had better hope not. Because if she is, you are going to be hanged in the public square at Foca. We'll send the photographs to your father.'

Angela clasped both hands to her neck.

Sasha lay beside him that afternoon; she was following his example and only moving at night. 'So Sandrine is alive. How long have you known this?'

'I learned about it the day before we left on this mission.'

'So I am no more use to you. You have had what I have to offer.'

'Hang around and find out,' he suggested. 'I owe you my life. And I'm not sure I don't owe you my reason as well.'

She considered this, then she said, 'You mean to exchange this girl for Sandrine. That is what this has all been about.'

'That is a spin-off. Destroying that train, capturing the governor-general's daughter – this will be a great propaganda coup. It was General Tito's aim to show the Germans, show the world, that we are still capable of offensive action. He had hoped to get Wassermann as well, but that can't be helped.'

'We would have had him, if you had not been so secretive.'

'I know. I did not wish to upset you. Anyway, he was probably killed in the crash, as he was already badly wounded. And we have the girl.'

'And if this girl does not survive the journey back to Foca?'

'I personally will have lost, but the victory will still have been gained. But she is going to survive, Sasha. I make that your responsibility.'

Sasha gazed at him for several seconds, then lay down, her head against his shoulder. 'So, she will survive,' she said enigmatically.

*   *   *

'Herr General?' Ulrich hovered in the doorway of the general's office. Although he had been summoned, he had no idea how to proceed. Blintoft sat at his desk with his head in his hands; his face was invisible.

But now he looked up; lines of anguish were etched across his face. Yet his voice was firm. 'Come in, Ulrich. Come in. Report.'

'We have recovered the body of one of the Partisans, sir. It is the man Brolic, who escaped from Belgrade in October following the arrest of his parents. The evidence indicates that he was shot by his own people. Our own casualties were fifteen dead and nine wounded. All the wounded are serious. However, Major Wassermann is alive; he survived both the explosion and the subsequent shooting. With him were the two nurses and the doctor, who apparently hid in the carriage until the gunmen left. They are the only unhurt survivors.'

'My daughter was with them,' Blintoft said. 'Why did she not survive with them?'

'The evidence suggests that she left the carriage, Herr General. There are pieces of material, which we have identified as coming from the Fräulein's clothing, attached to the door frame. There is also the dead body of her escort, which was found outside the train.'

'You mean the bandits hauled her out?'

'I don't think they hauled her out, Herr General. I cannot believe that the Partisans would have entered the carriage and not killed Major Wassermann and the medical staff; they killed just about everyone else. I think the escort helped her to leave the carriage in an effort to save her life, and then she was captured outside, while he was shot.'

'But she was captured.'

'I believe so, sir. We have not found her body.'

'So we must accept that radio message as the truth. They want to exchange her for Fouquet. And what do you think they will have done to her in the meantime?'

'Ah . . .' As usual Ulrich chose his words with care. He did not wish to distress the general further by telling him that the post-mortem on Brolic's body indicated that he had had sex very shortly before his death, and that his clothes were stained with semen. 'I believe she is unharmed, Herr General. She has to be, if she is to be exchanged for Fouquet.'

'Fouquet . . .' Blintoft nodded. 'You say she has been in our cells for more than two weeks?'

'Held incognito, sir. I did not know who she was. I obeyed Major Wassermann's orders.'

'I am surrounded by duplicity,' Blintoft said. 'Which has brought about my ruin.'

'I still have every hope of catching these thugs, Herr General. There is evidence that, apart from the man killed, at least one of the Partisans was wounded. From the amount of blood we found on the ground on the top of the culvert, it is presumed quite seriously. But we have found no body. That means they are carrying a wounded man. Or woman.'

'Do you not suppose the wounded person may be Angela?'

'No, sir. The blood, as I have said, is on the top of the culvert. Fräulein Angela's torn clothing was at the other end of the train, near to the track. There was no reason for her to be taken up to the embankment, as they were clearly in a hurry to get away, and the only blood near to where she was captured belongs to her escort and the man Brolic. No, sir, I believe they are travelling under great difficulties. If you would allow me to use all the men at our disposal, and really scour the country . . .'

'No,' Blintoft said. 'The radio message said they would kill my daughter if they were too closely pursued. This must not happen. We must accept that we have been defeated, on this occasion. Use the call sign they gave us, and tell them we agree to the exchange.'

Ulrich gulped. 'All of them? The man Kostic and the Brolics as well?'

'If that is their price, we must pay it. Your overwhelming – your *only* – responsibility is to have my daughter returned, unharmed. Understand that.'

Ulrich clicked his heels.

Angela sat beside Tony. It was now four days since they had left the train, and they were resting for the afternoon beside a tumbling mountain stream. They had left the plain behind and were now climbing, which had slowed their progress, although there was still no sign of any close pursuit. Tito had done his stuff.

As for the girl, Tony thought he had never seen a more forlorn waif. Apart from her tattered clothing, the very last remnants of chic had disappeared; she wore no make-up, and her hair was a tangled mess – rather like Draga and Sasha. But at least, although she was clearly exhausted, she had stopped complaining.

Now she looked from left to right. For the moment they were relatively alone. Draga was lighting a fire, Sasha was reconnoitring, and the two men were sprawled beneath the trees; they were more exhausted than anyone, as they were the stretcher bearers. 'How much further?' Angela asked.

It was the first time she had addressed him directly since he had first awoken. 'Another few days.'

'Are you in much pain?'

Since they had entered Bosnia, Sasha had allowed him more morphine, so he was able to reply, however drowsily, 'Not as much as you would like me to be in, Fräulein.'

Her face twisted. 'Did you shoot my mother?'

'No.'

'But you were there. In command.'

'Yes. I was sent to shoot your father. But your mother stepped in front.'

'So you shot her.'

'I told you, I did not. I would not have fired at all. But one of my people did so, against my orders.'

'Sandrine?'

'No.'

'The man Kostic?'

'You have seen him?'

233

'I have watched him being tortured.'

Tony tried to focus on her face, which remained impassive despite what she had just said. 'And have you also watched Sandrine being tortured?'

This time her nostrils flared. 'I saved her.'

'Why did you do that, Fräulein?'

'Because . . . because I wanted her for myself. I took her, for myself.'

'Did she not resist you?'

'I think she wanted to. But she was in my power.' Again the defiant look. 'She is very beautiful.'

'I think so. Is she still very beautiful?'

'More than ever. Do you not resent what I have told you?'

'No, Fräulein. Firstly because I know you only said it to hurt me, and secondly because Sandrine is Sandrine, and I will love her no matter what may have happened to her.'

Another flare of the nostrils, then she spat at him. 'I hate you.' Her hand moved, and it held a knife. But she had not noticed Sasha returning to the camp. Now Sasha struck her on the side of the head, tumbling her full length to the ground. Then she crouched over her, hitting her several times on the face; Angela whimpered with pain and fear.

'She must live,' Tony said.

Sasha looked at him; her expression was the same as when she had been crouching over the Cetnik prisoner on the retreat from Uzice, and this time he knew she was going to disobey him. But then they suddenly heard a sound on the far side of the stream. Sasha looked up, and saw men standing there. They were relatively clean-shaven. 'We thought we'd never find you, Captain Janitz,' one of them said. Tony gave a sigh of relief.

'He is quite distraught,' Ulrich said into the telephone. This was a private line, linking the Belgrade office to Berlin. 'Nothing matters save the return of his daughter.'

'He is not the man we once thought he was,' Heydrich said.

'Perhaps it was the murder of his wife. Perhaps it was the Russian front. Who can say? He will be retired.'

'And the girl, Herr General?'

'She has caused enough trouble. This whole business is setting up to be a colossal propaganda coup for these Partisans. This must not happen.'

'You mean, we just leave her with them? They may well execute her.'

'Of course. But it occurs to me that we could make this proposed exchange work to our advantage. You will agree to it, as Blintoft wishes. You will have the woman Fouquet with you. As she is the man Davis's lover, there can be no doubt he will be present when you meet. There is even a faint chance that Tito himself may attend. This will be your chance, Ulrich, to achieve great glory. You will have the opportunity to wipe out the leaders of this band of vipers at one blow.'

'Ah . . . I am only allowed to take six men with me, Herr General.'

'Six *soldiers*, Captain. But here is another thought. You still hold the man Kostic, do you not? Under sentence of death?'

'Yes, Herr General. He is to be part of the exchange.'

'Exactly. Have a talk with him. Remind him that if he is returned to the Partisans, as they wish, they will certainly execute him for treason. Whereas if he were to cooperate with us, his death sentence would be lifted. He will agree to this. Then give him a concealed weapon, and you have a hidden reserve.'

'It will still be highly dangerous.'

'War is a dangerous business, Captain. But here is another thought. You are in touch with the Cetniks, are you not?'

'Major Wassermann had a contact,' Ulrich said cautiously.

'Who is known to you?'

'Yes, Herr General.'

'Very good. Get hold of this contact, and inform him of the coming exchange, and the date given to you by the Partisans. Tell him that you would like him and some of his people to be present – perhaps under the guise of wanting to keep in touch with the Partisans – just to make sure there is no treachery. But if there is treachery, they will be required to support you. Then all you have to do is make sure there *is* treachery.'

Ulrich thought of his wife, waiting patiently in Hamburg for his return. 'Yes, Herr General. You understand that Fräulein von Blintoft will die?'

'I wish her to die, Ulrich, just as I wish Fouquet and Davis to die. Just make sure that the Fräulein is killed by a Partisan bullet. Have the shot fired by Kostic. That will further discredit them. Report to me when the mission is completed.'

'Yes, sir. May I enquire after Major Wassermann?'

'He has survived his ordeal very well. I am told that he will recover. Given time.'

'He will be very upset to learn of the death of his fiancée.'

'We will not tell him until he is stronger. And then . . . if what has happened makes him hate the Partisans the more vehemently, that will be for the benefit of the Reich. I will wish you good fortune, Captain.'

Ulrich stood in the doorway of cell thirty-one. 'Well, mademoiselle, you are to be set free. Does that not please you?' He held out a heavy coat, and threw a pair of boots on the floor. 'It is very cold.'

Sandrine did not move. 'Do you expect me to believe you, Herr Captain?'

'Yes. Because I am telling you the truth.'

'You are going to set me free? Just like that?'

'Well, actually, you are going to be exchanged. Your friends have captured Fräulein von Blintoft, and wish to exchange her for you. And some others.'

'You have agreed to this?'

'The general has, certainly.'

Slowly Sandrine sat up. 'Is Angela – Fräulein von Blintoft – all right?'

'The Partisans say that she is in good health. We shall have to see. They also wish you to be in good health. But you are, are you not, mademoiselle?'

Sandrine sat up, pulled on the boots, and then stood. Ulrich held the coat for her, and then the door. She stepped into the corridor, and faced Anke, who was also wearing a coat. Sandrine looked at Ulrich.

'She will accompany us,' Ulrich said.

Sandrine looked past Anke at Svetovar, also fully dressed.

'Him too,' Ulrich said jovially. 'And the Brolics. We will make a happy party, eh?'

Sandrine walked in front of them along the corridor to the steps. She knew this had to be a trap. But was it a trap for her, or for Tony? She felt the tension begin to grow. But she could do nothing until the trap was sprung.

'How do you feel?' Tito sat by Tony's bed.

'Bloody awful, sir.' Over the past couple of days he had been weaned off the painkillers.

'But, as usual, you will recover. You are like the cat with nine lives, eh?'

'Yes, sir. Have we heard from Belgrade?'

'Oh, yes. They have agreed to the exchange.'

'Just like that?'

'Yes. I feel the same. Obviously they are up to something. But we will be ready for them.'

'When will it happen?'

'In three days' time.'

'I would like to be there.'

Tito nodded. 'I imagine you would. I think it can be arranged. Captain Janitz will make the actual handover, and receive Sandrine and the others. That includes Kostic.'

'He is willing to do this?'

'I do not suppose he had any choice. We gave them a list of who we wanted in exchange for the general's daughter, and they accepted.'

'And when we have him?'

'Oh, he will be court-martialled. But really, his crime was

that of overeagerness and disobedience of orders. We cannot condemn him for anything he may have told the Gestapo under torture. Now, I have a visitor for you.'

Tony raised his eyebrows, and even more so when Curtis entered the room. Tito left them, and the major said, 'I see you have been in the wars again, Colonel.'

'It's my business. What brings you to Foca?'

'Actually, General Mihailovic has sent a small party, at my suggestion, to make his peace with Tito. He wishes to make it clear that the attempt to prevent your withdrawal from Uzice was not authorised by him, but was due to a misunderstanding of his orders.'

'And Tito has accepted that?'

'Well, I'm sure it is true. But there is another reason: this exchange.'

'You know about that?'

'Our agents in Belgrade reported it. Apparently, it is the talk of the city. It will be quite a coup – if you pull it off.'

'We'll pull it off.'

'Don't you suspect that the Jerries may have a trick up their sleeve?'

'We are prepared for that.'

'Well, do you mind if I come along, with my people?'

'You mean Mihailovic's people.'

'They are Cetniks, yes.'

'And why should you wish to be present?'

'Well, were there to be any treachery, we would hope to intervene. I understand you are limited to six soldiers. But nothing was said about us not being present. The Nazis cannot object to that.'

Tony considered. 'How many men do you have with you?'

'Six privates and a major. A man I think you know. His name is Matovic.'

'I remember Matovic. Not my favourite person. I'm surprised he had the cheek, or the guts, to come here.'

'He volunteered. And he's a good soldier.'

'Well, Major, I will discuss your proposal with General Tito.

But you need to understand that you will be held responsible for the behaviour of your Cetniks.'

'They are under my command, and will do as I wish,' Curtis said stiffly.

'I would not trust a Cetnik further than I can spit,' Sasha declared. 'They killed seven of my girls.'

'And you killed several of them,' Tony reminded her gently. 'What do you think, General?'

'Oh, they are up to something; their turning up here immediately before we make the exchange, and wishing to be present, indicates that.'

'You think Curtis is part of it?'

'No. He is an honest man. But as I said once before, he is also a dupe, because he believes all other men are as honest as himself. But I think it might be a good idea to play along for a while. If by any chance Mihailovic has decided to come off the fence and join forces with us, well, I do not think that is an opportunity we can afford to pass up.'

'And if he is going the other way?'

Tito grinned. 'Then I think it will be a good opportunity to find out.'

The general left, and Sasha would have followed him, but Tony caught her hand. 'I haven't seen much of you recently.'

'I would have thought you had seen far too much of me,' she said. 'And I have been busy, guarding our prisoner.'

'What have you done to her?'

'What she would no doubt have done to me, had I been *her* prisoner. Do not worry; she is not harmed, visibly. Does this make you angry?'

'I could never be angry with you, Sasha.'

'You are my commanding officer. I did my duty.'

'In everything?'

Her lips twisted. 'It is often a pleasure to do one's duty.'

'And now?'

'I will continue to do my duty as required. But I am assuming

239

that, once Sandrine returns, what you require of me will be less onerous than recently.'

She made to free her hand, but he tightened his fingers. 'I reckon you think I am all kinds of bastard.'

Now she did free her hand. 'Not at all. You are just a man.' She went to the door, looked over her shoulder. 'But it *was* a pleasure, sir.'

'What did you see?' Tito asked the captain in charge of the reconnaissance patrol.

'As they were instructed, General. Two command cars, six soldiers and a captain, one female gaoler, and six civilians.'

'And?'

'That is all, General.'

'You waited to make sure no one was following?'

'Yes, General. There was no one following.'

'Thank you. Dismissed.' Tito looked at Tony, who lay on a stretcher beside him on the hillside overlooking the shallow valley through which a rough track wound its way. The Partisan doctors had patched him up as well as they were able, and his life was no longer in danger, although it would be some time before he was again fit for duty. But this exchange was more Tony's business than that of any other man in the army, and Tito had had him brought to the rendezvous. 'What do you think?'

'I find it difficult to accept that they are not meaning to try something.'

'Agreed. So we must be prepared to meet them on the same basis. You understand this, Janitz?'

Sasha nodded. 'I will take my people, and the German, down to the rendezvous. I will make the exchange as arranged. If there is any treachery, I will engage the enemy, and be supported from up here.'

Tito gestured at the twenty men crouched or lying amidst the bushes on the wooded hillside. 'These are my best marksmen. But you understand that you will be risking your life?'

'Yes, sir.'

'Well then, good fortune.'

Sasha saluted, and went to stand by Tony's litter. He squeezed her hand. 'And from me.'

Sasha's mouth twisted. 'I will bring Sandrine back to you, my Tony.' She grasped Angela's arm, and pushed her down the path, followed by her women. Angela was handcuffed, and looked more like a waif than ever; she shivered at Sasha's touch.

'I will go down as well,' Matovic said. He had been strangely nervous all morning, Tony thought.

'If the Jerries see you they may pull out,' Curtis objected.

'We will stay concealed unless we are required,' Matovic assured the major, and signalled his men to follow him. Curtis looked at Tony, who looked at Tito, who shrugged. The general knew he held all the high cards, and was prepared to let events take their course.

'How much farther?' Ulrich had appropriated Albrecht as his driver.

'Another two miles, Herr Captain.'

Ulrich looked at Sandrine, who was seated beside him in the centre of the back seat; Anke sat on her other side, and there were two soldiers in the front beside Albrecht. 'Well, Fräulein,' he remarked, 'you are on the verge of another triumph, eh?'

'I will tell you tomorrow,' she replied.

'Do you have no feelings at all?'

'You never took the trouble to find out, Captain.'

Ulrich could understand how Wassermann had lost his temper with her; he was close to doing so himself. But that was at least partly tension; in only a few minutes' time he was going to have to kill her. And then kill Angela von Blintoft – or at least see that she was killed. Two of the most attractive women he had ever met.

He and Sandrine had spent the last night in Sarajevo, having taken the train from Belgrade, and he had entertained her to dinner . . . and wished so much that things could be different. Before he could stop himself, he squeezed her hand. She looked up in surprise, and actually smiled. He had not seen her smile before, and realized that she was, at last, beginning to believe that it was going to happen.

'I see them,' Albrecht said.

'What are you doing here?' Sasha asked Matovic as she and her squad descended into the valley.

'We have been given permission to oversee the exchange.'

'Well, do it from over there, and keep out of sight,' she told him.

'As you wish, Captain.' He and his men went off to hide amongst the trees and tumbled rocks.

'Check your weapons,' Sasha told her women. 'And remember, at the first sign of treachery, take cover and open fire. But do not hit Sandrine.' The women nodded and spread out, unslinging their tommy-guns. 'And you just do as you are told.' Sasha released Angela's wrists.

Angela rubbed her hands together. 'And if I attempt anything, will you kill me?'

'With pleasure.'

'Why do you hate me so? Is it because I tried to attack Davis? He killed my mother.'

'He did not do that.'

'He admits he was there to kill my father. I have every reason to wish him dead. But he is your lover.' Her lip curled. '*Was* your lover. His mistress is now being returned to him.'

'Yes,' Sasha said equably.

'Would you not rather she had been executed?'

Sasha considered her. 'I would rather you were to be executed,' she said. 'You are evil. Your regime is evil. You are creatures of the pit, and should be returned there. If I ever see you again after today, I will kill you.' She smiled. 'Very slowly.'

Angela gulped, and one of the women said, 'I see them.'

The two command cars came slowly down the rough road. Sasha stood up and levelled her binoculars, counting heads;

the second car was crowded. Fifteen people in all, of whom six were soldiers, as arranged. There were also a captain and his driver, and a large woman wearing uniform, but she had no doubt that she could cope with them, even without the support with which she was surrounded.

The car stopped, and Ulrich got out. He gazed at Sasha, and she gazed back; they had never seen each other before, and he was surprised to find himself facing a woman, when he had expected . . . 'Where is Davis?'

'That is not your business,' Sasha said. 'Bring your prisoners forward.'

Ulrich looked past her at Angela. 'Are you all right, Fräulein?'

'How can I possibly be all right?' Angela asked. 'I have been raped.'

Ulrich looked at Sasha. 'She was to be returned unharmed.'

'You will find no bruises on her body. We are at war. In a war, women get raped. If it will relieve your mind, I shot the man who did it.'

'You . . .' As with Sandrine, Ulrich found it difficult to relate this handsome young woman with the business of killing.

'So, bring our people forward,' Sasha said.

Ulrich looked from her to the six young women standing behind her, each armed with a tommy-gun, and his sense of sadness grew; all these attractive females would have to die. But there was nothing for it. He turned and waved his hand. The German soldiers got out of the command cars, as did Albrecht and Anke. The soldiers remained standing in front of the cars; like Sasha's women, they were all armed with tommy-guns. Then the six prisoners also disembarked, and started to approach Ulrich.

The Brolics moved slowly and uncertainly, the two children huddling against their mother. She was more interested in looking at Sandrine, who moved easily and confidently, as she always did. Kostic was behind her, and Angela held her breath; he would certainly remember her.

Sandrine returned Angela's stare; from both her torn clothes and her generally unkempt appearance, it was obvious that she had been having a hard time. Sandrine was also surprised, and disappointed, that Tony was not here to greet her. But he was surely somewhere close. When she reached Ulrich she hesitated. 'Go on, mademoiselle,' he said. 'You are free.' Sandrine drew a deep breath, and stepped past him. She watched Angela step past Sasha to come towards her, and heard Ulrich say in a low voice, 'Now, Kostic.'

Instantly she knew the trap was about to be sprung. Without hesitation she turned back and threw herself against Ulrich, still close behind her. Such was the force of her charge that she knocked him off his feet; he crashed to the ground, winded, with her on top of him, and before he could recover she had whipped his pistol from its holster.

For a moment no one reacted. Kostic had also produced a pistol, but Sasha naturally supposed he was on their side, and only reacted when he levelled it at Angela and squeezed the trigger. Angela gave a shriek and fell. Sasha dropped to her knees, shouting, 'Take cover,' as she returned fire.

The German soldiers now also opened fire, and, caught in the midst of it, Kostic was hit several times and went down. The Brolics were already on the ground, desperately hoping not to be hit. Anke drew her pistol, and Sandrine, still lying on top of Ulrich, shot her twice in the stomach. Ulrich tried to sit up, and was forced down again by Sandrine holding the pistol to his throat. 'Keep still or I will blow your head off,' she told him. He lay back, staring at her.

Two of the soldiers had been killed, and the other four, as well as Albrecht, were sheltering behind the cars, which were already riddled with bullet holes and now burst into flames. Sasha scrambled back to her feet, as did her women. Angela rose to her knees, her now bloody hands pressed to her body. 'They meant to kill me,' she muttered.

Sasha ignored her as she went forward. Kostic was dead and Anke was clearly dying, writhing on the ground and weeping and shrieking; the remaining soldiers were lost to sight behind the smoking cars. 'You are outnumbered,' Sasha called. 'Throw out your weapons, and then come out with your hands up.' She stood above Sandrine and Ulrich. 'That was quick thinking,' she said. 'Did you know they meant treachery?'

'I had a pretty good idea,' Sandrine said, getting off Ulrich. 'You can get up now.'

Slowly Ulrich pushed himself up, now more concerned with Sasha's tommy-gun, which was pointing at him, than with Sandrine's pistol. 'Tell your men to surrender,' Sasha said.

Ulrich hesitated, and then looked at the bushes to their left, from which Matovic and his Cetniks now emerged.

'What are they doing here?' Sandrine snapped.

Sasha shrugged. 'They were to oversee the exchange. Not that you have been much help,' she told Matovic as he came up to them.

'I am doing what I came to do,' Matovic said.

'Arrest this bastard,' Sandrine said.

'What has he done?' Sasha asked.

'He sold me to the Nazis. He will hang.'

Sasha turned towards the Cetniks, and looked down the barrel of a tommy-gun; her own was at the end of her fingers, hanging by her side. 'It is you who are under arrest,' Matovic said. 'I came here especially to deal with this bitch. Tell your women to lay down their arms, or you will die.'

'Are you stupid?' Sasha asked. 'Do you not know that you are overlooked?'

'They will not fire into us, and risk hitting you . . . and Sandrine,' Matovic said. 'Do it. And you, mademoiselle.'

Sandrine and Sasha looked at each other. They were entirely surrounded by the Cetniks, but, having got this far, Sandrine did not intend to be murdered, however much she was determined to avenge herself on this man. She gave the Luger back to Ulrich, while Sasha surrendered her tommy-gun to one of the Cetniks. 'Don't shoot,' she called to the women.

'That is very sensible behaviour,' Matovic said. 'Captain

245

Ulrich, prepare to pull out. We will take these two with us. And you, Fräulein,' he called to Angela.

Slowly Angela stumbled forward. 'I am wounded.'

Matovic tore away some of her dress to look at her flesh. Her face twisted in a mixture of pain and distaste. 'It is nothing more than a nick,' he said. 'You'll survive.'

Tito handed his glasses to Tony. 'I do not understand what is happening.' They had seen the various movements, and heard the exchange of shots, but had not interfered, as it had appeared that Sasha was in full command of the situation. But now that she had handed over her tommy-gun . . .

'That bastard Matovic,' Tony said.

'We will have to open fire.'

'You'll hit the women.'

'He is playing some game of his own.' Curtis had also been studying the situation through his glasses. 'I'll sort him out.' He got up, and ran down the slope, blowing his whistle and waving his arms.

'He's gone mad,' Tito said.

'I think he's just come to his senses,' Tony said. 'Christ, to be able to get down there . . .'

'Prepare to fire,' Tito told his marksmen. 'They cannot be allowed to get away.'

Tony swallowed; Sandrine and Sasha might just have been condemned to death. He watched Curtis stumbling down the slope, his revolver drawn, and gasped as Matovic levelled his pistol and shot the British officer in the chest. Curtis went down, the revolver flying from his grasp. But his appearance had distracted everyone, and Sasha and Sandrine were the first to react. Sasha wrenched her tommy-gun from the hands of the man standing beside her, spraying the Cetniks before they had a chance to recover. Sandrine struck Ulrich with a karate chop on the shoulder, and as his knees sagged she regained possession of the pistol. Matovic turned to face her, and she shot him through the heart.

The Cetniks, who had fallen away from Sasha's tommy-gun,

presented the marksmen on the hill with exposed targets, and the brief gun battle was already over. The Germans had tried to join in, and had been destroyed by the Partisans; only Albrecht and two of the soldiers remained alive, and they had their hands high in the air. Tito waved at his men, and Tony's stretcher was carried down the hill.

Sandrine was kneeling beside Curtis, whose eyes were open. 'Bit of a foul-up, mademoiselle.' He turned his head as Tony was placed beside him. 'I owe you an apology, Colonel,' he said, and then his face stiffened.

'He was a brave man,' Sandrine said.

Tony reached for her hand. 'As you are a very brave woman.'

'I cannot leave you alone for a moment without you getting yourself shot,' she complained.

'Do we shoot these people, General?' Sasha asked. Ulrich was sitting up and holding his shoulder.

'Please, not him,' Sandrine said.

'He tried to kill us all, treacherously.'

'He was only obeying orders. And before then, he did his best for me.'

'And this one?' Tito gestured at Angela.

'Her too, after her fashion.'

'I am wounded,' Angela said. 'Will you not help me?'

'Oh, bind her up,' Sasha told her women.

Angela gave a shriek as the women surrounded her.

'What is your name?' Tito asked Ulrich.

Ulrich stood up, and did his best to come to attention. 'Captain Hermann Ulrich, sir.'

'Well, Captain Ulrich, I suggest you return to Belgrade, and restore the young lady to her father. Tell him that we have found him out, as we shall do again and again until he, and you, and all of your filthy apparatus, have left our country.'

Ulrich looked at Tony. 'We haven't met,' Tony said. 'And I strongly recommend that we do not meet again. But I thank you for helping Sandrine.'

'How can we get back to Belgrade?' Angela asked. Her

247

clothes were even more tattered, and she now had a bandage round her waist. 'There is no transport.'

'That is quite true,' Tito agreed. 'You will have to walk, at least as far as Sarajevo. It is only thirty miles.'

'But I am wounded.'

'I am sure you will make it. Do you not belong to the master race? Now is your chance to prove that.'

Angela looked at him, then down at the ill-fitting boots she had been given to wear, and finally at Sandrine. Then she hugged her torn fur coat around herself, and set off along the road.

Ulrich saluted both Tito and Tony, and looked for a last time at Sandrine. 'They told me you had a sting, mademoiselle. And I did not believe them. I will wish you good fortune.' He followed Angela, with Albrecht and the soldiers behind him.

'I wonder what story they will tell,' Tony remarked.

'We should have killed them all,' Sasha said. 'I do not see how you could wish to spare their lives, Sandrine.'

'Because they saved mine,' Sandrine said.

Tito called the Brolics forward. 'Your place is with us now.'

Both the parents seemed to have aged a hundred years, Tony thought.

'Our son,' Brolic ventured. 'Is he . . . ?'

Tito looked at Sasha.

'Your son died in battle against the Germans,' Sasha said. 'Avenging you.'

They sighed, and hugged their remaining children.

'Bring the major's body,' Tito said. 'He will have a proper burial, and you, Tony, will personally report his death to Alexandria.'

'What about these others?' Sasha asked.

'Leave them. If Mihailovic wants to come looking for his people, he is welcome to do so. '

'That man tried to kill me,' Angela said as she stumbled along the uneven surface. 'How did he come to be armed?'

'I do not know, Fräulein,' Ulrich said. 'It is something I am going to find out.'

Angela considered for several seconds, then she asked, 'What is going to happen to me?'

'I am sure your father will be overwhelmed with joy to have you back, Fräulein.'

'But . . . all of those people, dead.'

'His orders were to bring you back, regardless of the cost,' Ulrich said. It was what was going to happen to him that was far more important, in his opinion. Heydrich had said that the girl had to be killed by either Kostic or one of the Partisans, so he could not now do the job, even if he had the stomach for it, in front of Albrecht and the soldiers.

Angela's shoulders hunched. 'It has been a disaster. My life has been a disaster. I am in such pain.'

Ulrich squeezed her hand. 'Do not take it so hard, Fräulein. You are alive, when you should – I beg your pardon, *could* – have been dead. You are on your way home to your father, and then you will be able to join Major Wassermann, and be married.'

Angela burst into tears.

'A message from Alexandria.' Tito entered the sick room. 'The most amazing news.' He looked at Tony and the two women. 'You will hardly believe this, but a few days ago Japan attacked the United States.'

'Good lord!' Tony remarked. 'Does that affect us?'

'Indeed it does, because Herr Hitler has declared war on America in Japan's support. That means we have America on our side. We cannot lose.'

Sandrine clapped her hands.

'They have also acknowledged Curtis's death, and recognised your existence,' Tito went on. 'Do you wish to be taken out?'

'Not if you still have use for me here.'

'I will have, once you are fit again, and now that the odds have changed in our favour. I think we still have a lot to do, convincing them that we are the people they should be supporting.'

'Will you tell them of Mihailovic's treachery?'

'I will let you do that. Hurry up and get well.' He looked at the two women. 'I will leave him in your care.' He left the room, beckoning the doctor and the nurses to follow.

Sasha and Sandrine looked at each other. This was the first time the three of them had been alone together. 'We mourned you,' Sasha said. 'And sought only to avenge you. But . . .'

'You thought I was dead,' Sandrine agreed. 'So did I, more than once. But as I am not . . .' She looked down at Tony. 'The decision must be yours.'

'The need for a decision never existed,' Sasha said. 'I always knew this.' She kissed Tony, and then embraced Sandrine. 'Summon me if you need me, sir,' she said, and left the room.

Sandrine sat down. 'Was she good?'

'Not as good as you.'

'You are obliged to say that.'

'So tell me about Fräulein von Blintoft.'

'She kept me alive. '

'You could say the same of Sasha.'

'And so, we are both alive.' She lay down beside him. 'What do you intend to do now?'

'As soon as I can stand again, go on fighting. Are you happy with that?'

'Oh, yes,' she said. 'Oh, yes.'